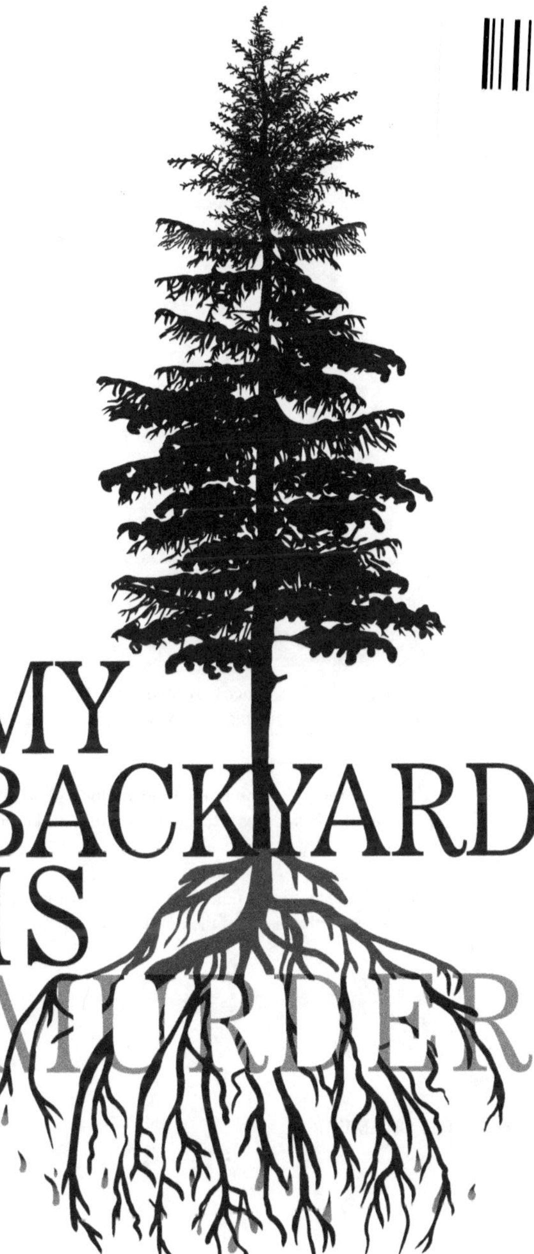

MY BACKYARD IS MURDER

JOHN R. SCANNELL

Wutherwood Press

ISBN: 978-0-578-25898-0

Cover Design by Jennifer Blair
Interior Design by Laura Eddings

PRINTED IN THE UNITED STATES OF AMERICA

Wutherwood Press

For my wife, Wendy,
the Mistress of Wutherwood,
who created a dog paradise for
Kaylie, Puggy, Aria, King, Baloo, Luigi, Beau, Wolfie, and Jackson.
One and all, they basked and bask in the beauty
of our tall, tall Wutherwood trees.

Trees are poems that the earth writes upon the sky.
— Kahlil Gibran

It is not so much for its beauty that the forest makes a
claim upon men's hearts, as for that subtle something,
that quality of air that emanates from old trees, that so
wonderfully changes and renews a weary spirit.
— Robert Louis Stevenson

Table Of Contents

Chapter 1	Epiphany	1
Chapter 2	It Was a Dark and Stormy Night	25
Chapter 3	Much Ado About Noting	59
Chapter 4	Enter, Stage Left	71
Chapter 5	Clueless	87
Chapter 6	Come Into My Parlor	96
Chapter 7	Sinners and Saints	111
Chapter 8	Big Brother	126
Chapter 9	Slowly I Turn	136
Chapter 10	The Most Dangerous Game	150
Chapter 11	Epitaph	158
Chapter 12	The Snowy Owl	171
Chapter 13	No Stone Unturned	183
Chapter 14	I Would Prefer Not To	196
Chapter 15	A Simple Question	210
Epilogue		220

Chapter One

Epiphany

Frank Hannigan
December 2019

I'd like to begin with a simple question. Could you be friends with someone who has killed three people?

I don't mean killed accidentally or in wartime. I want to eliminate the tearful laments, "He didn't mean to do it," as well as the stern edicts, "He's a soldier. He had to do it." Such comments make killing seem merely a matter of an unlucky fate or some military purpose.

No. I want to know if you could be friends with someone who had *murdered* three people. Deliberately. Intentionally.

I don't want you to answer immediately, okay? I want you to really think about it. As you think, I want to tell you a story.

If someone had asked me that very question four years ago, I would have responded with an immediate, emphatic "No!" Maybe even a "Hell, no!"

I would have responded with unbridled certainty, calling such a question absurd, ridiculous, deranged. I would have spat out my answer in exclamation points. "Be friends with a murderer?! Are you kidding me?!"

In four years, that unbridled certainty has evaporated. Circumstances have changed, and so have I. What I am sure I would have said—once upon a time—is not what I'd say now.

No one is more surprised than me.

When I was a youngster, my mother—a woman weaned on a diet of aphorisms—would always tell me that "Two wrongs don't make a right." As a child, I believed her. It never occurred to me to ask, "So what happens if you are the victim of a terrible wrong, and that wrong is never righted? What if it goes unpunished?"

If I could ask her that question now, I wonder how she would respond. Would she simply reiterate the lesson learned at her own mother's knee—*Two wrongs don't make a right?* Might she insist that *Forgiveness is the only path?*

I once asked my wife if an unpunished wrong is a tragedy, or merely part of the human comedy.

"That's just the kind of question an English teacher would ask," she said.

In my experience, the distance between comedy and tragedy is infinitesimally small. I'm certain you understand how small that distance can be. How else could anyone, standing on the bluffs high above the swollen Susquehanna River, laugh while watching a white, clapboard, two-story house—unmoored from its foundations by Hurricane Agnes—float by at a crazy angle atop swirling waters? Floating away to oblivion. Why would anyone find that funny?

From the shore, the spiraling house appeared to be completely intact, when someone in the gawking crowd casually remarked, "They should have just called a moving company." We all laughed. But only for a moment. The whole scene was surreal—comic and tragic all at once.

That's where my life is right now—trapped somewhere between comedy and tragedy. My wife keeps asking, "Do you ever wonder how this whole business will resolve itself?"

My stock response to her oft-asked question is, "I try not to wonder."

But I do wonder.

I don't know for sure the fate of the floating house, but when I wonder about it, the house never floats up to the river's edge and re-establishes itself on some previously poured foundation. Never. Although that would be delightfully comic.

I'm certain the house met a tragic end. Which is why I keep my wondering to a minimum.

Perhaps the house represents one of life's truisms: *Sometimes things just get out of hand.* Things get out of hand, and events spin out of control.

I recall an incident on a late March afternoon when I was a rookie teacher. My car hit an icy patch as I was driving to my high school for a rehearsal of the senior class play, *Lost Horizon*. Almost April, it shouldn't have been snowing. The calendar had already declared spring's arrival, so this snow and ice were officially unexpected. My mother called it an "onion snow," but I didn't care what vegetable it was named for.

I went into a spin.

I remember gripping the steering wheel as if I were on the whirligig at Dorney Park and thinking to myself, *So this is what the world looks like when life is spinning out of control.*

After a 540-degree spin, my car pitched over an eight-foot embankment into a freshly-plowed farmer's field, coming to rest on its roof in the soft mud. It could easily have been fatal, but it wasn't. As I climbed out of my inverted vehicle, I kept touching myself and laughing.

As I said, comedy and tragedy.

My point is simple. Things occasionally get out of hand, spin out of control, and assigning blame isn't so straightforward. There are always circumstances that account for what happened.

In this case, Mother Nature provided the circumstances—the snow and ice—and I'm unwilling to file a grievance against Mother Nature.

Stuff happens. Terrifying stuff happens. Sometimes it's comic, sometimes it's tragic. Sometimes both. Sometimes.

November 13, 2015

I'd fallen asleep in the family room—as I did so often—during the eleven o'clock news. Isabel, my lovely wife, was working in her office just down the hall, while outside, an ominous wind howled through the trees.

I was having one of those murky, half-awake experiences. Not awake, not asleep. Wondering if what I was hearing was a dream or reality. God, it was loud!

Still drowsy, I'm sure I mumbled. "What the hell...? What am I hearing?"

It's not the news, some inner voice cried out.

My mind sped from zero to sixty. Instantly. Wide-eyed, I sat bolt upright on the recliner. Completely awake.

I shouted, "What the hell is that? Isabel, what's that noise?"

I couldn't recall any noise like it. A loud crack. A collision...and then another and another. The ceaseless howling of the cold, November wind combining with a hundred cracks and snaps and swishes. A crescendo of noise that cancelled out everything, even thought.

The noise cancelled everything but fear.

"Trees are coming down!" Isabel screamed from her office. "Get to the north side of the house. Now!"

Isabel and I ran from opposite ends of our house to the living room. Then the house shuddered and groaned. Not like an earthquake. No, we heard a heart-wrenching, booming crash from overhead—somewhere in the rear of the house—accentuated by the sound of glass shattering, both near and distant. Two dogs cowered at our feet, wondering just like their humans, *What the hell is happening?*

As quickly as the terrifying noise arose, it ceased, leaving only the unrelenting, howling wind. Isabel and I stood for a moment in the living room, absorbing the reality of what we'd just heard and felt. Our black lab began to whine, so I knelt down and petted him.

"Where's Miss Aria?" Isabel asked. "Oh, my God, where's Miss Aria."

We had three dogs. Only two were with us in the living room.

"Wasn't she under the desk in your office?"

"No. I thought she was with you."

I shook my head. Panic suddenly gripped Isabel's sinking heart.

"She's probably asleep on our bed. Oh, my God, she's in our bedroom."

Isabel ran down the hallway and pushed the bedroom door open. I followed, but by the time I'd gotten to the bedroom door, Isabel was already curled around Miss Aria on the bed. Miss Aria, Isabel's most-beloved Flat-Coated Retriever, lay on her side on the bed. Tree branches, fir needles, rubber roof tiles, drywall, and heaps of unidentifiable detritus were strewn across the bed and on the floor. In the few moments it had taken us to get to the bedroom, a large stain of blood had already spread across the bedspread. Miss Aria lay motionless in Isabel's arms, washed in a flood of Isabel's tears. Isabel stroked her face, kissed her sweet head, and said between tortured sobs, "My sweet girl. Oh, my sweet girl. I'm so sorry. I'm so, so sorry."

Isabel was inconsolable. I knew better than to interfere.

In the dim light, I squinted at the ceiling. A large tree branch, the limb of a giant felled fir, had pierced our rubber roof—yes, a roof of recycled rubber—and had shattered our bedroom ceiling, filling our bedroom with debris. A gaping hole looked out into the night.

I must call 911, I thought. *The thought is father to the deed.* The 911 operator asked if anyone had been injured. Without hesitation, I said yes.

Perhaps that's why the fire department arrived almost instantaneously. I was standing on my front deck when the first emergency vehicle—sirens blaring—rolled down my driveway. Two fire engines arrived immediately behind.

"Where's the injured party?" an EMT asked as he strode onto the deck. The flashing, whirling red lights from all the emergency vehicles cast an eerie glow across the face of our home.

"It's our dog," I said. "It's Miss Aria."

"Your dog? Did you say your dog?" He seemed confused.

"Yes, sir." I suddenly felt guilty for having said that some*one* had been injured. "Our Flat-Coated Retriever is dead. She was killed when a huge tree limb smashed through our roof."

The scene commander joined the EMT and me on the front deck.

"So what's going on here?" he asked.

The EMT responded very matter-of-factly. "Their dog was killed when a tree hit their house."

"Are you the one who called 911?"

"Yes, sir," I said. "I'm Frank Hannigan."

"Because a tree fell, right?" the scene commander asked me.

"Yes, sir. But I'm pretty sure it's plural. I'm certain several trees fell." I gestured with my thumb, "Out back."

The wind still blew, and limbs from the two giant western red cedars flanking our driveway swayed across the tops of the emergency vehicles parked on the gravel.

"Let's see if we can find out exactly what's happened here," the scene commander said. He shouted to two of his crew. "Alex, you and Marie bring the search lights out back as quickly as you can." He turned to me. "Okay, let's go see what we can see," he said. "Stay behind me." He turned on his flashlight.

What I saw shocked me. Frightened me. Saddened me. In the narrow flashlight beam, I could see all was chaos.

If a tree falls in the woods, I thought.

"My God, what's happened here?" I asked.

The scene commander stopped and held his flashlight out as a road-block. "Let's wait for the lights."

What the lights revealed was what the scene commander described as the worst damage he'd ever seen in Snoquamish.

"This is awful," he said. "Trust me, I've seen a lot."

His team reported in to him by radio as we picked our away across my backyard, pushing limbs out of the way and shimmying over huge fallen tree trunks. I could hear chain saws whirring and grinding somewhere overhead.

"The count so far is five trees," the scene commander said. "Two firs and three hemlocks. You're lucky to be alive, Mr. Hannigan. We're removing the tree trunk that smashed into your bedroom, and we'll be putting a tarp over the hole—but that part of your home is structurally unsafe. It's gonna have to be repaired quickly."

I heard what the commander was saying, but I felt numb, confused. *I'll call Roger in the morning,* I thought. *He'll know what to do.* Roger was—what did Isabel always call him?—our go-to-guy. Whenever I think of Roger's own humble description of himself—he called himself "Your Handy Craftsman"—I had to laugh. Roger was far more than a mere handy craftsman. He was the man who had single-handedly remodeled our home. Outside and in. He could do damn near anything—decks, plumbing, electrical, carpentry, cabinetry, flooring, tiling...you name it. Or he knew people who could.

"Rain's expected tomorrow, I think," the scene commander said. "Just be glad it wasn't raining tonight."

Yeah, I'm glad. I should be grateful for small favors.

Another fireman joined the commander and me and pointed to the two-story custom shed that Roger had built shortly after Isabel and I met. The shed was only partially visible as we stood next to the crushed wall of my master bedroom. The wind was still howling, and I couldn't hear the conversation.

"What did your guy say?" I asked the commander.

"He said your shed is completely destroyed, Mr. Hannigan. I'm afraid it's a total loss. I know you'll be tempted to rescue your belongings that are in there, but I wouldn't, if I were you. A fir cut the whole shed in two. It'd be dangerous to go inside. I'm sorry."

I'm sorry, too, I thought.

Even as I stood outside in the howling wind, I could still hear Isabel sobbing over our lifeless Miss Aria. There was no comedy here—only tragedy.

There are few tragedies like the death of your dog. The fateful date—November 13, 2015—is inscribed on the box holding her ashes.

December 2019

My older brother insists that everything is cause and effect, and maybe he's right. We all understand cause and effect, right? A causes B...B causes C...C causes D...you get the idea.

For instance, somebody causes someone else's trees to fall. That's A. Then that somebody, who caused someone else's trees to fall, is found murdered. That's B.

Over a very short period of time, several more somebodies—people who are also responsible for felling trees that are not theirs, and equally responsible for a dead dog, a shattered roof, a crushed shed, and unrelenting nightmares—are also murdered. Let's call those unfortunate individuals B^2 and B^3.

The police begin an investigation to discover the someone responsible for pushing all those murdered somebodies into the hereafter. Let's call the police investigation C.

All of this plays out in the newspapers and television, and suddenly things have gotten out of hand. The newspapers speculate about a possible serial killer loose in the community, and fearful citizens pen letters to all the local papers demanding that the culprit—or culprits—be brought to justice. Television news anchors echo all the speculation, and while the police are conducting an exhaustive search for an unknown killer, everyone's locking their doors and eyeing everyone else with suspicion.

As I said, cause and effect.

Seattle's Eastlake suburb has been wrestling with three unsolved murders—even though one of those murders occurred well beyond their jurisdiction. The Seattle Chronicle recently weighed in with the head-line: *When Will the Dead Receive Justice?* In the article, the columnist described the dead trio as a "rash of murders."

I'm not sure what equals "a rash of murders," but all three murders remain unsolved. I'm particularly grateful for that because I tend to look at these events—these murders—through a radically different lens than the stumped detectives or the speculating journalists.

I don't call any of them murders. I think of them more as the adminis-tration of justice. Punishment for crimes. Harsh punishment, perhaps, but an arguably defensible punishment for dreadful crimes committed that would otherwise have gone unpunished.

Speculation in the media includes interviews with psychologists and psychiatrists offering armchair diagnoses. The police wonder if they should be looking for a sociopath or a psychopath…or maybe a recidivist, a prisoner recently released, now free to roam and free to kill. And oth-ers want to know how you'd recognize the killer if you crossed paths with him…or her…or them.

Here is what I know.

The police and journalists are looking in the wrong place for the wrong person. The person they're looking for isn't a psychopath or a sociopath. He isn't crazy or low-functioning. He's never been to prison.

The person the police should be looking for—but aren't—is a man who hopes to spend his golden years with his wife…at home…reading books…sipping wine…enjoying life with his dogs and cats…and rabbits and squirrels…and birds. He'd feel awful if he didn't mention the birds. He donates annually to the Audubon Society, the World Wildlife Fund, the ASPCA, and a host of animal rescue groups. Trust me, I know.

I can assure you, the bad guy the police are looking for is, in almost every way, a good guy.

What's the old adage? *This didn't have to happen?* Yeah, that's the one.

Until four years ago, Isabel and I lived in what we would both describe as "our sheltering woods" or "our little piece of heaven." Our acre of land had more than 35 very tall trees, and beyond our southern property line there lived two wonderful neighbors, Jack and Margaret. Much of their property belonged to nature—tall trees and untended growth.

A lovely forest surrounded both our properties, and it was inhabited by all the usual denizens—rabbits, chipmunks, raccoons, squirrels, hummingbirds, Oregon juncos, robins, Steller's jays, woodpeckers—Margie loved birds and placed feeders all over their two-acre property. Isabel and I loved the ubiquitous deer that nibbled our apple trees and came to the salt lick. And we were always pleasantly surprised by the occasional bobcat, and the once-seen mama black bear who gamboled across our backyard with her two cubs.

It was idyllic.

Then, four years ago, a developer bought that large tract of land along our southern boundary—including Jack and Margaret's home and two acres—cleared it of virtually all trees, and cut the holding roots of five of our 100-foot-tall evergreen trees. Deliberately, we're pretty sure, given that they did it right after our complaints about their destruction of the 20-foot vegetation buffer they had agreed would be left on their side of the boundary.

Isabel and I knew that Hemlock Hill—the new subdivision now standing south of our property line—would be built. *You can't stop progress, right?*

Isabel and I understood we couldn't stop progress, and we consoled ourselves with the belief that we could live our lives happily, undisturbed by Hemlock Hill. Truth be told, that was *my* hope—what Isabel described as "Frank's delusional thinking."

When construction began, destruction began. What had once been a forest was cleared. Almost all the trees disappeared, including the 20-foot buffer. Then the bulldozers arrived and harvested the top soil. Unfortunately, bulldozers have the ability to dig deep, and when the bulldozers dug along the common boundary line, the one where the Comstock-Hannigan property meets the Hemlock Hill property, the developer knew that our trees—the trees on our side of that boundary—might have their holding roots severed if he dug deep enough. How could he not know?

Guess what happened? Our holding roots were severed. These were big trees—each tree over one-hundred-feet tall—and cutting those roots would have consequences.

The day we discovered the compromised holding roots, I called Mick Walther, the developer responsible for Hemlock Hill. I must euphemistically confess that our conversation didn't go well. Then I made nineteen phone calls to the Snoquamish city planner—each with Isabel's permission, of course.

Her permission came in the form of *Goddamn it, Frank, just call her again. She knows this development. I just met with her yesterday about their schedule.*

Not a single call to the city planner was ever returned.

I tried to make each successive call more urgent than the previous one, explaining frantically that the careless developers had cut the holding roots of our trees.

As I left the 19th message—my 19th pleading phone call—my frustration boiled over. "If you don't respond to my messages," I said, "I'm gonna come up there and do a dance on your desk." I may have said "goddamn desk," but I really don't remember.

Less than an hour later, two police officers, one male and one female, arrived on our front deck. They wanted to follow up on our complaints, but not in the way I had hoped. They were very interested in knowing what I meant by "doing a dance on her desk." That struck me as an asinine question. Rather than call us back and assuage our fears, the city planner had decided to take my comment as some sort of actual threat. There's your comedy and tragedy.

"Really? That's why you're here? Is that the only thing Amelia Artaud told you about the messages I left? That I was going to do a dance on her desk? I left nineteen messages. Didn't she tell you about our severed tree roots?" I asked angrily.

I desperately wanted to show them what prompted my calls—all nineteen—but the cops refused to walk around the house to look at the severed roots of our trees. Their reluctance was maddening.

"I can see you're upset," said the female officer.

"No, officer. I left upset behind an hour ago. When the people paid to represent our interests ignore us, we don't get upset, we get furious."

"You need to calm down, sir. We're here because of an alleged threat..."

I interrupted. "So she didn't mention our trees roots being cut, did she? The threat is real, and it's to *our* lives, not hers."

"You really should accompany us out back," Isabel said in a calm steady voice. "Once you do, you'll have no doubt why both Frank and I are so upset at the city's complete lack of response."

They ignored both our invitations.

Just like the city planner, I thought.

I looked balefully at Isabel and shrugged. She walked to the far end of the deck where the male policeman stood.

Unmoved and unmoving, our pair of officers were rooted to our front deck. They had no interest in going anywhere to see anything. None. Our looming tragedy held no interest for the police at all. They didn't want context. They didn't want the whole picture. I don't know why. None of our concerns seemed to register; none of it seemed to matter.

They wanted me to answer their questions, but before I answered, they felt compelled to read me my rights. That alone should have signaled to me that this casual front-deck conversation had escalated to an interrogation.

"What did you mean when you said you'd do a dance on her desk?" the female officer inquired.

Explaining the obvious is always difficult. Nevertheless, I tried.

"You know, something to get her attention."

I might as well have been talking to the wall. My exasperated self decided some snarky elaboration might help. "I hadn't decided if I'd do a foxtrot or a tango."

The police were not amused.

Isabel's look warned me off, and I could see she viewed the confrontation with the police far more seriously than I did. So I decided to return to my own original request.

"Look officers, just come look at what has happened to our trees."

I was angry, but I don't believe my tone was threatening. I just wanted them to understand that my angry words, left on the city planner's voicemail—and now hardened into a police investigation—didn't just fall from my lips unbidden.

No, this was A causing B. I was upset that nineteen calls went unanswered. Not one response. Not one.

I suppose the police arriving was the response.

Despite our insistence, the two police officers remained manifestly disinterested in seeing our compromised tree roots. Worse, they actually stated that their visit was partly because my wife and I could be terrorists—well, one of them did. Mr. Policeman off-handedly remarked, "Who knows? You might be terrorists."

That's when I had my moment.

I stepped toward the officer. "What did you say? Did you say we might be terrorists?"

Emotional escalation is exactly what police don't want. I didn't want it either, but stupid, insultingly curt comments made on my deck, at my home, and embellished with the word "terrorist"...

"Sir, please step back," ordered his female partner.

"No sir, ma'am. Your partner just suggested we might be terrorists," I said.

"That's not what he said," she replied, attempting to intervene calmly.

"I'm afraid that's exactly what he said," Isabel reported. She never took her eyes off the male officer as she spoke.

While she'd been standing quietly during this entire front deck police encounter, Isabel was never a passive observer. She was completely capable of speaking up and speaking out.

I wasn't about to let the policeman's remark pass. "Yes, it is. He said 'you might be terrorists.' That's exactly what he said."

I glared at him over his partner's shoulder. "Well, I've got a hot flash for you, asshole. If we look like terrorists," I said, pointing to Isabel and myself, "Snoquamish must be crawling with terrorists. Mad bombers everywhere. Blowin' up Safeways and QFCs. You must be arresting terrorists every day."

"Sir, please calm down."

"I don't think so," I said. "I'll calm down when the two of you get the hell off my front deck. You come here to intimidate me because I had the audacity to get pissed off at the city planner after I phoned her nineteen times—nineteen times! On each message, I tell her the roots to our trees—*our* trees, the ones on *our* side of the fence—have been cut by the developers. That they now pose a danger to us. And she ignores me. So I say I'll do a dance on her desk if she doesn't call me back...and you two show up. And you ignore us, too."

I took a deep breath.

"Then your asshole partner here says we might be terrorists."

I paused, my gaze landing directly on the male officer.

"Go ahead, tell your partner the truth, asshole. That's what you said, isn't it? Just admit it!"

He said nothing.

I gotta hand it to Miss-Calm-in-the-Storm. She let me rant and then proceeded almost as if I'd said nothing at all.

"Sir, I don't know what my partner said, but he didn't mean to call you or your wife terrorists." Her face was irritatingly neutral. I imagine that's the "professional look," the same look she'd give me if we were both standing atop a rumbling, active volcano moments before an eruption.

"Really, officer?" I asked. "So now you're a mind reader? You know what your partner means and doesn't mean? Does he ever get to talk for himself or is he just window dressing for the Snoquamish police?"

I shook my head realizing that talking with the police—or to the police—was a dead end.

"I'm done talking with you." I looked at Isabel, and we both moved in unison to the storm door.

"We need to finish up here," the female officer said.

"Good, you do that," I said. "You finish up here, officer. And while you're at it, take a stroll out back. Take some pictures. That'll help you finish up."

I closed the front door and locked it. I walked to the kitchen and pulled down a bottle of wine and gave myself and Isabel a generous pour.

Their unwillingness to accede to a simple request to "look at the tall trees behind our house and you'll understand" made us realize that they weren't interested in understanding anything about what had happened. They weren't working on our behalf. They were doing the bidding of a city employee, who was doing the bidding of the land developer, who was filling city coffers with money.

The police were not playing for our team. They were playing on the developer's team—the developers had deeper pockets and more valuable turf to protect.

The day after our police visitation, Dean, our arborist, visited our property, giving us the worst possible news that our trees—and quite possibly our shed and our home and our lives—were in danger.

"Those five trees," he said pointing out each one as he walked the fence line, "they will fall. Their holding roots are compromised by whoever graded beneath the topsoil on the other side of the fence." He hopped the low chain-link fence, knelt on one knee and pulled up a severed root. He took a picture with his cellphone. "Look, you can see where the roots have been cut. This root belongs to that fir tree, Frank. The one just to your left." He shook his head. "Subgrading to this extent was completely unnecessary."

Dean stood up, rubbed the dirt off his hands, and stared at the barren, vacant lot, where once a forest had stood. He hopped back across the low fence, then looked up into the high branches of two of our threatened trees.

"I hate to tell you this. These two firs—they're at least seventy-five years old. Probably older. But they're going to fall. It's a matter of when, not if."

Dean's prediction was unambiguous...and emphatic.

"These trees could fall in the next big wind. You better get an emergency permit to have them taken down," Dean said. "I'd take them down for you right now, but these are heritage trees, maybe landmark trees. I can't remove them without a permit."

The "next big wind" hit the very next evening, before any permit could be obtained. Five gigantic trees—two firs and three hemlocks dominoed in the howling winds. In literally moments, we lost our dog, our master bedroom, our shed—and all its contents—five irreplaceable trees, and our peace of mind.

This wasn't a tragedy caused by Mother Nature. High winds or not, this tragedy was caused by severed tree roots. This tragedy was man-made, the entirely predictable result of the carelessness and indifference of developers and city planners.

This didn't have to happen! became our mantra.

I probably shouldn't be writing any of this, but I am. As a former English teacher, I feel that things achieve greater clarity when they've been written down. I need that clarity to sort things out, to decide what to do.

As a college freshman way back when, my English professor, Dr. Gable, would often quote author, E.M. Forster. "How do I know what I think until I see what I say?" That was Dr. Gable's bedrock belief.

"The writing process is the thinking process made visible," he'd tell us. "You can't know what you think until it's been recorded on paper—as a final draft—in ink."

Yes, I went to college in the pen-and-ink era, when I used a manual typewriter. What my students teasingly called "the olden days."

I discovered the truth of Dr. Gable's beliefs when I was eight-years-old, years before Dr. Gable and I would ever meet. It happened the day I scribbled "There is no Santa" on the last page of my school notebook. Almost immediately, I looked over my shoulder, hoping no one had seen me write it, and tore out the page and crumbled it up. I felt as if I'd committed sacrilege.

But sometime later I wrote it again—"There is no Santa." This time more carefully, with better penmanship. I realized that I'd written what I believed; written what I knew to be true.

Writing it down—"There is no Santa"—could not suppress the feeling of sadness that rooted me to my chair. *I've lost Santa,* I thought. Only later did I tell myself that I couldn't lose something that never existed.

In fact, that's what I told myself decades later when I sat at my computer and tapped out the message, "There is no God." That same sadness filled me once again. *No Santa? No God?*

Over the years, I've learned that life is simply a process of subtraction. The longer we live, the more we subtract, until one day all of us are reduced to zeros. By age eight, I'd lost Santa—and the Tooth Fairy and the Easter Bunny. Somewhere around age fifty, I lost God. And about four years ago, I lost my belief that "law" equaled "justice."

It's not as if I hadn't been warned. When I was in my thirties, my friend, Jack Dunnigan, told me that "law" and "justice" were not the same thing at all. He couldn't have said it more clearly or concisely.

Jack had just passed the Washington State bar exam, and all his friends were gathered together celebrating his achievement.

I raised a glass to toast his success. "To Jack," I said, "who will be fighting for truth, justice, and the American way."

Everyone laughed, realizing that I'd just plagiarized the catchphrase from the television show, *The Adventures of Superman.*

"Please, please," Jack said, as we all laughed and applauded. "I'm not Superman. I may act like it sometimes...but no one will ever mistake me for mild-mannered Clark Kent." More laughter. "I'm just a simple lawyer interested only in arguing the law."

"Well," I asked, "isn't the law the same as justice?"

Jack hesitated, always a stickler for exactitude. "Sometimes law and justice align, Frank," he said in a provisional tone of voice. "But only just sometimes."

I should have heeded Jack's cryptic comment. But I didn't. It was a party, I was a bit tipsy, and I was young—well, much younger than I am now—and hopelessly naïve. I believed they were the same.

Some delusions—like the law being interested in justice—die harder than others. My belief that the law was interested in "justice for all" is my most recent subtraction. One that saddens me more than losing Santa or God.

The week after our trees fell, as soon as the most urgent repairs were under way, and shortly after I visited Serrene Homes to see if reasonable people could reach a reasonable settlement, Isabel and I contacted a lawyer—but it proved to be a useless attempt to get justice.

"The law is on their side," our lawyer told us.

"But the law is unjust," we replied.

"Some laws are like that," was our lawyer's sympathetic, but pathetic, comment. "Pursuing this lawsuit is a dead end." It took four months and ten thousand dollars to realize the truth of what he said.

Apparently, the law permits developers to cut the roots of trees on neighboring properties if they are under the soil on the developer's side of the fence, unless those neighbors know to secure protections for their trees. The developer doesn't have to consider the consequences to the health or stability of trees on neighboring properties. Six-inch holding roots and heritage trees be damned.

Those were *our* trees...*our* belongings...*our* lives. I'm left to wonder if there would have been any consequences if the trees had killed us in our bedroom instead of Miss Aria.

Isabel and I have done our best to put our lives back together. The shed is rebuilt. The roof and master bedroom repaired. All the debris removed. And insurance paid for a lot of it.

But you can't rebuild tall, tall trees—the ones that brush the sky with their topmost branches.

You can't wave away the nightmares or restore peace of mind.

And you can't rebuild a dog—there is no canine resurrection. What price tag can you ever put on the death of an animal who has stolen your heart?

Adding insult to injury, if Isabel and I had undertaken the cutting of the five trees that fell in that wind storm—that is, if we'd cut down our own trees simply because we wanted to—we would have been subject to fines exceeding $150,000. The penalty for cutting a tree without permission in Snoquamish is $1,500 per diameter inch.

That's if *we* had cut the trees. But, when a third party is developing adjacent lands to build new homes for homeowners—homeowners who will enrich the city coffers—the trees on our property can fall without consequence.

That is, without consequence to the developer. Or to the city.

Only Isabel and I suffered the losses and the consequences.

I think that's when we had our epiphany. Isabel and I concluded we would no longer play by a set of rules written by and for the power players. After that infuriating encounter on our front deck with the police, we decided to be proactive.

Remember the question I asked earlier? Let me ask it again. Could you be friends with someone who has taken the lives of three people?

Isabel and I are reasonably average citizens who, in the past, occasionally scanned the headlines and wondered over our coffee and scones how anyone could commit murder.

But our wondering ceased when we found ourselves abandoned by the normal agencies of justice. When justice, in even the smallest measure, was denied. All legal pathways were closed. We needed an extralegal remedy.

In the end, our pathway through destruction, pain, and loss ended with murder.

It was an utterly unconventional destination that surprised us both.

Reading the newspaper articles about three murdered individuals or watching television coverage and listening to the broadcasters talk about the terrible tragedy of their deaths—and the mystery that still surrounds them—is disconcerting. I want to let them hear the voices inside my head.

Cause and effect! Our trees' roots were deliberately cut. Our trees fell. Our property was destroyed. We could have been killed. Our dog WAS killed! And yes, the law allows it.

Any number of friends have offered their sympathy and commiserations. "This isn't right." *We know.* "There should be consequences." *We agree.* "Well, if that's the law, there's nothing you can do."

I'm sure our friends thought we should simply forgive everyone and move on.

I must admit, I've struggled with that advice. I've searched my heart to see if forgiveness was possible, probably because both my religion and my literary background spoke eloquently about forgiveness. Every high school English teacher I've ever known has dealt with the concepts of forgiveness and redemption during discussion of the great literary works.

Consider forgiveness.

Shortly after Aria's death, a former high school colleague, who was also a dog-lover, called me to express his condolences. Soon after that phone call, I received a letter from him. I'm sure he'd written because, when he phoned me, I was angry. He'd heard the bitterness in my voice—a bitterness he could not assuage—and decided to use our shared literature background to help me heal. His letter began:

Dear Frank,
To err is human, to forgive, divine.

I appreciated that he reached out that way—it was such an English teacher thing to do. *To err is human* is probably Alexander Pope's most famous, oft-quoted poetic line.

Interestingly, I remember one surprising classroom discussion revolving around Pope's declaration that, *to forgive [is] divine.* You can only imagine my surprise when one of my students asked me, "Isn't vengeance equally divine?"

"What do you mean?" I asked.

"Well, the pastor at my church is forever talking about how we must forgive those who have wronged us. I get that—at least I think I do. I suppose it depends on what kind of wrong it is. And Pope is saying that to forgive is divine. Alright. Forgiveness is what God does, right? Well, if forgiveness is God's thing—and we're all expected to do what God would do and forgive—why was there ever a Sodom and Gomorrah? Or Noah's Flood? Why is there a Hell? Why would God need a Hell if everyone is forgiven?"

Whenever my English class became a theology session, I always fell back on my Catholic school upbringing. I realized that discussing divine wrath—the expulsion from the Garden, Sodom and Gomorrah, the Flood, the plagues visited on Egypt, all those Old Testament blockbuster moments—was above my pay grade. Instead, I wanted to make this discussion more human, more humane.

"I think all God wants is that those who wrong us take responsibility for wronging us, and ask for our forgiveness. We forgive when those who cause us harm show us they are contrite—that they feel responsible for what they've done—when they acknowledge their guilt."

"What happens, Mr. Hannigan, if they don't show contrition or acknowledge their guilt?" my student asked.

I was stumped. I shrugged, and said, "I don't really know." That was true. I didn't know. Not then.

But I do now.

Serrene Homes hadn't shown any contrition, hadn't asked for forgiveness. They hadn't even expressed any sympathy.

But now I know the answer to that student's question. I'm not happy with the answer, and perhaps I'm now in need of redemption.

When friends suggest we *move on and forgive*, or tell us, *There's nothing you can do,* we listen patiently. Even as we pretend to agree with their point of view, the voice in my head calmly declares, *Yes, there is.*

We hear them cautioning us, "You can't take the law into your own hands. People who do that are vigilantes."

Vigilantes? No. Wrong word. Neither Isabel nor I know what the right word is, but it's not vigilante.

Truthfully, our new role doesn't need a name, because we never intended to take the law into our own hands. Taking the law into our own hands—like the bad law that victimized us—just makes our hands dirty. We wanted no part of any law that permits the perpetration of an injustice.

So we never took the law into our own hands—we took justice into our own hands. That's a very different thing.

Most recently, it's the developers who've experienced tragedy. Where once the developers could laugh and avoid responsibility for the misfortune they caused us, now we have some old-style satisfaction in rebalancing the scales of justice. As I said, the distance between comedy and tragedy is infinitesimally small.

When we listen to the news, we occasionally hear some pundit spouting that "We are a country of laws." And I reflexively sneer, *Right, a country of laws, some of them bad. What are we supposed to do when confronted with laws that deny justice or permit injustice?*

Isabel and I have our own answer to that question.

We don't expect everyone to like our answer.

So this is the story of a married couple that I believe you might like to know, perhaps even have dinner with. They could easily be your friends.

The woman is my wife, Isabel Comstock, and the man is me, Frank Hannigan. She's an accountant, and I'm a retired English teacher and publishing consultant—she's eleven years younger than me. We live on a little piece of heaven that Isabel named Wutherwood long before I arrived.

Until recently, we were two good, even exemplary, citizens. In fact, we were more than that. We were two good, and even exemplary, human beings, who were proud to be our brother's keeper, as well as keeper to dogs and cats, and the numerous creatures that dwell outdoors.

Then we lost our dog, our master bedroom, our shed, and five irreplaceable trees...and our peace of mind. And everyone told us there was nothing to be done.

The emerging theme from friends, developers, city planners, and anyone willing to give us an audience seemed to be, *What happened was an accident. It's nobody's fault.*

But they're wrong. This man-made tragedy wasn't an accident.

I recently commented to Isabel, "When needless tragedy strikes, you can't always see what people lose."

Isabel agreed.

Isabel and I decided we could NOT do nothing. Doing nothing would be surrendering to injustice.

This is the story about the ineffable somethings we lost that November day. We lost many things besides our trees, our shed, and our dog. We lost our belief in the law, our sense of community, our innocence.

This is the story of the path we took to restore our devastated psychological equilibrium.

This is the story of the *next* somethings that we did. The somethings that didn't have to happen.

But did.

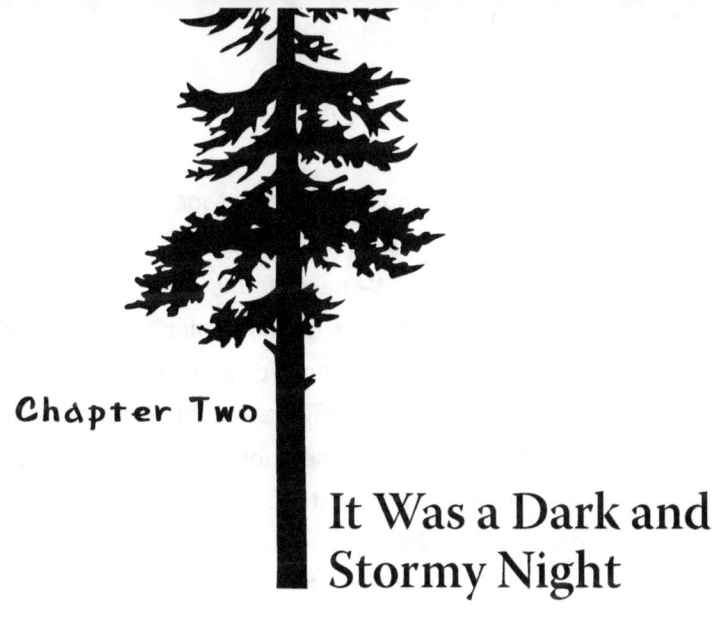

Chapter Two

It Was a Dark and Stormy Night

Frank Hannigan
December 2018

Around noon the police came to our front door. Isabel and I were alerted because our security system worked as designed. It barked.

We have an ever-alert, three-dog security system which erupts into relentless barking when anyone approaches our home. Isabel calls it our barkophony. The dogs don't settle down until the stranger is identified as a familiar friend, or proves to be someone we need to talk with, or is revealed as a delivery person—who usually dashes off the deck as quickly as possible.

We take a great deal of comfort knowing no wise person would ever think of entering our home without an invitation. Fools approach at their peril.

As I reflect on this moment, I recall thinking nothing of the police cruiser I'd seen from my office window a few moments earlier. It was moving slowly down our unpaved lane. No siren. No flashing lights. Nothing to grab my attention.

A few weeks earlier there had been some kind of disturbance at one of our neighbors. Isabel and I had been at the theatre that evening, but our next-door neighbor, Annette, reported she'd seen three police cars in the neighbor's driveway just as dusk faded to dark. Annette didn't know why the police were there. We never found out.

When our dogs erupted in their full-alert mode, I walked to the front door, pulled it open, and pushed open the storm door the slightest bit. Two Snoquamish police officers—a woman and a man—stood on our deck a few steps back from the door. The female officer held a small envelope, and her male partner stood just behind her shoulder with his thumbs hooked over his belt.

My dogs crowded in the small niche at our front door, pushing me from behind. Barking frantically at the police, the dogs wanted to run outside, but I wasn't going to let them get near anyone with a gun. I think the officers were introducing themselves, but as Wolfie's threatening bass blended with Luigi's soprano yip, I could barely hear a single word.

"Excuse, me, officers. I'll be with you in a minute," I said as loudly as I could. "I'm going to put my dogs in the garage."

It took just a few moments, while the dogs eagerly followed me into the garage where Isabel and I kept their treats. But this wasn't a time for treats. I returned to the front door.

Once again, I pushed the storm door open a few inches. I apologized. "Sorry, officers, we can talk now."

"Could you please step outside, sir?" the female officer asked. "We'd like to ask you a few questions."

"Could I step outside?" I said, deliberately repeating her question, and remembering my last encounter with the local police. I gave her question some thought and replied, "No, ma'am. I could, but I won't."

They had come to my home for some unknown reason, so I decided to ask, "What's the problem, officers?"

"We'd like you to please step outside, sir," she repeated calmly.

I've often wondered if a police officer's calm insistence, that you do what you just said you wouldn't do, has to do with the exercise of power and control.

"I heard you, officer." I spoke politely. "Perhaps you didn't hear my reply to your request, officer. I said, 'No.' I thought I'd said that clearly, but apparently I didn't. Let *me* repeat *my* question. What's the problem, officers?"

She took a moment to evaluate what was going on. "I don't understand your reluctance to come outside," the officer said in a level tone.

"And I don't understand your reluctance to converse where we are," I replied. "I'm quite happy talking to you from here. Besides, it's a bit chilly outside—and I'd really rather not have you come in."

I pulled the storm door shut and locked it to emphasize my refusal to join them out on the deck. Then I lowered the storm door's upper window pane so we could more easily talk through the screen—the chill December air immediately hit my face.

"Let me ask you again. What's the problem, officers?" I stood behind the screen and folded my arms against the cold. I watched the two officers trade glances. Clearly the female officer was in charge.

"Are you Frank Hannigan?" she asked.

"Is that a relevant question?"

"I'm simply trying to ascertain who you are."

"And I'm trying to ascertain why you're here."

Silence descended for just a brief moment.

"Are you Frank Hannigan?" she repeated.

"I'm the man who answered this door when my dogs alerted me that someone had arrived. That's who I am."

I could hear my favorite canine trio—Wolfie, Luigi, and Jackson—barking in the garage.

"Are you Frank Hannigan?"

"Is Frank in some kind of trouble?"

"I just want to know if you are Frank Hannigan."

"I understand that. You want to know my name. You also want me to come out on the deck. Three times now I've asked if there's a problem...I suppose that's four times now, isn't it? I also asked if Frank—whoever he may be—is in some kind of trouble."

Neither officer spoke.

"It seems none of us is any good at answering the other's questions," I said before lapsing into silence.

"May I see some ID, sir?" This female officer was nothing if not persistent.

"Why?" I asked. *Why should I have to identify myself to anyone except my wife when I'm in my own home?*

"I'd like to see some ID, if I may," she said. Her tone was flat, direct, and unemotional, but I could see her colleague working himself into a lather.

"No, officer, you may not. For the moment, my identification seems quite unnecessary. I am in my home, on my property, with two uninvited police officers standing on my front deck. Besides, I don't have my ID on my person, and I have no intention of fetching it for you. If you'd like to call me something other than 'sir,' you may call me 'Mr. Anonymous.'"

The male officer stepped over to his colleague and whispered something in her ear.

I felt an impish impulse.

"Officer," I said, directing my comment at him while wagging my finger in parental disapproval, "Officer, no private conversations on my front deck," I said. "Would you care to whisper confidentially in my ear, too?"

His eyes darkened. He looked irked, but I couldn't be sure.

I looked directly at the female officer. "Look, officer, either tell me why you are here, or I'll bid you both a good day and close my front door. I don't like paying to heat the outdoors."

We stared briefly at one another. As I stepped back and began closing the door, she suddenly spoke up.

"Sir, a boy has gone missing," said the female officer, pulling a folded piece of paper from the small manila envelope she was carrying. She held up the paper. "This boy. We're going door-to-door and asking everyone in your neighborhood and other nearby neighborhoods if they've seen this young man."

She approached the door offering to hand the piece of paper to me. I wasn't going to open the door.

"Please hold it closer so I can see it," I said.

She pressed the paper against the screen. Two color photographs filled the 8½ x 11 sheet of paper. The picture on the left was clearly a school photo. A young man with a thick, bushy, red mane, looking pensive, probably posing for his senior yearbook picture. The other was a casual photo of a smiling boy in profile—dressed in full football pads, his red hair disheveled, and his helmet dangling from his right hand. He wore a Snoquamish Catholic jersey with the number 82 on the sleeve. The bottom of the page explained that he was eighteen years old, six feet two inches tall, and 195 pounds.

"Who's the wide receiver?" I asked.

"What?" asked the female officer.

"Are you a football fan?" I asked.

"Not really," she admitted.

"Well, any boy playing football at that height and weight and wearing number 82 is an end. Probably an offensive end. I'm guessing he's a wide receiver. So, who is he?"

"He's the missing boy," piped up the male officer, his impatience clearly on display.

"I didn't ask *what* he is," I said, "I asked *who* he is. You do understand the difference, don't you?"

Mister Officer cocked his head to one side, his face radiating annoyance.

The female officer spoke up. "Jacob Forrest. The missing boy is Jacob Forrest, a senior at Snoquamish Catholic. He's your neighbor. He lives in the subdivision just behind your home."

"Okay," I said nonchalantly. I looked intently at the two photos. "Don't know him," I said. "Runaway, maybe?"

"We don't know. Our job is to find him," said the female officer, explaining the obvious.

"How long has he been missing?"

"His parents don't remember seeing him after 11:30 p.m. this past Friday night."

"Well, I haven't seen him."

The male officer stepped closer to my locked storm door.

"Is that 'haven't seen him lately' or 'haven't seen him ever'?"

There was that tone again—the tone and demeanor that kept me from joining them in friendly conversation on my front deck, as I might have done in years gone by. I was tempted to ask the female officer how often she let her partner off his leash, but I surmised that wouldn't be helpful. I took a deep breath.

"We try not to have anything to do with the folk in Hemlock Hill—that's the subdivision behind us." I motioned with my head.

"But you did have words with Mr. Forrest this past Saturday morning, didn't you? Jacob's dad? He said he came to your door to ask about his son and that you were rude to him."

I stood there silently. I wasn't inclined to answer any of this man's questions.

"You did talk to him, didn't you?"

"Him who? I don't have the foggiest notion who I talked to. Some tall, red-headed man in a blue windbreaker came to my door around ten Saturday morning. I was watching a soccer match on television when my dogs alerted me that someone was at my front door. I answered the door, but I could barely hear what he was saying until I stepped outside. He said he lived in the house nearest my fence. Over in Hemlock Hill."

"And you talked with him?"

"Not really, I don't talk to people from Hemlock Hill."

"Why not?"

"Long story. Besides, it's none of your business." I was tempted to unload all my pent-up feelings about Hemlock Hill—a place they could just as easily have named Treeless Slope.

Wouldn't that be a great name for a subdivision? I thought. *They should have named it Treeless Slope, which is what it really is.*

"Did he say what he wanted?" the male officer persisted.

"Yeah. He wanted to know if I'd seen his son late Friday night."

"What did you say?"

"You can ask him."

"I'm asking you."

"Well, apparently he's already told you I was 'rude' to him. So let's leave it at that. Barely a single word has passed between us and our *neighbors* in Hemlock Hill. We like it that way."

I freighted the word "neighbors" with sarcasm.

"That goddamn development has been a thorn in our side since the day developers decided that parcel of acreage really needed two dozen new homes. And there it stands," I said pointing out my back window. I paused, mulling over what to say next. "We decided that if they left us alone, we'd leave them alone. We don't consider them neighbors. It takes more than proximity to call someone a neighbor."

"Is that the way things are? Right now?" the female officer asked.

"Pretty much."

The lead officer glanced at her partner. As she folded the photograph, she said, "Mr. Forrest mentioned that you accused his son of stealing wine from your shed. Did you do that?"

"No, officer, I did not."

My mind was racing in another direction entirely.

I should have told this Mr. Forrest his son was a wine-stealing, foul-mouthed teenager who decided he'd rather shoot me than sign a confession. I should have told him I was about to give his son the gift of a lifetime before he came back and threatened me with a pistol. I should have told him the last time I saw his son, he was soaking wet and completely dead.

"Even if I had seen his son, officer," I explained, "I wouldn't know who I was seeing, would I? He didn't have a photo. He described his son as a tall, redheaded, high school senior. That's when I asked Mr. Forrest if it were possible that his son might be the person stealing wine from my shed."

"What did he say?"

"He got all defensive. Told me there was no way his son could be a thief. So I told him I was overjoyed to hear that his son was such an angel."

"Then what happened?"

"Nothing. He just scowled at me, and said, 'They told me you'd be a lousy neighbor,' and stormed off. That's when I said something rude."

"What did you say?"

"I'd rather not say," I said.

A moment of silence intervened.

"Do you have proof his son stole your wine?" the female officer asked.

"Do you mean, was I standing next to Mr. Forrest's son while more than a case of wine mysteriously disappeared from my shed since August? No. I wasn't. From the day we built that shed, we never locked it, and we never had to. We stored wine in it because it stays cool in there even during the summer months. For eight years, no wine ever disappeared. Never. Then Hemlock Hill is erected on our southern boundary, and bottles of wine begin disappearing. You think maybe it's a coincidence?"

Both officers seemed content to hear me out.

"My wife and I went on vacation last summer, came home, and—*voila!*—empty slots in a previously full wine rack. Six empty wine slots to be exact."

"That's not proof," said Mr. Officer Unfriendly.

"Yeah, officer," I said with as much snark as I could muster. "You are so absolutely correct. That's NOT proof. No one could be more correcter than you. I bow to you, sir. Your correctivity is undeniable."

"Why didn't you call the police?"

I stared at the officer who just asked me that question. He was young—early thirties—maybe 6'1" and physically fit. And an imbecile. Sometimes you just have to take a deep breath. This was one of those sometimes.

"Didn't you just say that I had no proof?"

"You still should have called the police."

"And say what? 'Gosh, officer, this wine rack was full when we left for vacation, and now it's missing six bottles?' That would have proven what? You'd have come here and taken a report, and that report might make you feel good, but we'd still be left empty-handed. No thanks, Officer Krupke. No thanks. Someone—probably someone from across our southern fence—has been stealing our wine."

"So you say."

"That's right. That's exactly what we say. We don't know who stole our wine, but using a process of elimination, we excluded adults and youngsters under ten-years-of-age, just on general principles. We narrowed the field of likely suspects to one particular category—teenage boys. I don't know how many teenage boys live over there, but I'm betting one of them is our wine thief."

"And now a boy is missing," said Officer Unfriendly.

"So you say."

I could tell he didn't like his own words being parroted back at him.

"Like I said, we don't have anything to do with the Hemlock Hill folk. However, when Mr. Forrest?—that's his name, right?—arrived at our front door, unexpected and uninvited on a Saturday morning, looking for his son—a teenage boy—I shared our suspicions about the missing wine."

"You keep saying 'we' and 'us.' Does anyone else live here?" Officer Unfriendly had seized on another line of questioning.

"Yes," I said, "but unless you speak dog or cat fluently, I doubt if you'd get anything out of them. They're not big on English."

"Do any other humans live here?" he asked, brushing aside my sarcasm with some of his own.

"Hmmmm," I said. I decided to be even less forthcoming. "You'll have to define exactly what you mean by 'human' and 'live here.'"

I could see that remark finally stepped on his last nerve.

"Why is it so hard to get a straight answer out of you?" he growled.

That's when Isabel came to the door.

"Hello, officers," she said in an extraordinarily calm voice. "You were asking about other humans who live here?"

"Yes, ma'am." The female officer stepped forward. "May I ask your name, ma'am?"

Isabel threw me a wicked glance—one with just a trace of a smile. "I'm Mrs. Anonymous...married to Mr. Anonymous." She looped her arm through mine. "Come on, officers. I'm sure you looked up everything about us before you even pulled into our driveway. Your computer's already given you our names. Stop playing your silly games. You know who we are."

"Did you..."

Isabel interrupted. "And no, I haven't seen the missing boy." She turned her gaze on the male officer. "Not lately...and not ever."

"What is it with you two?" the male officer asked. "A kid is missing. His parents are frantic. They're worried sick. We come here looking for a little help, and all we get is attitude."

For a moment, Isabel and I traded glances, and I wondered if I should say what had been on my mind for way too long. I surrendered to the impulse.

"You really want to know? Here it is. You're cops. You're the boys... and now the girls"—I pointed at the female officer—"in blue. Three years ago, my wife and I were Mr. and Mrs. Good Citizen. We were good guys and we thought of the cops as good guys, too. We'd gotten a few speeding tickets—who doesn't?—but the cops were good guys just like us. We all belonged to the Fraternal Order of the White Hats."

"What about the Maternal Order of the White Hats?" Isabel asked pointing at the female officer.

"Okay. We belonged to the Universal Order of the White Hats," I said to Isabel. "If people needed help, we'd help. We wanted to help whenever possible. We rescued animals; helped our neighbors; donated to charities; cooperated with the police—all the usual White Hat stuff. But three years ago, we found out that the cops had changed clubs. They'd switched over to the Universal Order of the Black Hats. Apparently, it's far more lucrative."

The police on my deck stared at me as if I were talking gibberish.

"We found out that the cops are NOT our friends; they're NOT our advocates, and they're definitely NOT interested in the concerns of private citizens. The cops—that's you two—work for the city and do the city's bidding. And the city does the bidding of the developers because it means money."

I pressed on, uninterrupted. "Three years ago, five of our one-hundred-foot tall trees hurtled to the ground when their roots were severed by the Hemlock Hill developer—you know, the guy who built the place with the missing kid. Those trees destroyed our custom-built shed, hit our home, and killed our dog. But the cops weren't at all interested in helping us. So...three years ago, we lost all respect for the cops. Now you know why we feel the way we do. As for Jacob What's-His-Face, we don't know him, and frankly, speaking for myself, I don't give a damn about where he might be. Probably drunk on our wine somewhere. He's not our problem, officers, and I won't let you make him our problem. Tell Mr. Forrest that."

"Sir, I'm sorry you had that kind of encounter..."

"Don't," I said, looking directly at Ms. Officer. "Don't even go there. We're not the least bit interested in a boilerplate, insincere, way-too-late apology. So save your breath. If the city wants to apologize, have them send us a check for $150,000. That's the cost we're assessing for the city allowing *our* trees to be cut down without *our* permission. Maybe then we'll feel differently. Three years ago, the cops weren't the least bit interested in helping us when we needed help. But here you are, knocking at our door, wanting our help and the help of all the other fine, upstanding Snoquamish citizens."

She nodded.

"Here's the thing...Officer...Officer..."

"McGuire...it's Officer McGuire."

"So here's the thing, Officer McGuire. We're no longer interested in being civic-minded. While neither of us is planning on robbing any banks, or burglarizing our neighbors, or starting a ruckus in a local bar, or even running red lights, we're sure as hell not the least bit interested in helping you or your colleague, Officer Unfriendly, or any of the nameless, faceless residents who moved into Hemlock Hill. We'd be okay if the earth opened up and swallowed them whole...and put back our trees...and gave us back our dog."

I thought I'd concluded with a tone that said, *We're done now, right?* I began closing the door.

"The neighbors behind you said they heard some muffled noise coming from your side of the fence two nights ago," said Officer Unfriendly, ignoring the finality of my tone.

I didn't respond. Nor did Isabel.

"That's what the neighbors said," Officer Unfriendly repeated. "Did you hear anything?"

"What time?" I asked.

"1:30 a.m. Maybe two."

"Two? Who the hell is up at that time of night? That's way past my bedtime, I'm afraid. And if I wasn't in bed, I was asleep on the sofa. Sorry."

"So neither of you heard anything?"

"Only his snoring," Isabel said. "He's keeps everyone up except himself."

"Very funny," I said to Isabel. I turned back to the police. "I make it a policy never to hear things when I'm asleep."

He came right up to the screen. "So you didn't hear anything?" he said, repeating his question.

I smiled at him. "How long have you had this hearing problem, officer?" I asked snidely. "I can recommend a good doctor to help with that."

The female officer could see her colleague was increasingly annoyed. She pulled him by the shoulder as she began moving off the deck. "Thank you, sir. Sorry we took your time."

"Good day, officers," I said as I began closing the door. I just couldn't resist a parting shot. "Maybe you should ask the Hemlock Hill folk what *they* meant by 'muffled noises.'"

I turned to Isabel and loudly asked, "Do you think they could hear my farts from that distance?" Then I shouted to the departing officers, "Were the muffled noises followed by a rancid smell?"

We watched as they climbed into their police cruiser. Officer Unfriendly cast several glances in our direction, and I'm sure he would have loved to flip us off. But he was in uniform. There are a few real advantages to being a civilian when confronted by the police.

I knew the police might come back—maybe later the same day. They'd want to look in my shed—look for evidence—look to see if Jacob had *ever* been in my shed. If they saw my surveillance cameras, they'd want to see the videos from Friday night. So I removed the cameras, the ones that had warned us that some larcenous teenager had picked the lock—again—and was back in our shed trying to steal wine. Isabel made certain any stored video files were erased.

That's right. We lied.

Jacob had paid us a visit two nights earlier. I didn't know his name when I first encountered him, but I knew someone had been paying visits to our property several times over the previous few months. Apparently, our wine cache—about forty-five bottles kept in our eight-year-old, now-rebuilt, custom shed—proved an irresistible temptation to at least one teenage boy.

I'd discovered the pilfering in late August after Isabel and I had taken a brief vacation to Cannon Beach, Oregon. When we returned, there were a half-dozen notably empty slots where I was certain we had put some Cabernet and Syrah one week earlier.

Neither Isabel nor I had ever felt the need to lock the shed, but that was before twenty-five new homes were built just beyond our southern fence. Where once there had been a forest of tall timber—where once birds and squirrels and deer had held court—now 25 homogenous, unexceptional, very vanilla but very large homes filled the clear-cut land. The sign on the street laughingly described them as affordable luxury homes. Affordable? With prices that began at $1.4 million?

The progression from forest to human community was both maddening and saddening. Early in the development process, the whole forest was razed. That's when our trees near the boundary line had their holding roots severed by the developer's bulldozer. That's when we called the developer, and he hung up on us. That's when we called the city planner and were ignored. That's when we asked the police for help and found they were wholly disinterested. That's when those compromised trees fell in the blink of an eye, crushing our shed, hitting our home, killing our dog, and shattering the stability of our days and nights.

The once-forested, now-barren land was graded and regraded. Pipes were laid. Underground wiring, concrete foundations, streets, and community mailboxes installed. Ever so slowly, a crammed-together community of cheek-by-jowl homes arose. Moving vans crowded the garage doors to disgorge families—with kids and pets in tow. They took possession of their new 4,000 sq. ft. homes, complete with miserly twenty-square-foot lawns. You know, the ones you can mow with a pair of scissors.

Now that families had arrived, their kids were like kids everywhere—curious and wondering what was just beyond that low chain-link fence to the north. What's on the property that has all the trees? The one with the shed? Well, the answer to the "What's beyond that fence" question was—and is—"us."

I told Isabel that the real answer to that question was, "None of their damn business," but she said that sounded too curmudgeonly.

"The people buying those homes aren't at fault for what the developer did, Frank," she said.

"Our lives and property are still none of their business. We don't have to be 'good neighbors' because Hallmark decided 'Welcome to the neighborhood' makes a great greeting card slogan. I don't plan to be a bad neighbor, but I'll be damned if I'll be a good one. The best they can hope for is that I'm an invisible neighbor. And they'd be well-advised to be as invisible as possible, too."

Isabel and I had lived happily together for more than a decade on our side of the fence—on our one acre of timbered, blackberry-bramble-occupied heaven. Isabel had moved in 15 years before I arrived. Our home, and the area we keep mown, comprises about half the property. The other half belongs strictly to nature and the wildlife—the rabbits, squirrels, birds, owls, deer, coyotes, and the occasional bear—whose nearby habitat was sacrificed for "affordable housing."

We love our acre and so do our dogs. They wear collars that respond to an invisible fence that runs around our property's perimeter. It keeps them safely on our acre.

I'd love to put an invisible fence perimeter around Hemlock Hill, and give their kids collars that would zap them whenever they decided to investigate anything on our side of the fence. Nothing fatal, just a reminder. But we can't.

So, when wine began disappearing, we started locking the shed. I suppose we could have moved all our wine into the house—no one would ever dare enter our house when they heard the threatening vocalizations produced by our trio of dogs—but why should we?

Then one night, someone picked the shed's lock. Picking locks may be the regular stuff of cop dramas on television, but it was a real first for our backyard. Another four bottles of wine disappeared. Nothing else. No garden implements. No holiday decorations—no wreaths or garlands or ceramic villages. Just wine.

A friend suggested I get a dye that I could paint on the necks of my bottles, so when someone handles the bottle, that person's skin turns a bright blue. That was a non-starter because I wasn't interested in turning my own hands bright blue, too.

Again, I considered moving all the wine into the house, but I wasn't ready to capitulate.

I refuse to surrender to a thief, I thought. *I want to catch this clever thief bold enough to pick the lock on our shed. I want him to feel caught.*

Finally, I consulted with a security company. They recommended battery-powered, motion-activated, remote cameras. Whenever those cameras were activated, an alarm would sound, and my cellphone would emit a distinctive tone. Activities in the shed would be recorded—audio and video. Now, if someone picked the lock, we would know and be watching.

That's how I met Jacob, face-to-face on a dark, chilly, rainy Friday night in December. Isabel and I were watching the 11:00 news in the family room when my phone's alarm went off. The phone said it was 11:06.

"Someone's in the shed," I said to Isabel as I stood up and moved to the kitchen. "My phone just buzzed me."

"The shed's locked, isn't it?"

"Yeah, it's locked. But someone's in there. Locking the shed didn't keep our Thanksgiving thieves out two weeks ago. Could be our thief picked the lock again."

"What do you want to do?"

I heard the worry in her voice.

I cautioned her to be quiet, putting my finger to my lips, while I opened the kitchen drawer where we'd begun keeping Isabel's pistol.

"I'm going out there. Keep your phone ready to call 911, okay?"

I quietly scooted out the front door. The dogs wanted to follow me out but Isabel did her utmost to keep them quiet.

"Shush," she whispered. "Stay."

The dogs quieted down.

As I closed the front door, I heard her say in a loud whisper. "Be careful, Frank."

I quickly crossed the front deck and moved around the east side of the house to the backyard, keeping in the shadows. I avoided the west side because we have an action light that would alert anyone in our backyard.

Fortunately, it was a typical Northwest December night, a cloudy, drizzly evening—quite dark except for some spill from one of the Hemlock Hill streetlamps a hundred feet away.

As I moved across my back lawn, I saw a dark figure, silhouetted by the distant streetlamp, emerging from our shed, his arms laden with what appeared to be wine bottles. Isabel's gun felt cold in my hand, and I scolded myself for not wearing gloves.

I spoke from the shadow of the Hawthorne bushes to the stranger standing on my shed's porch barely ten feet away.

"I see you managed to pick the lock, again."

My voice surprised him. Whoever it was suddenly stood stock still. From the glow of the streetlight beyond the fence, I could see the chiseled features of a teenage boy's face. Yeah. A teenage boy wearing a hooded sweatshirt, his arms gathered to his chest.

"Don't move," I said. "I have a .45 caliber pistol pointed right at you. I'd hate to shoot those bottles of wine you're cradling in your arms."

A young man's voice growled his disbelief. "You're bluffing. It's dark. You don't have a gun."

"You may be right." I moved out of the shadows directly in front of him. I chambered a round, and nothing sounds as ominous in the dreary black night as the steely slide and clunk of a chambered round.

"But I don't think you want to bet your life on that," I said.

The glint of something metallic in my hand quieted his surly response.

"What do you want?" he asked sullenly.

I motioned for him to walk toward me—away from the shed and toward my house, putting the shed between us and Hemlock Hill. I wanted to be sure no homeowners from his side of the fence would be able to see anything, even on this dark, rainy, December night.

"Looks like you've got your arms full, my unknown thief," I said. "I want you to kneel down. Slowly. I don't want any broken bottles."

He stood ten feet away, unmoving, his wine-filled arms still drawn to his chest.

What's going on in this young man's mind? I can't say. He can see the pistol. He knows I have a gun.

Was he wondering if I'd actually shoot if he started running away? Was he wondering if I had lousy aim? Was he wondering if he could simply overpower me? He was over six feet tall and appeared to have an athletic build, so I decided to keep my distance.

"Let me repeat, young man. Get down on your knees. And gently place those bottles on the ground."

"Okay, okay," he said, dropping to his knees. He sounded annoyed. Although he was wearing a dark hoodie and jeans, he wasn't dressed to be kneeling in wet grass in cold, rainy weather.

Almost as soon as his knees touched down, he whined, "Shit, old man, this grass is soaking wet...and freezing."

"That's too bad. Maybe you should pick better weather before you decide to steal my wine. Count yourself lucky you're not kneeling in a pile of dog shit."

Only the susurration of steady rain broke the silence. The kneeling young man shifted his weight from one cold wet knee to the other.

"Are you waiting for me to ask you again to put my wine bottles down?"

"Okay. I'm freezing. Give me a fucking break."

"Should I say 'pretty please?" I asked.

"Alright, Jesus, alright. I'm putting the bottles down, alright?"

He unloaded his arms and then struggled as he pulled several bottles from beneath his hoodie. Altogether, he'd taken eight bottles. I counted them as he placed each one carefully on the ground.

"Move back, away from the bottles," I said, motioning him to back up. "And stay on your knees."

I moved a bit closer to get a glimpse of what he'd taken.

"Wow! That's quite a haul. Were you planning to drink it all yourself or were you planning to sell some of my exquisite wine to your teenage friends who don't have a neighbor with dozens of bottles of wine in a nearby shed? One with a lock you know how to pick."

He didn't utter a word.

"You have a name?"

He maintained his stoic silence, shivering as he knelt in the rain, his arms wrapped around himself.

"Are you the one who's been stealing wine from my shed since summer?"

He didn't answer.

"You're going to tell me what I want to know," I assured him. "Sooner or later, you'll be too wet and too cold to keep quiet. You know that, don't you?"

He still didn't respond. He was a determined young man.

"I've got all night, kid. Even better, I'm retired. You can keep quiet for as long as you want. If I get uncomfortable, I'll just ask my wife to bring me a big, comfy blanket and umbrella. We'll tag team you until you decide to tell me what I want to know…or until you catch pneumonia. Your choice. Trust me when I tell you, it's either answer my questions now and go home, or get arrested for theft when I decide to call the police."

"Jesus Christ, old man. I put all your bottles on the ground. Just like you asked. Okay? Can I get up now? I'm freezing," he said.

"That's what I'm counting on. But you're going to stay there until I get answers to my questions. Until that happens, you're not going home or anywhere else. If you move, I'm afraid this gun will go off. I'll just be following those handy *Stand Your Ground* laws."

He didn't respond.

"Unless you'd rather I just call the police now…?"

"Come on. You don't have to do that."

"No, I don't, but everything now depends on you. Let's start with you raising your hands as high above your head as you can."

"Raise my hands?" asked my thief. "Christ almighty, I'm freezing."

"That's a shame. You're going to keep freezing until I get what I want. Now, get your hands up."

"Or what?"

"Wow. You're just a bundle of hostility and noncompliance, aren't you? Let's start again. What's your name?"

"None of your goddamn business."

"Okay, Mr. None of My Goddamn Business. That's what I'll call you. Okay?"

"I don't have to tell you anything."

"No, you don't. You have the right to remain silent even though those bottles of wine—my bottles of wine—are shouting, 'Look, everyone! Here's my fingerprints!' I bet your fingerprints are all over my wine rack, too. And my shed. Am I right?"

I have to hand it to this kid. He's stubborn. A freezing, teeth-chattering mute.

"You don't have to tell me anything," I said. "But here's how the police are going to see it: Your fingerprints are all over my wine bottles. It's a dark and stormy night. I confronted you. There was no way I could know you weren't armed. But here you are with your gangsta hoodie, in my backyard, with your arms loaded with my wine. You threw the wine on the ground, I became frightened for my life, and I shot you in a fit of panic. I was so scared I emptied a whole clip into your chest."

Light from the distant streetlamp clearly glinted off the barrel of my pistol. He could see it was no imaginary gun.

"Now, for the last time, raise your hands."

As the rain picked up, he raised his hands. He was completely soaked. "I'm freezing my ass off in this rain, old man," he said. "I'm standing up."

"Nope. Standing up will be the last thing you ever do. Understand?"

I decided it was unwise for me to mention that I'd never shot a pistol before.

"I don't care where the first bullet hits you. After this old man empties the entire eight-shot clip into you, I'm pretty sure you'll be plenty dead. I don't think that's what either of us wants."

"What the hell do you want?" I could hear the anger in his shivering voice. "You got your wine back, didn't you?"

"Yeah, I did. But I want to make sure you don't come waltzing back here when we're gone. So, I need some solid information."

"Like what?"

"Name?"

There was a brief pause.

"Jacob," he said.

"Can you prove that?"

"What? That my name is Jacob?"

"How do I know you're not a Josh or a Jed?"

"'Cause my name is Jacob."

"Prove it," I said. "Give me your driver's license. And before you give me a ration of crap, Jacob...you'll stay right where you are until I have that proof. Once I get that, I'll consider letting you change your posture. I want your wallet."

"I bet that gun isn't even loaded." He was visibly shivering.

"Really?" I asked.

I thought a brief demonstration would move things along. I ejected an unspent bullet onto the grass, picked it up, and held it out in the palm of my hand. The distant light glimmered off the metal casing.

"I'll trade you, Jacob. This bullet for your wallet."

"This is an unlawful search and seizure."

"Imagine that. An educated thief demanding his Fourth Amendment rights. Good for you. Did you learn that in school?"

He didn't seem inclined to answer my question.

"Don't worry, Jacob. It is Jacob, right? You can sue me in federal court for denying you your Fourth Amendment rights. Your wallet, please."

"It's in the pocket of my hoodie." He reached in the deep hoodie pocket and retrieved his wallet. He threw it at me.

"This makes you a thief," he growled. "You've just committed a felony."

"Oh, my. Do you have something against robbery? I've always thought a little larceny is good for the soul. Haven't you heard? Or is breaking into my shed and stealing my wine a different category of larceny?"

He returned to his sullen silence.

"Now your cellphone."

"I don't have a cellphone."

"Of course, you don't," I said with all the sarcasm I could muster. "A teenage boy out on a cold, rainy, December night, and you don't have a cellphone. Right. Let me repeat: I want your cellphone. Toss it gently in my direction."

He found his cellphone in his hoodie pocket, too. He tossed it toward me, and I snatched it up as it hit the wet grass.

"Thank you, Jacob. Now here's what's going to happen. You're going home. I'm keeping your wallet and cellphone until you come back tomorrow morning. Let's say around ten? I'll be photocopying everything in your wallet. Your license. Your credit cards. Everything. Knock on our front door when you come by. The dogs will alert us, but we'll be expecting you. I'll get you a cup of coffee and have you sign a confession about what happened here tonight, and about the wine you've previously stolen. After I have what I need, I'll give you your wallet and cellphone back, and we'll all go back to living our lives. The police won't be involved at all. Unless of course, my wine begins disappearing again."

"Can I stand up? Jesus, I'm so damn cold."

I stepped back a few more feet.

"Stand up. Go, ahead. Stand up. Now when are you coming by tomorrow?"

"Ten o'clock."

"Very good. And how do you like your coffee? Black?

"Stop fucking with me. I'll show up at ten."

"That's right, Jacob. You do as I ask or you're screwed. I caught you in the act of stealing my wine. I've got you on video breaking into my shed and walking out with the evidence. I don't want to involve the police— and I don't think you do either. I don't think you want to risk an arrest record. You get a felony on your record, you can kiss getting into a good college good-bye."

It was dark, but I could feel the heat of his anger radiating.

"You don't have video." Jacob grumbled, but his bravado was slipping.

"That's another bet you'd lose, Jacob. How do you think I knew you were out here? Modern technology. I saw you stealing our wine and I came out to stop you."

"You won't get away with this shit, old man," Jacob growled. "My father's a lawyer—a defense attorney. He doesn't take shit from anybody. You're gonna regret this. My father will make sure you spend the rest of your life in prison."

"The rest of my life? For what? Robbing you while you were robbing me? Is that right? You know, Jacob, I'm really getting tired of you. You decide to steal from me—to take what doesn't belong to you—and now that you're caught, you decide you can threaten me. You want to hear a real threat?" I lowered my voice into a threatening whisper. "What if I just post the video of you in my shed on Facebook with a simple narrative? 'Teenage Burglar Caught in the Act.' I'll use your name, too. Ain't modern technology grand?"

We stood silently in the cold rain.

Then Jacob mumbled, "I'm cold." It was practically a whisper.

"We're almost done. Let's see what we've got in here," I said. I opened Jacob's wallet. I saw a driver's license, a Snoquamish Catholic HS ID card. It was too dark to read any of the smaller print. There was also quite a bit of cash.

"There's $620.00 in my wallet. It better be there when I come back tomorrow morning."

"Oh, Jacob. I'm so disappointed that a good Catholic boy—like you—thinks I'm a thief."

"You don't know shit about ne."

"Maybe. Maybe not. Let's see what I do know. You live in Hemlock Hill. You are a student at Snoquamish Catholic. I'm guessing you're seventeen or eighteen years old. You are a thief carrying $620.00. Is this money all yours? And you need to go to confession for stealing wine that doesn't belong to you. How'm I doin'?"

"Fuck you," Jacob said.

"Really? I also know your mother would probably be disappointed with your foul mouth. A good Catholic boy like you? Cursing?"

"Fuck you."

"You should try expanding your vocabulary a bit, Jacob. You'll need to add cursing to your growing list of sins when you go to confession." I made the sign of the cross in the hopes of amusing Jacob, at least a little.

I suddenly felt terribly tired.

"Go home, Jacob. Get warm. I'll see you tomorrow morning. Ten o'clock. If I don't see you by eleven, I go to the police. They won't have any doubt when I hand them your wallet, cellphone, and show them the video. Not only that, I'll make sure you're a star on Facebook."

Jacob didn't waste a moment. He turned and loped stiffly to the rear of our property and hopped across the low fence that defined the boundary between Hemlock Hill and us. It was clear that the cold affected his mobility.

I returned my wine to the rack in the shed, pulled the shed door closed, and went into the house to dry off and warm up.

Isabel had been watching the two of us from the darkness of our dining room bay window. She'd caught a few words, but the rain and the distance hadn't allowed her to hear much.

As I walked in the door, she offered me a towel as I handed her Jacob's wallet and cellphone. I toweled my face and hair as we sat down at the kitchen table.

"I want to make copies of everything in his wallet. His license, his school ID. Everything. He's coming by tomorrow morning at ten to retrieve his things. I told him I'd give him everything back if he signs a confession. If not, I go to the police with his wallet, his cellphone, and the uploaded video of him breaking into our shed."

"Does 'he' have a name?" Isabel asked as she opened Jacob's wallet.

"Oh, sorry. He said his name is Jacob. Check his driver's license. Is his name really Jacob?"

"Yep." She pulled out his Washington State license. "Jacob Grosvenor Forrest—that's forest with two r's."

She pushed the license across the table for me to inspect, as she continued looking through his wallet.

"Oooooh," she said in a mock swooning girlish tone. "Lookey here, he's got a bunch of hundreds in here."

She pulled the cash out and spread the bills on the table.

"Count it, Isabel. He said he had $620.00. That's quite a bit of cash for a high school student."

I watched Isabel count the money. "He's off by a dollar. He's got $621.00."

"We'll just tell him that's the interest he made on his money overnight."

We were asleep—well, I was asleep—when my phone beeped another alert. It's not a noisy tone, but any tone at all tends to wake Isabel. Her difficulty in falling asleep is superseded only by her inability to remain asleep.

"What's that?" she asked.

"It's the surveillance cameras in the shed."

I rolled out of bed and walked to the bedroom window. My phone said it was 1:23 a.m.—simultaneously very late and very early.

"Maybe I didn't completely shut the shed door. I know I didn't lock it. It's windy. Still raining. If the door is swinging open, the motion sensors might pick that up."

"You don't think Jacob came back, do you?" Isabel asked.

"I doubt it. We have too much evidence already. He'd have to be a first-class jerk."

I put on my white chenille robe.

"I'll be right back. I'll zoom out, close the door, and zoom back—the rain will never touch me."

That night I discovered that I should never underestimate the irresponsible behavior of a first-class jerk.

As I stood at the sliding door to the back deck, the dogs all crowded behind me.

"Get back," I said. "Get back. I'll be right back."

I moved quickly across the sodden grass to the shed—getting wet along the way. The door was open just as I suspected. I looked inside and satisfied myself that there was no one in the shed and that all the wine was there. I stepped outside, made certain the door was locked, and began walking back to the house.

"Not so fast, old man," said a voice from the shadow of the shed.

I recognized the voice...and the "old man."

"Jacob," I said. "Shouldn't you be at home getting your beauty sleep?"

When Jacob stepped into the dim light cast by the distant streetlamp, I saw he had a pistol.

"Does your father, the lawyer, know you're out roaming the neighborhood with a gun?"

"Shut up," he said. "The shoe's on the other foot now, isn't it, old man? You forget to bring your gun? Modern technology got you out here earlier, and I knew I could rely on modern technology getting you out here again."

He was mocking me.

"What can I do for you this fine evening, Jacob?" I tried to sound confident and cool but I could feel my stomach knotting up.

"It's your turn to kneel down on the wet, freezing grass. I want to see how you like it."

He gestured with the pistol, pointing to the ground. I knelt.

"So, you came back tonight to make sure I'd get wet?" It was damn cold.

"Fuck you," he said. "I came back for my wallet and my cellphone. I want that video, too."

"Good luck with that, Jacob. It's not as if I've got your wallet and phone in my pocket. Get real. They're in the house. I don't have them on me."

"Phone your wife."

"Really? See what I'm wearing? It's called a bathrobe. Something old men wear. And when I come out to my shed in the dead of night, I don't carry my cellphone with me. I'm not like you, Jacob. I don't carry my phone everywhere, all the time. So, I can't phone her. I'll be happy to call her if you've brought another cellphone."

He was hovering over me, standing much closer to me than I ever did to him. Clearly, he was younger and stronger, and he knew it. I was wondering if he'd formulated any real plan at all—except to come back here with a gun. Perhaps he figured everything would be *ad hoc* from that point.

"Tell you what, old man," Jacob said angrily. "Call to her. Get her out here."

"She'll never hear me from here, Jacob."

"Stop using my name."

"You don't like your name? Jacob. Grosvenor. Forrest." I landed and paused on each of his names. "How'd you get Grosvenor as your middle name?"

"None of your goddamn business."

If I could keep him talking, take more time outside than I should have, Isabel might get curious.

"Jacob Grosvenor Forrest. Born on January 17th. Hey, Jacob. Quick quiz. What famous disaster happened on your birthday?"

"How the hell should I know?"

"You've studied US History, right?"

"I never found it very interesting."

"You didn't find the Los Angeles earthquake of 1994 interesting?"

Jacob just flashed me a "Who cares?" look.

Apparently not, I thought.

"Never mind," I said. I was wondering if Isabel was watching any of this from the bedroom window.

"If you want my wife to hear us, we'll have to go over to the bedroom window. She's probably still asleep. She's a heavy sleeper. She'd sleep through the Second Coming. I got up because I heard the shed's alarm go off."

He wasn't happy about it, but he gestured for me to get up and walk over to the bedroom window. I stood up and walked. The bottom of my sodden robe weighed a ton. I stopped about ten feet from the window.

"Let me go over and knock on the window. That'll wake her, okay?"

"Do it," was all he said.

I stepped forward and banged on the window. No response. I banged on it again. A minute or so later, the window slid open.

"What do you want?" asked an invisible voice. The bedroom was pitch black from the outside.

"I want my wallet, my cellphone, and that damn video deleted," demanded Jacob in a loud whisper. He stood about fifteen feet behind me in the middle of the yard. "You've got one minute to get them. One minute. I want everything, or your husband's dead. Now back up, old man."

As I backed away from the window, Jacob stepped forward and kicked me just behind my knees. I sank down to the wet grass and I could feel the barrel of his pistol pressing into my scalp.

"Clock's running," Jacob said. "Your husband will be dead in less than a minute."

Suddenly, I heard two muffled shots above my head. Jacob fell backwards. It all had happened in the blink of an eye. Literally. Jacob lay in the darkness on the cold, wet grass only an arm's length from where I was kneeling. I reached over and searched for a pulse. Isabel had always bragged that she scored well at the shooting range—and now I had proof.

"Thanks for saving my life," I whispered from the darkness.

"Happy to help. I knew that silencer would come in handy someday.

But I still ruined the screen," she said, noting the bullet holes in the mesh. "He was an even bigger first-class jerk than you thought." The shakiness in her voice betrayed her calm words.

"What the hell was he thinking?" I asked. "I was ready to give him a break. No police. No problems with his parents…"

"What do we do now? Call the police?" Isabel wondered as she pulled on her bathrobe.

"Not if I can help it. You know what kind of luck we've had with the police. We're terrorists."

I can hear the police.

You had to shoot him? Couldn't you just be happy calling the cops when this good Catholic boy had a momentary lapse in judgement? Jacob was just a kid. He had his whole life ahead of him. Stealing wine is just teenage hijinks, isn't it? Threatening you with a gun wasn't a good thing, of course, but you didn't really believe he'd shoot you, did you? Why did you feel you had to shoot him?

Suddenly, we'd be the ones in trouble. The burden of proof would be on our shoulders, against a dead kid with a lawyer father. This could turn on us in so many ways.

"If the police do come here, Isabel, the first thing they'll do is arrest us. What about our dogs and cats?"

"Good point," she said. The animals have always been our highest priority.

Feeling trapped, we made our decision.

"I don't think we'll get a lot of sleep tonight," Isabel said. "Get Jacob's pistol. Come inside and get out of those wet clothes. We've got some work to do."

In a few minutes, I was dry and dressed in heavy flannel. We went out to the garage, and Isabel threw me a pair of heavy-duty gloves. "At least our hands will be warm," she said.

We both grabbed shovels, and I pulled the pick down from its hook.

"Are we ready?" she asked.

"Upper woods?" I asked.

"Yep. That'll be Jacob Grosvenor Forrest's final resting place. The Forrest forest. Out of sight, out of trouble.

"You hope."

"We both better hope," she said ruefully. "Let's go."

We walked out into the night.

"No flashlights," was all she said.

We worked throughout the night, wrapping his body up into a large blue tarp, putting him on my hand truck, and rolling him into the wooded area of our property. The ceaseless December rain had formed pools in the low spots in the backyard, reflecting light from the distant street lamp. As we buried him in the woods, the evergreen canopy offered us some small shelter from the rain.

I dug and Isabel dug until our arms ached and we just couldn't dig anymore. The grave was four feet deep, maybe four-and-a-half-feet, when we dropped Jacob's tarped body into the hole. I scattered what remained of a 20-pound bag of lye that I'd kept in the shed as fertilizer, and then we covered him up. A newly-buried body normally leaves a mound of dirt, so I used my wheelbarrow to spread the excess dirt amidst the ivy that covered the floor of the forest where no one was likely to see it. Finally, I heaped two to three feet of yard waste all around the burial site. It looked like part of our summertime dumping ground, full of fallen branches, withered blackberry vines, and grass clippings. I threw the skeleton of an old Christmas tree on top for good measure.

I left the hand truck and all our tools on the porch of the shed. If they had Jacob's scent, it was in the same place where he'd pilfered our wine.

We went inside, stripped off our drenched clothes, and dried off.

This didn't have to happen, we thought.

We threw all our sopping clothes into the washer with bleach, and Isabel reminded me that we still had Jacob's wallet and cellphone sitting on the kitchen table right where I'd tossed them after my first confrontation.

We removed the phone's battery and sim card, then threw every-thing—wallet and cellphone—into a sink full of hot, soapy, bleach-filled water. We washed everything. License. Credit cards. Cash. Everything. Three times. Finally, we swabbed the tabletop with alcohol. We wanted to be careful.

We decided to stash Jacob's 9mm pistol behind the storage reser-voir in our well house, and tuck his wallet and disassembled cellphone in a large plastic bag that we shoved into the back of one of the three wine refrigerators we keep in the garage. Who's going to look in a wine refrigerator?

I took a hammer to the sim card and recycled the battery.

Neither Isabel nor I are monsters, despite what you may think. We're not.

We're just ordinary people who have learned that the police and the legal establishment—lawyers and lawmakers—don't have our backs. They're all about order and tranquility as long as it's their order, their tranquility. When our order and tranquility disintegrated three years ago, the police demonstrated that they could and would do nothing to restore it. They would do nothing to give us justice. Apparently only developers or entrepreneurs with the ear of city hall—and the money to fill its cof-fers—receive that kind of proper attention.

Isabel felt sick about shooting Jacob, but he'd be alive right now if he hadn't returned with a gun...and threatened to kill me.

I can only speak for myself. I harbor no illusions about what my fate may ultimately be. I've read enough crime thrillers and watched enough cop TV to know that the police and detectives are a pretty savvy bunch. While it's not my intention to try to outwit them, I have no plans to saun-ter into the local police headquarters and confess. I also have no plans to help the authorities find the culprit when they come to my home with photographs of "a missing boy from Hemlock Hill." Doing either of those things—confessing or helping—is what ordinary people who see themselves as good citizens do, but that whole good citizen routine is now in my rearview mirror.

My wife and I gritted our teeth while being victimized by forces more powerful than us—the police, the city, and the developers—but I'll be damned if we'll be victimized by some foul-mouthed teenager who acts as if he's holding a royal flush when he doesn't even have a pair of deuces. He was all bluff and bluster—until he had a gun. Then Isabel shot him through the heart. I wonder if his final thought was *I should never have come back. I should have done what I was told to do.*

I'm pretty sure what we did is against the law—the burying part, not the shooting part. That was self-defense. But the burying part was definitely a gray area, and really good citizens don't wander into the gray areas.

And we don't want to hear any of that "boy" nonsense. Some boy. He was a thief, and worse, he was a man who came back with a pistol in his hand and murder on his mind. He decided to rob us—for the third or fourth time—and decided he could be surly and snide when we caught him. Now he's dead.

One thing's for certain: his robbing days are over.

We plan to help the police as much as they helped us. When we needed help, all we got was a chorus of police and lawyers singing, "Too bad, so sad. No one broke the law."

Here's what we want to know: What law allows the destruction of someone else's property? As far as we're concerned, there's the law written by powerful interests, and then there is the real law. The real law should say we must be compensated for trees destroyed by developers. The real law should forbid being insolent and insulting when caught stealing wine from a stranger's shed. There are consequences—even when the developers and teenagers think otherwise.

Since the police don't seem capable of obtaining justice for us, we've decided to step in and do what needs to be done.

It's been a day since the police came to our front door. I've contemplated what's next—Isabel may be thinking the same thing, but she still has her work to do. I'm retired and have plenty of time for contemplation, and I lead a fairly solitary life except for Isabel, and our dogs and cats.

Maybe someday soon there will be a knock on our door. It could be police with search warrants, or police dogs sniffing around to see if the scent of the missing boy can be detected. Certainly, the shed will smell like him. Probably the hand truck, too. I wonder sometimes if dogs can smell blood when the rain has washed it into the soil. I wonder if handcuffs, mug shots, iron bars, and orange overalls will be my future—our future.

I can imagine the boy's father looking at us as if we were some strange, alien creatures—some atavistic humanoids with murderous tendencies embedded in our primordial DNA.

I've imagined Jacob's father asking me if we actually killed his son "over a few bottles of wine?"

And I've imagined my answer.

"No, sir, we didn't just kill him because he's a thief. Nor because he said, 'Fuck you' when we caught him stealing from us. We killed your thieving, cussing, arrogant, gun-toting, thug-of-a-criminal son because he was planning to murder me in my backyard in the wee small hours of the morning."

I've also imagined newspaper headlines speculating about *The Hemlock Hill Disappearance*, and I see the faces of my own children filled with disbelief and disappointment when they discover what Grandma Isabel and Grandpa Frank have done.

C'est la vie.

What I've been unable to imagine is not being caught. Not being prosecuted. I believe the cops are smarter and more resourceful than me—but I hope I'm wrong.

I can't imagine myself not being in handcuffs, not living the rest of my days behind bars. Then I wonder if that's just the limitations of my earlier, civic-minded self. My old, civic-minded self definitely sees me going to jail. We'll just have to wait and see how my new self—the "evolution of justice" self—makes out.

As our new selves wait for resolution, we are planning to deplete the wine reserve we have stored in our shed.

Oh, yeah. One last thing. When I saw Jacob's birthdate on his license—January 17th—I had to laugh. I remembered that date specifically because I'd been working as a consultant in the San Bernardino School District on that day in 1994 when the ground began shaking. I still remember growing fearful and slightly seasick watching the overhead lights in my hotel room swaying back and forth.

Out of curiosity, I googled January 17th and discovered it's also the day Carnegie Hall held its first jazz concert in 1938, and the day of the Great Brink's Robbery in Boston in 1950. As it happens, January 17th is also the feast day of St. Anthony, the Abbott. He is the patron saint of gravediggers.

Chapter Three

Much Ado About Noting

Jimmy Brautigan
January 2019

Murders in the Seattle suburb of Eastlake were "as rare as hen's teeth." That's how Jimmy Brautigan put it...or rather, how his mother put it.

"Always one of my mother's favorite expressions," Jimmy would say. "Mom had a saying for everything. She used to tell me, 'Jimmy, keep your eyes on the stars and your feet on the ground.' Then I became a detective, and now I find myself with my eyes on the ground—the whole damn time. That's where most of the clues are when someone gets murdered."

Assigned to the very infrequent Eastlake murder cases were two detectives who'd been partners, "Since Jesus Christ was still in short pants." The senior member of this detective duo was James Brautigan—a tall, lean man with steely gray hair and a droll sense of humor—who everyone called Jimmy. Whenever he'd introduce himself, he'd say, "My name is Jimmy—I used to be a locksmith." Sometimes it got a laugh—sometimes it didn't. But that never deterred him.

Only slightly less senior than Jimmy was his partner Steve Olson—a tall, broad-shouldered redhead who always sported a crew cut. When he and Jimmy first met, Jimmy's first comment was, "That's about the red-dest hair I've ever seen." Lately, Jimmy had kidded him about the silver gathering at his temples.

Each morning—or whenever they were meeting to work together on a case, as they did last night around midnight—Jimmy always greeted his partner with a "Hi-ho, Stevarino"—a catchphrase that comedian Louis Nye created for The Steve Allen Show in the 1950s. None of the younger detectives or police colleagues understood the reference.

Once Jimmy commented to Steve that "Anyone who understands the reference 'Hi-ho, Stevarino' is either ancient or dead. I guess that makes me ancient."

Jimmy Brautigan made no apologies for who he was. "I'm an old-school detective in a new-school universe," he'd tell anyone willing to listen. "Probably none of you remember when the television world was only VHF and UHF—or when you actually had to stand up and walk over to the TV to turn it on or change the channel. Of course, even back then, you never had to turn the knob very far because there was only ABC, NBC, and CBS."

A new detective once asked Jimmy derisively, "Your TVs had knobs?" That detective promptly received an obscene response from Jimmy that included the words "knobs" and "your sister."

"Christ, Jimmy, you need to retire. Knobs on TVs? Pretty soon you'll be telling us about the day the wheel was invented..."

"Go ahead," Jimmy would say, "Make fun...but yeah...yeah, I was there when they invented the wheel. And you should be glad I was. The wheel wasn't always round. You know that, right? I'm the one who sug-gested that a wheel with right-angles was a bad idea."

Jimmy Brautigan, old-school detective, kept a handwritten daily jour-nal which he carried everywhere. He had little use for iPads or tablets or any of the other electronic digital gadgetry that had taken over so much of the police world.

"I'll always have my notes," Jimmy would say proudly to his fellow detectives. "One electromagnetic pulse, and you're all back to square zero."

Nevertheless, he'd sat in on all the digital training sessions that the department required.

"Yeah," Jimmy would say, "I was in the room. It was a training session for dinosaurs—for guys like me who survived the meteorite extinction. Did you see any young guys there? I didn't. Nope. Just the guys with one foot in the grave and the other on a banana peel."

Jimmy still preferred the pen and paper universe, although he grudgingly acknowledged the value of the camera feature on his tablet and cellphone. The pen and paper universe would always be his comfortable domain.

Younger colleagues were always curious about the stories that fellow detectives were fond of telling about the legendary Jimmy Brautigan.

"He's always carrying his notebook—not the digital one, the hardcopy one. He's got more than 400 rubber-banded volumes filled with his scribbled observations and suspicions. More than 400, covering three decades of police work. Swear to God," the lieutenant would explain—usually over a beer or two. "I've seen them."

When his story was met with incredulity, the lieutenant would raise his right hand as if that offered additional proof. "You think I'm kidding? They're all stored chronologically. More than four hundred volumes crammed side-by-side in two oaken bookcases down in his basement. Each book has the date Scotch-taped to its spine. Brautigan's chronicles cover three decades of bad guys."

On this Thursday morning, Jimmy sipped his coffee as he sat with his latest journal reviewing his handwritten notes from the previous night. His was a very legible hand. "Not like the friggin' bird-tracks you guys call handwriting," he'd tell his younger colleagues. "Didn't they teach penmanship when you were in school?"

Once, a newly-minted, smart-ass detective shrugged at Jimmy's question and said, "Who needs handwriting when you've got two good thumbs and a cellphone."

Every day, Jimmy's first order of business was to reread the carefully-composed, handwritten notes he'd made the day before about any ongoing case. The Walther murder was today's ongoing case.

Wednesday/Thursday, January 30/31, 2019

It's shitty weather. It's been a lousy, cold, rainy winter, and last night was a cold, rainy night. A bad night to die. Worse, it's never good to die in a grocery store parking lot. Doesn't anybody die in grassy fields and sunshine anymore?

The victim is Ms. Kelsey Walther, age 44. She was found dead next to her truck in the Factoria QFC parking lot around 23:30. Another shopper—a Ms. Victoria Karpov, a nurse at Evergreen Hospital who was on her way home after her shift—saw Mrs. Walther's body as she was driving toward QFC's front door. Ms. Karpov says she stepped out of her car when she saw Ms. Walther's body, but she neither approached nor touched the body. Ms. Karpov did call 911 as she parked her own car 50 feet away in an area that was better lit. She locked her car doors and waited for the police.

Detective Steve Olson and I arrived on the scene at 23:47; a patrol car was already at on the scene. Officers Markowski and Carter said they found Ms. Walther lying face down near the right rear wheel of her white 2019 Dodge crew cab pickup truck. The back of her head was bashed in. She was wearing a light-brown, puffy, down jacket, a cream-colored blouse, two-inch heels, and tailored jeans. A black knit cap was found about five feet from her body. I'm guessing it was hers. The CS folks will let us know. There was blood spatter on the rear panel above the wheel, ruining an otherwise spotless vehicle. The pool of blood around her head was three feet across and getting diluted as the rain kept falling. I congratulated Markowski for putting a tarp over her body to keep it out of the weather.

The right rear tire of the victim's pickup truck was flat, and that may account for Ms. Walther being found immediately next to that wheel. Officer Markowski checked Ms. Walther's cellphone to see if she had contacted AAA or someone else to help change that tire. Apparently not. Her cellphone has been taken in evidence.

I asked Ms. Karpov why she didn't approach the body, after all, Ms. Karpov is a nurse. She said, "I know a dead body when I see one. You see that much blood and...well...there was way too much blood for her to be alive. You can't be too careful, Detective. Besides, it's dark, rainy, and some killer might still be skulking about. Who knows?" I took Ms. Karpov's contact information, gave her my card, and thanked her for calling 911. Other than Ms. Karpov, there were no witnesses that we know of. No video either.

Officer Carter said she found a bag of groceries—it was so cold that the ice cream she'd bought hadn't melted—and Ms. Walther's large purse on the passenger side seat, both apparently undisturbed. This doesn't seem to be a robbery. The purse and groceries have been bagged and tagged for prints. Officers Carter and Markowski said we'll have to wait on the Medical Examiner's report, but it looks like Ms. Walther's COD was blunt force trauma.

The ME's office arrived at 23:51, and, after the scene was photographed and inspected, Ms. Walther's body was taken to Harborview Hospital for autopsy. Officer Carter called for a tow truck to take Ms. Walther's vehicle to impound. CS investigators will go over it to see if there is anything that might point us in the right direction.

Olson and I inspected the interior of the pickup. Other than the groceries and her purse, we found the registration in the glove box and some gym clothes behind the passenger-side seat. Nothing unusual. Except the truck cab was spotless. I mean, really clean. There is a "Serrene Homes" logo on both front doors and the tailgate, but the truck is registered in her name. We also found a light-green Post-it note on the driver's seat. The note said, "The most dangerous game." That's all. I have no idea what it means. We'll run the note for prints, and do a handwriting check to see if Ms. Walther wrote the note. If not, we'll see if anyone in her circle knows who wrote it. We don't know what it means, if it means anything at all. It might be a clue; it might be nothing.

Detective Olson and I went to the address on Kelsey Walther's license, and her husband, a man named Mick, answered the door. I hate this part of the job. We asked him if he knew where his wife was, and I watched his reactions closely. Like I always say, that's what we're paid for. He told us she'd just run down to the QFC to pick up some ice cream for him and some dog food—and something quick for dinner, too. He said she'd left maybe an hour ago...maybe longer. He wasn't sure. He'd been watching a basketball game he'd taped.

We informed him that we believed the woman we'd found was his wife, that she appears to have been murdered, and that he would need to identify her. We handed him the driver's license we found in her purse at the scene. It took him a moment to realize we were serious. When he did, he burst into tears. As I said, I hate this part of the job. A black and white took him over to Harborview to identify the body.

Mr. Walther owns the construction business—Serrene Homes—the name we observed plastered all over the truck. His company builds single-family homes in new subdivisions. His wife ~~does keeps~~ kept the books for Serrene Homes and worked with clients.

Well, that's it for now. I hate late nights. I hate late, cold, rainy nights most of all. (Who the hell decided to spell Serrene with two "r's?")

Detective Jimmy Brautigan's crime scene journal always made interesting reading—if you could get past the dirty fingerprint smudges and coffee stains on almost every page. He was finicky and voluble—and often sloppy. Physically, not mentally. When you finished reading his journal, you knew what had happened and how he felt about what had happened. You might also realize that his wife had been an English teacher before she died of pancreatic cancer. Commas were usually where they belonged, and verb tenses were carefully checked, and the right words were always capitalized. He didn't hesitate to carefully cross out an incorrect verb or preposition. Jimmy wanted exactness and precision in his police prose. There were no shortcuts.

"Just say it," he'd always tell fledgling detectives. "If you're feeling shitty because it's rainy and cold, say so. Feeling shitty changes the way you look at a crime scene. Remember, it was probably rainy and cold for the victim and the perpetrator, too. Put everything in your notes when you're working a crime scene. You never know what'll be really important later on."

"First impressions count," Jimmy would emphasize. "*Your* first impressions count because you are trained to look. But here's the difference. Everybody looks, the world is full of lookers. But you're paid to understand what you're looking at. So everything counts. You're trained to connect the dots; create timelines: what happened first, what happened next; interview the casual lookers to see if they can help you see what they couldn't see for themselves. That's why we call you detectives."

He always concluded with the same advice. "Being a detective is a science and an art. We have forensic folks who'll help you with the science. Your job is to get in touch with your artistic side."

When Brautigan typed up his notes, he usually transcribed them directly from his journal, vivid details and all, leaving nothing out—except the smudges and stains.

His lieutenant always gave him a bad time about that. "It's a public record, for Christ's sake, Jimmy. People can request these kinds of documents. Keep the foul language out of it. We all feel shitty, sometimes, but we don't write that in our reports. We write 'crappy.' Can you do that for me?"

"Sure thing," Jimmy said. "From now on, I won't write '*The weather was shitty*.' I'll write '*The weather was fuckin' crappy*.'"

Brautigan sat down at his desk and turned on his computer. He'd only gotten four hours sleep last night.

No, he corrected himself, *I spent four hours in bed but I slept maybe two-and-a-half.*

After rereading his notes from yesterday, Jimmy's second order of business was to check emails so he'd be up-to-date on what everyone else had done with the case. Today's first message, however, was from his oldest daughter reminding him that his birthday dinner would be at 5:00 p.m. that Saturday. She never sent emails to his police address unless she was worried that he'd forget to check his personal emails—which he often did. He still had his original AOL account. Mandy once suggested he at least get a Gmail account.

"Why?" he had replied, "I can ignore a Gmail account as easily as I ignore my AOL account. You know that, right? Once upon a time all anyone had to do was check their mailbox to see if anyone had sent them a letter. You remember letters? And stamps? And mailboxes? And grammar?"

He'd already turned 62 last December on Christmas Day, but he never celebrated his birthday on his birthday.

"Jesus always manages to suck all the oxygen out of the room," he said, "so we celebrate my birthday on almost any day except Christmas. That Jesus is a pretty popular fella. I was thinking maybe we should shoot for the 4th of July?"

So, this year, he'd be celebrating his 62nd birthday forty days late, on February 2nd of the wrong year. His daughter selected the date.

"Be on time, please," the email admonished him. "Mom used to say you'd be late for your own funeral."

He replied. "Got it. Saturday. Five PM. On time. You realize I turned 62 *last* year...not this year?"

His terse style online was at complete variance with his talky report style.

The next email was the Medical Examiner's report. Maureen, Jimmy's favorite ME, confirmed that Kelsey Walther's cause of death was blunt force trauma, a single blow to the head, probably from a heavy piece of metal.

"Did you see the email from Maureen?" Jimmy asked.

"First thing this morning. Probably a tire iron," said Steve Olson. Jimmy and Steve had been partners for more than twenty years.

"Did we find a tire iron at the scene?" Jimmy asked leaning back in his chair.

"Well, Walther had a flat tire, but her spare and her jack and tire iron were still in the truck."

"So, if it was a tire iron, it wasn't *her* tire iron."

"Probably not."

Jimmy looked idly at his journal. "Did we find out why she was parked so far out in the parking lot?"

"Her husband says she's been trying to do that ten-thousand step routine. You know, ten-thousand steps a day? Said it was part of her New Year's resolution. He's guessing she needed the extra steps."

"I wonder if she'll have that on her cellphone," Jimmy said as he got up and walked over to Olson's desk. He pulled on some latex gloves and pulled a cellphone out of a clear plastic evidence envelope and searched for the Exercise App.

"Looks like she got to 8,747 steps before she met her maker," Jimmy said.

"Proof, yet again, that exercise will kill you," Olson commented.

Olson and Brautigan had a reputation for dark humor—the lieutenant was always hassling them about their "inappropriate humor"—but Olson and Brautigan both knew it kept them sane in a world gone mad.

"The whole world's not mad, of course," Brautigan would say, "just the part we're assigned to. Sane people should never be assigned to a homicide detail."

"Damn straight," Olson would say. "Homicide investigations are killers."

The lieutenant's general state of mind always perched on the edge of exasperation. "If it weren't for you guys actually bringing in the bad guys all the time, I'd have to fire you."

"Dead bodies don't pop up too often in this part of town," Detective Olson said with a wry smile. He began scribbling a list of *"Things I Gotta Check On."*

Like Brautigan, Olson believed in paper. Steve Olson was a veteran list maker, and he preferred making hardcopy lists on a piece of paper rather than typing it into his phone.

Things I Gotta Check On

* ~~Find out where her husband was when she was killed.~~
* Check her insurance coverage.
* Interview everyone at her workplace. Friendly? Unfriendly?
* Check her phone. Texts. Emails. Social media accounts.
* Check her computer at home.
* Check to see if there's any direct threats against her, her family, or the company.
* Find out if she was fooling around on the side.
* What does "the most dangerous game" mean?

The initial investigation lists were always the easiest, and in most cases, led the detectives in the right direction. For instance, when a wife dies, one can easily look at the still-living-and-breathing husband as suspect number one. In this case, Olson had already begun considering moving the husband down the list. Down, but not off. Husbands were always suspects.

Jimmy was curious. "What makes you think Mick Walther was a doting husband?"

"Come on, Jimmy. When his wife went grocery shopping, Walther was at home watching a basketball game he'd taped."

"At 11:00 at night? Who goes shopping at 11:00 at night?"

"Everyone doesn't keep your hours, Jimmy. Some people actually do things late at night."

"Late nights are for sleeping. Always have been."

Jimmy and Steve had had this very discussion way too many times—and it always came up when they had to begin their investigations in the dark of night.

"You saw the look on his face when we told him. How many guys do you know can break down and cry on cue unless they're really broken up?"

"Okay. But that doesn't mean he didn't have someone do it for him. The husband's always on the hook—or the boyfriend. We can't rule him out until we look at the company books and review the whole insurance angle," Jimmy pointed out.

Olson underlined item number two. Lots of spouses are killed for the insurance money, especially when there might be personal insurance policies and company insurance policies. Maybe Serrene Homes was in financial trouble. Insurance policies often proved to be quick fixes for a lousy cash flow.

Solving a murder is always easier when the spouse does it, Olson thought. *Guilty spouses usually act guilty and often do other stupid things. They might as well put on a t-shirt that says, "I Did It."*

Even if her husband didn't kill her, it was a good bet that someone she knew—work colleagues, friends, family members—had decided they'd be better off with her dead. In most cases, most people are murdered by loved ones or friends, not strangers. It's one of life's great darkly-comic ironies.

You always kill the ones you love, the ones you shouldn't kill at all, Olson quietly hummed the familiar tune to himself.

Chapter Four

Enter, Stage Left

Frank Hannigan
January 2019

In case you were wondering, killing a person is really not all that difficult. It takes time and patience, particularly if you are planning to kill someone without being caught—or if you want to avoid even being suspected of doing the deed. That's the real challenge. It's important to kill someone quietly, without alerting neighbors or passersby with excessive noise. Gunshots and screams—they're the real problems. When it comes to murder, silence is golden. It pays not to advertise.

As I reread that, I know that it sounds callous, almost as if I enjoy killing people. I don't. But anything worth doing—including exacting a justice unavailable by other means—is worth doing right. My wife and I have each killed one person to date—of course, she was defending my life while I was seeking a personal justice that had been denied by the powers that be. One was self-defense, and the second death was, admittedly, murder.

However, it's vital that I point out that both these deaths were completely avoidable. Completely.

If only Jacob and the Serrene Home folks realized that their actions have consequences. Making foolish demands at gunpoint in the middle of the night has consequences. Killing someone's dog, putting lives at risk, and destroying property and trees without any apparent remorse, has consequences—as Jacob and Kelsey now know for sure—although they may be, as Isabel says, "well beyond knowing."

It occurs to me that far too many folks—and Jacob and Kelsey may be among them—no longer believe that a crime merits punishment. Falling trees and dead dogs are just the cost of doing business. Nothing personal here, they think, and certainly nothing criminal. The same with getting caught stealing wine. If the wine gets put back, no harm, no foul, right?

A week after Jacob's death, I asked Isabel if she thought that these folks felt as they do because their money had essentially shielded them from consequences—*i.e.*, punishment.

Isabel pointed out that, historically, crime brings punishment most often to the poor or middle classes. Anyone who reads a newspaper or watches television understands that wealth and negative consequences are often inversely proportional. That is, the more money you have, the fewer consequences you'll feel.

"There's nothing new or novel about that," Isabel said. I heard the resignation in her voice.

Isabel reminded me that consequences are not an egalitarian concept. Consequences seldom apply equally to the wealthy, if at all. "Wealthy folk," she said, "are clever enough to pass laws or regulations that legalize actions that should clearly be illegal."

She's right, of course. Money can do that. For instance, the wealthy folk craft regulations allowing developers to do what they damn well please to the property of neighbors. Magically, those illegal actions—heretofore called crimes—morph into innocent, legal actions. And *voila*, no consequences.

No crime. No punishment.

Please understand, we tried our best to get Serrene Homes to do the right thing. A week after our trees fell and our dog died, I went to their offices to voice my...my...my what? My objection? My anger? My amazement and frustration that no one from Serrene Homes came forward to apologize?

I questioned the wisdom of going to Serrene's offices, especially since even I could not properly gauge my mood. If asked to describe it, I'd be hard-pressed to respond. My mind was a jumble of anger, hurt, sadness, confusion, and righteousness.

Serrene's corporate offices were a two-story, lots-of-glass office building—pure, unmistakable suburbia—and bright fall sunshine illuminated the lobby as I approached the receptionist at her desk. I could see she was intent on reading whatever was on her desk while sipping coffee from a bright-red Serrene Homes mug. She didn't see me.

I stopped in front of her desk and waited. Finally, I cleared my throat and introduced myself. "I'm Frank Hannigan. I'd like to speak with Mick Walther."

She looked up suddenly. I'd startled her, and she spilled coffee on the documents. She grabbed a tissue, wiped the documents, and dabbed drops of coffee from her chin. She composed herself and asked, "Can I help you?"

"I'd like to speak with Mick Walther."

"Do you have an appointment?"

"No. But I need to speak with Mr. Walther about one of his current subdivisions."

"May I ask which subdivision?"

"Yeah," I said, "The one behind my house." My tone probably revealed some latent hostility.

She stared at me in silence, slowly placing her coffee cup off to the side. I believe she was trying to assess my mood. After a moment, she said, "Mr. Walther is not here at the moment, but I'll see who's available. Please follow me...Mister...Mister...forgive me, I've forgotten your name."

"Hannigan. Frank Hannigan."

She ushered me into a conference room dominated by a long mahogany table with eight well-padded chairs on either side. I sat opposite a wall filled with smiling portraits of all the main corporate players at Serrene Homes. The wall behind me was all glass, looking out onto a largely empty parking lot.

When she reappeared at the door, the receptionist said, "Kelsey will be with you momentarily, Mr. Hannigan. Can I get you anything? A cup of coffee, perhaps?"

"No, thank you," was all I could say.

Kelsey arrived a few moments later. Dressed in a tan business suit, her hair pulled back in a ponytail, her eyeglasses hanging on a chain. She took the chair opposite me rather than the one next to me. I thought the distance between us was appropriately symbolic.

"How can I help you, Mr. Hannigan?" Her tone was polite but distant.

"That's a very good question, Miss...?"

"Walther. Mrs. Walther. You asked to speak to my husband, but he's not here."

I took a moment to collect my thoughts.

"I'm not sure where to begin, Mrs. Walther." I took a deep breath. "You're familiar with the Hemlock Hill subdivision?"

"Yes."

Another deep breath. "My home is literally the next house north of your subdivision. While your folks were clear-cutting and preparing the plot, they cut the holding roots of five of my trees—trees that were each over one hundred feet tall. Each of those trees stood along our common boundary line. Now they're firewood."

Remarkably, she said nothing. I was wondering what she might be thinking.

I continued. "Apparently you didn't hear me. A week ago, those five trees—three hemlocks and two firs—fell in a wind storm. They crushed my two-story storage shed, crashed through the roof of my home above the master bedroom, and killed my flat-coated retriever. I've written out a full report of the damages done to my home and property—inside and out—as well as the death of a member of my family."

I placed a manila folder on the table.

"It's all in there, Mrs. Walther. The dates. The phone calls we made to your husband and the city planner concerning our compromised roots. The report of our arborist about the likelihood of those trees falling. Lots of photographs. It's all in there. I'd like you to give this document to Mr. Walther and have him contact me as soon as possible. My contact information is all there, too."

I thought I'd been succinct and direct.

She didn't reach for the folder. She sat at the table, looking down as if she were inspecting its mahogany top.

"I cannot accept these documents, Mr. Hannigan," she said, still looking at the table top. "Nor will my husband." She looked up. "To date, everything we have done at the Hemlock Hill development has been properly permitted. We have adhered to all the rules, regulations, and statutes concerning construction. If you wish, you can have your lawyer send these documents to our lawyer. We don't handle legal matters out of this office."

I could hear the defensiveness in her voice.

"Those trees fell because your people cut the roots of my trees. My trees."

"I heard you the first time, Mr. Hannigan." The politeness was gone. Only a tired indifference remained. "Now, if there is nothing else…"

"So that's it? You killed my dog! No concern? No consideration? No apology? My wife and I could have been killed." I felt frustrated and terribly alone.

"I don't know what you want us to do, Mr. Hannigan. You weren't killed, were you? We can't bring back your dog. Dear Lord, Mr. Hannigan. Just go get a new dog. People get new dogs every day. Your insurance will repair any of your buildings."

Her dismissive attitude about Aria hit me hard, hurt me in a way I never anticipated. A quiet fury filled me. *She doesn't care. Not today. Not tomorrow.* I didn't want to give voice to my fury. That would not help.

I spoke slowly and deliberately. "I want you to give these documents to your husband." I pushed the file across the table.

Her answer was swift and short. "No." She pushed back her chair and walked to the door of the conference room. "I'll have my receptionist give you the name of our lawyer."

I had resisted calling a lawyer, foolishly hoping that reason among reasonable people might prevail. That's why I'd gone there. That's why I went for the next two days.

On the second day, the receptionist—whose name I finally discovered was Madelaine—told me she'd been expressly instructed not to allow me to proceed anywhere past the lobby...if indeed I arrived a second time. Which I did. Madelaine also said she'd been instructed to call the police if I attempted to move past her.

"I'm sorry, Mr. Hannigan. But I have my instructions," she said.

"Do you know why I'm here?" I asked.

"Not exactly."

"For starters, I'm here because your company killed my dog."

Madelaine said nothing but her face spoke volumes. Clearly, she hadn't known that.

"At the very least, I'd like them to acknowledge what they did—to me, my wife, my home...my dog."

"I'm so sorry, Mr. Hannigan."

Are you the only person here with a heart, I wondered.

"You tell Mick Walther or Kelsey Walther that I'll be back tomorrow. Ten o'clock. With my complete complaint written out for their inspection. You tell them that I expect them to be here. You tell them that. They can't do what they've done and act as if nothing has happened. That's despicable. That's cowardly. You tell them I said so."

On day three, at ten o'clock, I'd no sooner entered the sacred precincts of Serrene Homes when I was confronted by the local police. Apparently my message had been delivered by Madelaine, and the police delivered Mrs. Walther's "No" in their own particular way.

"If you come here again, Mr. Hannigan," one of the officers said as he held open the door for my exit, "you'll be arrested for trespassing. Do you understand?"

I understood only too well.

But I could write letters to Serrene Homes. My letters might shame the Serrene folks, but they would never threaten. No one could ever return and say that my letters threatened anyone with vengeance if they didn't respond to my entreaties. So I began sending letters. I sent the same brief letter on the first day of each month for almost two years. All I did was change the date.

Dear Serrene Homes Folks,

We truly wish you'd take responsibility for the pain and suffering you have caused my wife and me. Your carelessness in preparing the Hemlock Hill subdivision cost us not only five of our beautiful trees, it cost us our beloved dog, our shed, as well as our piece of mind. Worst of all, your behavior in this matter—that is, your unwillingness and failure to make us whole for the damage that you inflicted—has made us wonder if anyone at Serrene Homes has anything approaching a conscience. Where are your morals? Where are your ethics?

We ask again, as we have asked each month, that you accept your responsibility in this matter and meet with us and discuss how you can properly reimburse us for our loss.

It would be the moral thing to do. The ethical thing to do.

We look forward to hearing from you.

We never heard from them. Not once. Except when we received a letter from their lawyer asserting that our letters constituted harassment. We stopped writing.

When Isabel lamented that "It's not fair," I agreed with her.

"You're absolutely right," I said. "Life isn't fair." I paused and smiled and said, "It's just fairer than death that's all."

"Fairer than death? Is that your idea?" she asked me.

"No," I confessed. "I stole that line from *The Princess Bride*"—a book I once taught to my high school students. "It's the last line of the book."

I think it was at that moment when we realized the depth of our pain and the white-hot anger that would illuminate all the details of our story.

Isabel turned to me. I could see she was mulling over the "fairer than death" idea.

"What they did to us—to Miss Aria—was unfair. And immoral. And it's still unfair and immoral," she said slowly, talking to no one in particular.

"Unfair and immoral...but legal," I countered.

"Well, maybe we should return the favor," she said, breaking out of her reverie. "Maybe we should give them the one thing that is less fair than life."

"That would be death," I said.

"Precisely," she said. "When a law is grossly unjust—when a just law simply does not exist—perhaps the only remedy is to inflict another injustice to balance it out. Let's call it illegal, but fair."

"An eye for an eye?" I asked.

"Maybe. But that sounds so Old Testament. We could call it a *quid pro quo*." She seemed amused.

"Too legalese," I said. "How about tit for tat?"

"Too suggestive," she said wryly. "How about like for like?"

"I have one better. How about measure for measure?"

"Leave it to an English teacher to quote a Shakespearean comedy before setting the stage for a tragedy."

Most of us desperately want to believe that the words "law" and "justice" are equivalent. But they're not.

Nevertheless, these laws—the ones legalizing what should clearly be illegal—fail to account for human nature. Just when the wealthy begin congratulating themselves because they have successfully rewritten the laws—twisting them so the words "justice" and "injustice" become interchangeable—just when they believe they have successfully made themselves immune to consequences, human nature enters, stage left.

Human nature, you see, understands the idea of natural justice. Perhaps the law can redefine justice, but it can never redefine—or re-engineer—human nature.

Imagine this. You just passed a law permitting murder—that is, making what was previously an injustice permissible. If no law prohibited the taking of a human life, then murder would have no consequences. That is, murder would have no *legal* consequences.

However, if that one law were changed, I'd predict an incredible surge in murders everywhere. Grudges and scores would be settled *en masse*. But things would not end there, because natural justice— through the agency of human nature—would manifest itself in a tragic barrage of revenge murders. Tit for tat murders. *Quid pro quo* murders. Revenge is a very natural instinct. After the first round of revenge murders, there'd be another round of revenge murders, and then another, and another.

Laws are designed by civil societies to intercept and placate human nature. Laws are intended to stop people from ruinous, destructive paths, giving them an alternative. The law is the community in action. But, the follow-up question should ask, *What if the alternative somehow becomes perverted*—what if the law, i.e., the community, tips the scales of justice against you?

That's our dilemma.

Isabel wanted me to know that she believed her killing Jacob was, above all, the defense of my life, but perhaps it was also some misplaced aggression. She might be right. Jacob was just one teenager doing what many other teenagers have done—stealing wine in the night.

Sometimes I ask myself if we overreacted, but then I realize we gave Jacob a chance to confess without incriminating himself publicly. We wouldn't even have had to tell his father. His little secret—his late-night forays to our shed for wine—would have been our secret alone. If he'd just signed his confession, I wasn't going to the police. I told him that. But Jacob was defiant...and arrogant...and vile. He upped the ante—coming back with a gun to somehow get himself out of trouble. Instead, he got himself killed.

Next time, I'll just call the cops and let them handle it. What could be easier than handing the cops both the culprit and the proof at the same time—along with indisputable video evidence? Next time.

Isabel was right. Neither of us was really angry at Jacob. Jacob was simply one unfortunate consequence of all the new homes in Hemlock Hill. Built by Serrene Homes—the company that shattered our lives without consequence or apology. Our anger would only be properly aimed when we had the good folks at Serrene Homes in our sights.

Dear God, I just said "good folks." Just shows you how a once-upon-a-time decent and upright person thinks about the world and the people in it. Once upon a time, everyone fell into the decent folk category, the well-intentioned folk column.

Since the developers have inflicted the crime, the "legalized crime"—the one that has led me to become a less-than-stellar citizen in the eyes of the law—I decided that I would no longer misplace my aggression. I'd put it right where it belonged.

Serrene Homes has a lovely website. It explains what they do and how well they do it. It also details the names and the lives of the people who have caused such mayhem and destruction to the once quiet existence my wife and I share. Maybe that should be "shared"—past tense.

Unfortunately, for the world at large, the beautifully appointed website avoids discussing any unpleasant or negative topics—like murdering dogs or killing trees on neighboring properties, destroying other people's property on adjacent land, or stealing indispensable habitat from the local wildlife. Or robbing us of our serenity.

Fortunately—for me, anyway—the Serrene Homes people think they're untouchable, and legally, that's true. My visits and letters got me exactly nowhere.

When Isabel and I tried bringing a lawsuit against Serrene Homes for the killing of our trees and the loss of our property, we found only an expensive dead end. Those were our lawyer's exact words. Do you think he saw the irony? Dead end?

Let me say for the record that those responsible for inflicting misery on us are not untouchable. The law may offer them legal protection, but human nature can secure justice when the law fails in its sacred duty.

If Serrene Homes had made some sincere effort to address our loss, even informally, a lot of pain could have been avoided. They would have shown that they were good corporate citizens, interested in the well-being of the community and not just their wallets. But that all hinged on a big "if," one that was never fulfilled. Never. Not in any way, shape, or form. As my mother always said, "If wishes were horses, beggars would ride."

It was left to Isabel and me to get justice for our dog, our trees, and ourselves.

A succession of Seattle Chronicle headlines readily revealed the available facts, without any hint of how justice may be obtained via alternative, extralegal methods.

January 31, 2019
Eastlake Woman Found Bludgeoned to Death

February 1, 2019
Factoria QFC Parking Lot Murder Yields Few Clues

Apparently, the death of Kelsey Walther—the administrative assistant and wife of Serrene Homes principal owner, Mick Walther—was worthy of the front page for the first two days. Despite public assurances from Detective James Brautigan of the Eastlake Police Department, subsequent articles, relegated to the deeper pages of the paper, revealed only the increasing frustration of the police as this excerpt from the February 3rd edition indicates:

> Eastlake police seem genuinely stymied. James Brautigan, lead detective, says there are few clues, but the most baffling feature is the lack of motive for Ms. Walther's murder.
>
> "She wasn't robbed or sexually assaulted," he pointed out. "No one stole her vehicle. The keys were still in her purse on the front seat."
>
> Brautigan refused to speculate that this might be a thrill killing—a random murder.

"Usually, people kill other people for a reason. I have no reason to believe that Ms. Walther's death is unusual in any way."

But Detective Brautigan is reaching out to the community to solve this mystery. "Someone out there knows something. Someone out there saw something. This murder took place in a grocery store parking lot—not in the middle of Timbuktu."

Unsolved murders don't get much press. Viewers tend to turn the channel when the police investigators declare, "We got nothin'."

Isabel researched the web and discovered that 37% of all murders in the United States remain unsolved. That's more than one in three. That statistic surprised me. I guess I've always thought that the closure rate for murders would be higher than that, but it's not. I didn't delve into the article too much. I think I just wanted to hope that most murderers are so careless and angry that they just don't give a damn about their own safety. They probably don't worry about getting caught while they're walking right up to their victim and sticking in the knife or pulling the trigger. Killing is the only thing on their mind.

Well, that wasn't me. I'd carefully plotted and planned Kelsey's demise. I don't know if she realized her daily habits made her easy prey for anyone who might want to kill her.

And, unbeknownst to her, there was someone who wanted to kill her. I'm sure she was completely unaware.

You could set your watch, almost to the second, when the front door closed on her always-washed, bright-white, crew cab, Dodge pickup. She'd back her truck out of the driveway at 7:45 a.m. every morning. Her daily drive took sixteen minutes—portal to portal—except Wednesdays when she'd stop at Starbucks and get four cups of coffee. She also got some pastries, but I have no idea what kind.

She kept Serrene's books—at least that was part of her job—and she was married to one of the two principal owners, Mick Walther. Mick's the one who said Isabel and I threatened to "shoot over his property." That was a lie. The truth is Mick and I argued over the phone the day I discovered our tree roots had been cut. After that phone call, he emailed a note to the city planner—the woman who didn't respond to my nineteen phone calls—that we had threatened to shoot at him. As I said, it was a lie. But hell, when your business is filling the city coffers, lies that should be ignored or dismissed are readily believed.

Isabel and I had given Serrene Homes plenty of time to do the right thing. To try to make things right. Isabel suggested that maybe they'd been doing the wrong thing for so long that it felt right. I thought about what Isabel said. When I decided to do the "wrong" thing, it didn't feel right, it didn't feel great, but it did feel just.

I remember being keenly interested in Kelsey's obituary which appeared four days after her death. The obituary said the funeral was to be held the following Wednesday at an Eastlake mortuary.

I decided to ask Isabel, "You want to go to the funeral? Pay our respects?"

Isabel peered at me over the tops of her glasses. Such looks were always a warning

"I thought not," I said. "Sorry I asked."

I don't normally read obituaries, but I'll admit a curious attraction to this particular obituary. Kelsey's life and mine had intersected for a few brief moments—but they were critical moments. Fatal moments.

The day after the funeral, Mick Walther offered a $50,000 reward for information leading to the arrest and conviction of the person or persons who had murdered his wife.

We were having our morning coffee when Isabel read about the reward. She started laughing.

"What's so funny?" I asked.

"It appears that Mick Walther is offering fifty thousand dollars for anyone who finds his wife's killer."

"Fifty thousand?"

"Yeah. Fifty thousand. Kinda paltry for a wealthy guy, isn't it?"

"What else would you expect from a man who kills and thinks nothing of it himself? Generous he is not."

"Well, Mr. Hannigan, that means you are safe...for now. I won't turn you in for less than a cool million dollars. If the bounty ever gets stratospheric, I may rethink the whole 'love, honor, and respect' thing.

"I thought it was love, honor, and obey."

"I don't do obey. But you are permitted to obey me whenever you like."

"Damn decent of you to tell me," I said. "However, I doubt if the reward will increase at all when the next body turns up. After all, the man currently offering the $50,000 will be dead, too."

"Alas," said Isabel standing and walking to the kitchen, "who speaks for the dead?" She often asked rhetorical questions. "Red or white, tonight?"

"Let's open the Syrah."

As she was uncorking the wine, she stopped for a moment.

"You never know. Perhaps Serrene Homes will ante up a sturdier sum when one of their owners ends up dead. After all, Kelsey may have been important, but Mick's a money guy. Somebody indispensable."

She poured two glasses of wine and handed one to me.

I took a sip of Syrah and considered Isabel's words before I responded. "Well, I'd like you to consider something closer to two or three million before turning me over to the authorities. Okay?"

Isabel sipped her wine, smiling that Cheshire cat smile.

Two more people were on my list. Kelsey's husband and the city planner who'd made me *persona non grata* with the Snoquamish police force. If you ask why, I've got an easy answer. Neither of them thought the death of our dog or the loss of our property and peace of mind worthy of response. Isabel and I, however, found their lack of response worthy of our response.

Kelsey "Just go get a new dog" Walther was the first. Now we have two to go. I'm anxious to proceed, but I must always counsel myself against doing things in haste. When it comes to achieving justice, I'm remembering my mother's sage advice: *Easy does it, Frank. Don't rush. One thing at a time. One thing at a time.*

Chapter Five

Clueless

Jimmy Brautigan
February 1, 2019

Kelsey Walther. Why?

Jimmy Brautigan had scribbled those three words on the whiteboard in the squad room. A full-color picture of Kelsey, downloaded from the Serrene Homes website, was taped below the question. His partner and several other detectives—a woman named Caroline and a third man, their tech guru named Ben—joined the early morning session.

"What do we know?" Jimmy asked.

"Not much," Steve admitted.

"There's no video coverage of that part of the QFC parking lot," Caroline pointed out. "We looked for cars traveling in that general area that night, and there is nothing unusual. Of course, it didn't help that there was a hard rain that night. We'd have been better off with snow."

"Yep. But we didn't have snow," Jimmy said. "Okay, Ben, you're our tech Houdini, tell us something we don't know."

Ben suddenly realized he was up to bat. He opened up his laptop and offered his summary.

"I looked through her cellphone, both her computers—the company computer and her personal computer—and there's nothing there that would indicate that anyone wanted her dead. She's on Facebook and Instagram, and I didn't find even a whiff of anything bad. She's worked at Serrene Homes since her husband founded it in 2005, and there's absolutely nothing to indicate that anyone doesn't like her. She's their bookkeeper. No grudges, no threats. All in all, her digital life is about as ordinary as it gets."

"Were there any messages or phone calls the night she died?"

"She called her husband as she left the office. As far as I can tell, the only thing on her phone was her grocery list. Nothing else," Ben said.

Steve had his notebook open and decided it was time to throw in a few missing pieces.

"Her husband said she went to the store because he wanted some ice cream," Steve said, "and that they needed dog food. She hadn't gotten home until around 10:30 because she'd been working late on a proposal for a prospective client at the office, and finished up a little after ten o'clock."

Jimmy jumped in. "So she went home, kissed her husband, and went to the store?"

"Yep," Steve admitted, "but apparently she often went grocery shopping late at night. Shopping at 11:00 at night wasn't anything unusual."

"Did she always go to the QFC?" Jimmy asked.

Everyone seemed stumped.

"I don't know," Steve said.

"I bet we can find out how often she was there—and when she was there—from their computer system," Ben said. "Most people input their customer number or phone number whenever they shop. Grocery stores rely on that data."

"Okay, Ben," Jimmy said, "you find out if she was a regular night owl, and if that's the case, we'll have a look at CCTV tapes on those other nights."

Everyone made some notations and then Jimmy asked, "So, what else do we have?"

Jimmy looked at a sea of blank faces.

"She loves her husband, loves her job, and everybody loves her?" Jimmy asked. He wasn't being sarcastic.

"Pretty much. Anyway, that's what the digital universe tells me, Jimmy," Ben said.

"No grudges, no threats?" Steve asked.

"None."

"So why would someone kill her?" Jimmy asked.

"She wasn't robbed," Steve reminded everyone.

"Or sexually assaulted," Caroline offered.

"Her truck was pristine—and it's not as if she'd had an accident in the parking lot and pissed off somebody," Jimmy pointed out.

"Could it be a random killing?" Ben wondered out loud.

That had been on everyone's mind. Random killings are both rare and very difficult to solve. Most murders happen for a reason. Finding that motive is usually the key.

Ben stared at his computer as if it would supply him with an answer.

"Hey," he said.

He turned his computer so everyone could see his screen.

"The company logo is plastered all over her truck—on the sides, on the tailgate. Any chance someone has a beef with Serrene Homes? Someone sees the truck. Flattens the truck's tire. When Ms. Walther returns to her vehicle, she sees the flat and she gets whacked while she's looking at her right rear tire. Someone could have come over and even offered to help her."

"That's cold," Caroline said.

"So, maybe, we're dealing with a Bad Samaritan?" Jimmy asked.

"Someone who doesn't like Serrene Homes?" Ben asked.

Steve pushed himself back from his desk. "It's as good a starting point as any. Let's go ask the good folks at Serrene Homes who that may be."

Steve and Jimmy called ahead to talk with the folks at Serrene Homes. Millie, their office manager, welcomed them as they walked in. The office was extraordinarily subdued—not just quiet, but somehow, beyond quiet. The death of a colleague tends to have that effect.

"Detectives, I think we've told you all we know on the phone, yesterday," said Millie. "Certainly I have, anyway. Everyone loved Kelsey."

"I'm sure that's true, Millie, and we're sorry to have to interrupt any of you..." Jimmy's voice trailed off. "Especially now. You have the sympathies of the entire department."

Steve could see that Jimmy was struggling. "But here's the thing, Millie. We were wondering if anyone might have it in for Serrene Homes. We're wondering if someone killed Mrs. Walther because she was in a Serrene Homes truck."

"But that truck is her personal vehicle," Millie said. "Her husband bought it for her when she began working directly with clients. He finally figured out that clients seemed more malleable and amenable when Kelsey was conducting the negotiation."

Millie cast a look around as if she was worried someone might overhear what she was saying.

"Mick," Millie said in hushed tones, "is a hard-ass in negotiations. I know this is a cut-throat business, but you can't be all take and no give. After a couple of clients walked away, the other principal partners had a 'come to Jesus' meeting with Mick. They all decided that maybe somebody else might be more effective. That turned out to be Kelsey. Everyone here loved her." Millie's voice began to crack with emotion. "In a lot of ways, she saved our bacon."

"Was Mick happy that his wife 'saved his bacon'?" Steve asked.

"I think he was happiest of all. His real love is digging in the dirt, or sawing a two-by-four in half. He's never had much patience with people.

If you ask me, he hated being the designated negotiator. His wife loved it."

Millie began crying.

"I understand, Millie. I truly do." Jimmy could sense the gravity of her loss. "So, it makes no sense that anyone would want to kill her. No one here would want to kill Kelsey."

He let Millie collect herself and take a few deep breaths. Jimmy reminded himself that interrogating people after they've lost someone close is always difficult.

"But Serrene Homes has its name on both doors and on the tailgate. Anyone seeing Kelsey's truck could easily conclude that it was Serrene's truck. If someone has a score to settle with Serrene Homes, they may not have paid much attention to who was in the truck. It could be that Kelsey just happened to be in the wrong truck at the wrong time. We think that whoever killed her might be aiming at Serrene—not at Kelsey."

"Oh, dear God," Millie said.

"We're not absolutely sure that's the situation," Jimmy said, "but right now, Kelsey's death makes absolutely no sense. She wasn't robbed. Whoever did this wasn't after her truck. Apparently, everyone loved her. All she was doing was grocery shopping." Jimmy paused.

"And still someone killed her in that parking lot," Steve added. "You can see why it doesn't make sense unless..."

"Unless whoever killed her was mad at Serrene Homes?" Millie added.

"That's the only thing that does make sense," Jimmy said.

"Did anybody at Serrene get fired or leave under a cloud over the last six months?"

"No. The folks who work here love it. I've been here fourteen years, and I've seen folks come and go—but they're always moving on and moving up. Mick's written a dozen letters of recommendation. I'd bet my life that it wasn't anyone who ever worked for Serrene."

Jimmy tapped his notebook with his pen. "Have you had any lawsuits lately? Are any lawsuits pending? Any unhappy homeowners?"

"There's always unhappy homeowners."

Jimmy laughed. "Okay, *really* unhappy homeowners."

Millie motioned for them to come with her.

Jimmy and Steve followed Millie into her office and she offered them seats next to her desk. She sat on the edge of her desk and pulled her computer keyboard onto her lap. As she typed, she explained how things had changed in the home-building industry.

"Twenty years ago—heck, ten years ago—everything we're about to look at would have been crammed into manila folders and kept in filing cabinets. Today, everything is digital. Everything. Any document that crosses my desk or the desks of the principals is scanned and filed. We're not a paper-free office...not yet. But we're pretty close."

"I'll be paper-free when I'm dead," Steve joked holding up his dog-eared notebook. "I just don't trust this...this digital everything. When I write something down, I've got it, and no one can change it. No one can hack into this notebook."

Jimmy leaned conspiratorially toward Millie. "Just call him Linus. That notebook is his security blanket." Jimmy didn't mention that this was the pot calling the kettle black.

Millie laughed. "That's just fine with me. My mom is in complete agreement with you, Linus. She still makes lists and leads a strictly cash life. No plastic for her."

"See, Jimmy, someone else agrees with me."

"Of course, she's 90-years-old."

"Ah, well," Jimmy said. "So what do we have?"

"Let's look at the complaint file together," she said, pointing toward the 40" screen that hung in the corner of her office. Everyone shifted to watch the screen.

"How many complaints are there?" Steve asked.

"That's classified," Millie said in a teasing tone. "I don't think my bosses would want me to admit to any number—even if it was only one."

"Well, we'll offer our apologies to your bosses after we've caught whoever's responsible for Kelsey's death. Can we look at the most recent complaints? Say, the last three years?

"Yes, we can."

"Hey," Jimmy said, suddenly animated. "Can you search for 'threats'?"

"I suppose," Millie said as she typed the word *threat* in her search engine.

Three files popped up with the word threat embedded in the company's description of the letters. Two files used the word as a dissatisfied homeowner might use it. "The owner threatened a lawsuit." But the third file indicated a threat against one of the company owners—Mick Walther. Apparently, someone on a neighboring property had threatened to fire a gun at Mick Walther if the developer chopped down any more trees.

"A threat with a gun?" Steve scratched his head and looked over at Jimmy. "Someone threatened Kelsey's husband?"

Millie teared up. She nodded and reached for a tissue.

"Sorry, Millie. It's gotta be hard. It's a place to start, Jimmy."

"Do we have a name?" Jimmy asked. "Who made the threat?"

"I have two names. Same address." Millie said. "Isabel Comstock and Frank Hannigan."

"Did they make this threat in writing?" Jimmy asked.

"No. Mick came back to the office fuming, saying somebody had threatened to punch his lights out. I've seen him mad before—but this was worse."

"Someone said he was going to punch Mick's lights out? Did this guy have a gun?"

"I don't know. I really don't. Mick stormed into his office, slammed the door, and sent an email to the Snoquamish City Planner. He sent her a note saying a nearby homeowner threatened to shoot him...or something like that. Mick never wanted to talk about it. All I could get out of him was that the homeowner was a crazy SOB."

"Can we see the email?" Jimmy asked.

Millie clicked her way to the file and selected an email dated

November 2015.

"That's more than three years ago," Steve commented.

Jimmy read the email aloud.

Date:	November 11, 2015
From:	mickwalther01@serrenehomes.com
To:	Amelia Artaud, Snoquamish City Planner
Subject:	Threats

A homeowner, I believe his name is Frank Hannigan, whose home sits just north of the plat currently being prepared for the Hemlock Hill subdivision, threatened to punch me in the face today. He also threatened to shoot over my property. I don't take such threats lightly.

"Doesn't say why Hannigan made the threat, does it?" Steve asked.

"I don't believe so," Millie said. She scrolled down to see if there might be more. "That's the whole email, and it's Mick's. But I have almost two dozen letters from an Isabel Comstock and Frank Hannigan that they wrote to Serrene Homes. We got one a month for almost two years."

"Can we see those letters?" Jimmy asked.

"Sure," Millie said. She clicked onto another file and hit the print button. "You'll only have to look at one of their letters. They kept sending the same letter every month—all they did was change the date. Finally, our lawyer told them to cease and desist or be charged with harassment. That's when the letters stopped."

Millie retrieved two letters from the printer and handed one to Steve and one to Jimmy.

Steve quietly read the letter and turned to Jimmy who was still reading.

"Doesn't read like a threat to me, Jimmy. How about you? They start out by saying, 'We truly wish you'd take responsibility for the pain and suffering you have caused my wife and me.' Apparently, they think Serrene was responsible for causing their trees to fall, is that right? Then they tell Serrene Homes that they should do the moral and ethical thing."

"Well, Steve, it's not a happy letter."

"True, but there's a long distance between being unhappy and being a killer," Steve said.

"Frank Comstock and Isabel Hannigan?" Jimmy asked. "Who are they?"

Everyone shrugged. Another small mystery. Steve scribbled down the names in his notebook.

"Would they be home? It's the middle of the day?"

No one knew.

Jimmy turned to Millie. "Different last names. Married? Housemates? Friends with benefits?"

"No idea," Millie said. "But I'll print out this file for you. It has their address. They live on the north end of the Snoquamish plateau—right next to Hemlock Hill, a subdivision we just finished."

"Oh," said Jimmy in a mocking tone, "plateau folk."

Millie pulled two pages from the printer as Jimmy stood up and extended his hand. His tone was gentle, tinged with sadness. "Thanks, Millie. Again, we're really sorry about Kelsey."

"Just find the person who killed her," she said handing the pages to Jimmy. "That'd be the best possible end to all of this."

As they left the Serrene Homes office, Jimmy suggested they call their tech specialist, Ben, and have him find out whatever he could about Comstock and Hannigan.

"Good idea. Let's put those digital folks to good use."

Chapter Six

Come Into
My Parlor

Frank Hannigan
February 1, 2019

It was mid-morning, and I was watching a pretty good episode of *Law & Order*. Isabel insists that a person anywhere in America could turn on the television at any time, day or night, and find an episode of *Law & Order*—or if not that, then another Dick Wolf production.

Suddenly, our eighty-pound Chow Chow, Wolfie, let out a preliminary bark, and then Jackson, our Black Lab/Coon Hound began baying, while Luigi added his soprano bark to the chorus. I paused *Law & Order* just as Detective Lennie Briscoe was about to make some wise-ass remark about the dead body. He always did that before a commercial.

Clearly someone was either in our driveway or already at the front door. That noisy canine cacophony is meant to keep strangers at bay and give potential troublemakers something to worry about.

Isabel loves it, too. "Our lovely barkophony is music to my ears, Frank."

I stood up and walked to the door, suddenly aware that I was still in my bathrobe. Two men, one in a rumpled blue suit and the other in a brown tweed sports jacket, stood shoulder to shoulder just outside our door. I couldn't say if they'd rung the doorbell or knocked. I keep promising to get a new doorbell—but I've been promising that for years. The barking drowned out any noise from the front door.

I pushed past my canine trio crowding the area by the storm-door. "Can I help you gentlemen?"

Each lifted his credentials. Eastlake Police Department. The dogs continued to bark.

"I'm Detective Brautigan, and this is Detective Olson."

"You'll have to speak up," I said. "Sorry."

The detective in the rumpled suit shouted, "I'm Detective Brautigan—and this is Detective Olson."

I looked at their badges and photographs and smiled. Our front deck is apparently a popular gathering place for the men in blue. Okay, tweed, too. But cops, all.

I knew I couldn't shush the dogs, so I stepped out on the front deck after pushing the dogs away from the door. We stood together on my front deck, each of us experiencing one of those moments when we wanted to say, *Okay, whose line is it?*

Detective Brautigan broke the silence. "Are you Frank Hannigan?"

"I am."

"May we come in?"

"May I ask why?"

"We'd like to ask you some questions."

"About?"

"Serrene Homes."

"You mean Hemlock Hill?" I asked.

"Same thing, I suppose. We come in peace," Jimmy said. "Are your dogs detective-friendly?"

"Mostly. Friendly is as friendly does," I replied.

I looked at both detectives and decided to declare détente with the Eastlake police. The Snoquamish police would have to wait.

"Come in. Let's sit at the kitchen table."

I pushed the door open in a welcoming gesture and wondered if they had come to play for my team or to play for the bad guys. Wolfie barked, backing away but never turning away, while Jackson and Luigi just wanted to be petted. We moved to the kitchen table and I offered to make them coffee. They declined.

"You sure? Best coffee in Snoquamish," I said. "But then I'm a biased individual with a really good espresso machine. In addition, we have the best water you'll find anywhere. Well water. We are plateau folk, after all."

"You still have your Christmas decorations up?" Jimmy said as he sat down at the table.

"Very observant. But that's why you're detectives, right? Yes, Detective Brautigan, we keep Christmas going as long as possible."

"Call me Jimmy."

"Thanks, but I'll stick to using 'Detective Brautigan.' Jimmy sounds friendly, and well, the police of late have proven to be anything but friendly…Detective Brautigan."

We had another *Whose-line-is-it-now?* moment.

"Well, I'm having some coffee," I said.

I walked into the kitchen and pulled a Christmas coffee mug from the cabinet. "Christmas is still in my coffee, too," I said holding up a cup with a fully decorated Christmas tree embellishing the sides. "Thanks for noticing all Isabel's beautiful decorations. My wife is a world-class decorator—or is that decoratrix?"

The machine began filling my cup.

"How long will you be leaving your decorations up?"

"Don't know. Last year they were up until the end of February. It's legal, isn't it? There isn't a date when they have to be down is there? Like taking off your studded tires? Detective Olson?" I asked.

"No, no. This is strictly idle chatter. My wife takes everything down by January second. It's like Christmas never happened."

"Well, wives do what wives do," I said as I sat down at the dining room table.

"Speaking of wives, is your wife here?" Jimmy asked.

"Yes, she is, but unlike me, she works for a living. She's an accountant with clients and deadlines. We are smack dab in the middle of tax season. Fortunately, I'm a man without deadlines."

"You're retired?"

I looked down at the chenille bathrobe Isabel had purchased for me a month after I moved in. Some days I never take it off once I put it on. My neighbors enjoy honking and waving when they see me walking to my recycling bin or mailbox in my white robe. Isabel says it make me look like Father Time.

"Retired?" I asked. "Does it show?"

Detective Brautigan smiled. "I'm hoping that's me in a few. Maybe next year."

"So. I'd love to talk with you guys all day, but I've paused my episode of *Law & Order* to entertain your questions. So, ask away."

Detective Olson reached into his tweed jacket and took out a faded gray notebook.

"Let me get right to the gist of it all," Detective Brautigan said. He opened his notebook, too.

"Did you threaten to shoot Mick Walther back in 2015?"

"The developer?"

"Yeah. Did you threaten to shoot him?"

"No."

Detective Olson consulted his notebook. "Did you threaten to shoot *at* him or *toward* him or shoot *over* the property he was developing?"

"No."

"Did you threaten him in any way?" Detective Brautigan asked.

"Yeah. I told that son-of-a-bitch that, if I ever saw him, I'd punch him right in the middle of his fat face."

"And what did he say?"

"Nothing. He hung up on me."

"This happened over the phone?"

"Yeah. The bastard's clear-cutting crew cut the holding roots of our trees, and those trees fell. I called him as soon as I saw the roots had been cut. I told him that the next time I saw him I'd plant a fist on his big, fat nose."

"And..."

I looked at both detectives. "And what? That's it. And I still plan to plant one in the middle of his kisser for what he did to our property here."

"What did happen?" Detective Brautigan asked.

It occurred to me that these cops might actually want to see what had happened. "You guys have a few minutes?"

I opened the back door and all three dogs dashed into the back yard while the three humans walked out across the back deck and onto the grass. As we walked toward the five giant stumps—all that was left of our majestic trees—I warned the detectives to watch where they stepped.

"There are dog bombs everywhere."

They both laughed...and then looked carefully at their feet.

I explained how the developer had knowingly severed the holding roots, how there hadn't even been time to get the emergency permits to safely remove the doomed trees, how the five trees had fallen together in a terrible wind storm—wiping out our newly-built, two-story, custom shed, shattering part of our roof, and littering our property with giant tree trunks and broken branches.

"Oh, and one of the trees killed our Flat-Coated Retriever, Miss Aria. She was asleep on our bed in the master bedroom. Everything happened so quickly, and she was asleep when one of the trees smashed the roof and collapsed the ceiling. She couldn't have seen it coming. She was dead when we got to her."

"Shit," Detective Brautigan said. "Your dog. I remember you mentioning that in your letter." Brautigan shook his head. "I can't say I blame you for wanting to punch the guy. Anyone who killed my dog—well..."

He walked toward the fence and the Hemlock Hill development as his partner and I trailed behind. He stopped and looked closely at the massive stumps.

"Dogs are special," Jimmy said. "I've always said that they're better than people. Still think that's true."

He walked carefully over the uneven ground where the ancient tree roots had pulled free from the topsoil. He touched each vast remaining tree trunk as if it were an old friend.

"What kind of trees were these?" he asked.

"The one you're touching was a hemlock. We lost three hemlocks"—I pointed to each hemlock stump—"and two firs. That fir's the tree that destroyed our shed, smashed through our roof, and killed Miss Aria," I said, pointing to the largest of the tree stumps. "One hundred and twenty-five feet tall and twenty-five thousand pounds."

Detective Brautigan turned toward me and gave me a wan smile. "I'm sorry about your dog, Mr. Hannigan. No one at Serrene seemed terribly concerned with what happened to you."

"Serrene? Why would they? They don't seem to care about anything except their bottom line. Dead trees, dead dogs. It's all the same to them. Just make sure nothing interferes with business."

"I can see you love your dogs," he said as he walked toward the fir.

"What's not to love? They're all rescues."

"Rescues? Wow. That's even better," he said as he traced his finger along the ridge of the bark on the Douglas fir stump. "Five trees? All at once? Must have been one hell of a mess."

"Yeah, it was. One hell of a mess. Want to see the pictures? Got them on my phone. Pictures of Aria, dead on the bed and then her poor body lying at the vet's office. I've got pictures of our once-proud heritage trees, all now fallen. If Isabel and I had decided to cut down those trees, the nice folks at City Hall could have fined us $150,000. Can you imagine that? $1,500 per diameter inch. But since the developer cut them down, there's no fine."

We walked along the property line. "Let me be clear, detectives. These trees were our trees—mine and Isabel's. They all stood on our side of the property line. But apparently the developer can cut any of our tree roots that happen to grow underground on his side of the property line."

"That's legal?" Detective Olson asked.

"Yeah. It's legal. Just one of the laws you guys are charged with enforcing. Makes you feel proud, doesn't it?"

"What are you going to do?" Detective Olson asked.

"I'm gonna punch Mick Walther's lights out if I ever see him."

"Really?"

I shrugged.

"Probably not."

"You don't look much like a punch-your-lights-out kind of guy," Detective Brautigan said.

"Not in your handsome chenille bathrobe, anyway," said Detective Olson.

"Yeah, but it feels good to say it. Maybe one of you guys could punch his lights out for me. You do that sort of thing with your job, right?"

"That's old school, Mr. Hannigan. The new approach stresses intervention—non-lethal intervention."

"What's that exactly?"

"Talking."

"Well, I can tell you that no one here ever threatened Mick Walther with a gun or threatened to use a gun. But that didn't stop him from making that accusation in an email to the city planner. Unfortunately, not only is cutting our trees' roots not a crime, lying to the city isn't a crime, either."

As we returned to the house, I asked them to check their shoes.

"I know, I know," said Detective Olson. "Dog bombs."

I couldn't see any of the dogs, but I could hear the occasional bark from the front yard. We walked back into the house, and resumed our seats at the dining room table.

"Let me see if I understand why you're here. You actually came out today to ask me about something I reportedly said more than three years ago? Something I never said, by the way."

The two detectives looked at one another, and then they looked at me.

"Do you subscribe to a newspaper?" Detective Brautigan asked.

"Yeah. I get the Seattle Chronicle online. Isabel gets the Washington Post and the New York Times. Strictly online. Isabel loves her tablet, and I use my computer. We're a paperless newspaper household. We're the Evergreen State, after all. Save the trees. Even my wife's office is mostly paper-free. Why?"

"Have you read anything lately about Kelsey Walther?"

"Don't think so, but the name's familiar. I met her at Serrene Homes when I went to talk with her husband Mick. I went right after our trees fell. He wasn't there, so she pinch hit for him. She's a real piece of work. She didn't give a damn about what happened here. Even when I mentioned the death of our dog. She told me to have our lawyer talk to their lawyer."

"You haven't seen or heard the news?"

"What news?" I asked.

"Kelsey Walther was murdered. You must have seen it. It's been front-page news in the Chronicle—and on all the local stations."

I shook my head—as if I couldn't believe my ears. "Well, I didn't read or hear anything about it. I'm pretty much a Sudoku fanatic with the Chronicle. That and the editorials. I'm a national news junkie. I don't do much local news—and the local broadcast teams on TV are just too damn cute for me, and when they stop being cute, they're too damn depressing. People getting killed close to home is just not my cup of tea."

What would you ask if you didn't already know? asked the voice inside my head.

"When did all this happen?" I asked.

"Last Wednesday."

"Here in Snoquamish?"

"No, Eastlake."

"How'd it happen?"

Detectives Brautigan and Olson traded glances. I decided I'd just let the question hang out there like a slow curve ball coming over the plate. Neither detective seemed interested in swinging.

My mind was racing. *Don't look guilty*, I said to myself. *Look interested. Look curious. Look as if you don't know.*

Of course, I knew she how she died. I was there. I'd watched all the local broadcasts, followed the online articles in the Chronicle. Read her obituary. Reporters used the word "bludgeoned," and that sounded so primitive. I was grateful that one good swing was all it took. I'll admit I wasn't sure if I'd killed her until I heard it on the news. The awful sound when my tire iron and her skull connected was so distinctive—something akin to hitting a cantaloupe with a hammer. Not loud. A soft, liquid *thwop*.

I wondered why the detectives didn't simply say, *Kelsey Walther was bludgeoned to death in the Factoria QFC parking lot.* They could have said that...but they didn't.

"I only met Kelsey Walther briefly, at Serrene's offices. It wasn't a happy encounter. And frankly, I don't know Mick except on the phone." I paused. "Kelsey Walther murdered? That's a shame."

Should I say I'm sorry? I'm sorry that the Walthers believe they can make a living while killing other people's dogs and destroying their property and serenity, I thought. *If the police are expecting me to have a crisis of conscience and blurt out a confession, they're gonna have a long, long wait. I'm never gonna blurt out, "It was me. I did it. I followed her to the QFC parking lot, flattened her tire while she was in the store, and killed her with the tire iron I took along for the express purpose of bashing her head in." That'll never happen.*

"Did I say something wrong?" I asked.

"No. You're fine," said Detective Brautigan. "We're just following up any lead that comes our way."

"Wow," I said leaning back in my chair. "A lead brought you to my door?"

They didn't seem inclined to respond to my question.

"May I ask: Where did you get the lead that brought you here?"

Both Brautigan and Olson ignored that question, too, while Detective Brautigan pulled out several pieces of badly-folded paper. I decided to let them take the lead.

"I have a report here," Brautigan said as he unfolded three sheets of paper, "that says the local police have been here three times in three years. The police reports aren't very flattering."

"So, let's see, you didn't get any earlier reports? Reports of times when Isabel and I got involved to help other people—plain, regular people—with problems ranging from lost pets to stolen purses to domestic violence? You don't have the flattering reports?"

Nothing.

"Well, I guess I'm not surprised," I said after a pause. "Two days before my trees fell, I called the city planner nineteen times. Left a message every time. Told her that my trees' roots had been cut—and that our lives and property were in danger. She never returned a single phone call. Not one. I got pissed off about her lack of response and left a final message saying I'd come to her office and do a dance on her desk if she didn't get back to me."

I think I saw Brautigan and Olson smile.

"Well, I never did a dance, but that comment brought two police officers to our door. I'm guessing that Mick Walther's email probably shoved them in my direction, too. When I asked those officers to look at my backyard—I wanted them to see how huge the trees were that Serrene Homes had sentenced to death—they basically said they weren't interested. They even read me my rights as if my phone call made me some kind of criminal. And one of them suggested that my wife and I could possibly be terrorists. No kidding. Possible terrorists. It all went to hell after that."

"What do you mean 'Went to hell?'"

"I told them to get the hell off my front porch and off my property. If they didn't have the decency to actually look at what provoked my calls to Mick Walther or the city planner—they could just...well...just leave."

"Is that what you said to them?"

"I don't remember exactly what I said. Check their police reports. I'm sure they've got it all written down somewhere. Whatever I said, I'm sure they got the feeling they were no longer welcome. If they didn't come here for all the facts—and they didn't—they could stick it up their royal blues. Let's just say it wasn't an amicable departure."

"What about the second visit?"

"That was this past December. About a week or so before Christmas. Pretty sure. Local police wanted to know if we'd seen a missing teenage boy. He lives in Hemlock Hill, the development that cost us our trees. The kid's dad came knocking on my door worried about his son—apparently his son had been out all night and hadn't come home—and instead of being properly empathetic, I wondered aloud if it was his son who'd been stealing wine from my shed. That was probably the wrong thing to say to a worried father."

"Why's that?"

"The dad told the police I was rude to him. That's probably true. I tend to be rude to anyone from that side of the fence. Of course, I've only met one person from Hemlock Hill—the worried dad with the missing son. Occasionally someone waves when I'm standing at the fence, but I do my utmost to ignore anything that even feels like a friendly gesture."

I paused, as if I wanted Brautigan or Olson to join the conversation. They just listened.

I was tapping the tabletop with my fingers. "I'm a dad, too. So I think I know how he feels. I think his son is still missing. Is that true?"

Detective Olson nodded.

"Sorry to hear that."

Brautigan looked at me. "The second police report says you refused to come out on the deck or identify yourself."

"That's not entirely true. As I recollect, I told them to call me Mr. Anonymous."

"Why would you do that?"

"Why?" I wondered how much I should say, and then I decided to just give it to them straight. I looked directly at Detective Brautigan.

"Any police force that suggests my wife and I are terrorists can kiss my ass if they want any cooperation at all. Any police force that would rather hassle than help its citizens—especially when those citizens need their help...like when tree roots have been compromised..."

I stopped talking. I took a deep breath. I was angry, but I needed to finish what I wanted to say.

"I told'em I'm done being helpful. If one hand washes the other, why am I the only one with dirty hands? They want me to be civic-minded? Well, screw civic-mindedness. If they won't help me, I won't help them."

I wondered if I'd overstepped some line of propriety.

"Sorry to dump on you guys," I said. "At least you had the decency to walk out to my backyard so I could show you what happened. The local cops never did. The first time any of them even walked into my backyard was last December, right after that kid disappeared. That's the third visit. They came looking for Jacob—I think that's his name—with dogs and a crime scene crew. The dogs picked up the boy's scent trail. Practically a straight line from his front door to my shed. Then, somehow, the scent trail went dead in the middle of my yard. However, they found Jacob's fingerprints all over my storage shed and on lots of my wine bottles. I'm guessing Jacob had been the one breaking into my shed and stealing my wine. My wine had been disappearing a few bottles at a time since last summer, and I was pissed. That's why I said something to his dad. I know now I shouldn't have. I really thought Jacob's dad might hit me, he was so distraught."

We lapsed into momentary silence.

"I'm curious," I said. "Did the police ever tell Jacob's dad what they found after they searched my property? His fingerprints in my shed and on my wine bottles?"

Steve and Jimmy looked at one another. This was the first they'd heard of it. They both gestured and made a face that said, "We don't know."

Another momentary silence, and then Jimmy got things moving again. "Let me ask again about that threat you made three years ago..."

"Damn it, Brautigan, there was no threat. That's bullshit. It never happened. I never threatened anyone at any time—not with a gun, anyway. I was angry about my trees—and that's when I told Walther I'd punch him in the face. Nobody here ever threatened anyone with a gun. Never. Mick Walther told that lie to the Snoquamish City Planner so the police would have to come out here. And apparently that same lie has brought you to my front door, too. All the way from Eastlake."

The detectives sat across from me without saying a word. They were listening and watching me.

"Do you own a gun, Mr. Hannigan?" Steve asked after a minute of silence.

"Excellent question. No. That whole gun-threat business is a lie. A damn lie. But it's still got legs, doesn't it? What was it Mark Twain said about a lie? 'A lie gets halfway around the world while the truth is still putting on his pants?'"

"Mark Twain said that?"

"Pretty sure it was Twain."

Detective Olson tucked his notebook in his jacket pocket and turned to me. "Sorry we took so much of your time, Mr. Hannigan."

"I'm just glad you could see what that son-of-a-bitch did to our trees—to the life Isabel and I share here. Sure wish one of you would volunteer to punch his lights out."

"I'm afraid that's not possible," said Brautigan as he and his partner walked out the front door.

I stood there and waved. "Watch out for the dogs," I shouted.

Isabel emerged from her office, and we watched as the detectives backed out. The dogs ran along the fence line as they departed.

"Do you think they suspect anything?"

"Don't really know, Isabel, my love. I hope not."

"Did they ask about Jacob?"

"A little bit. Nothing to worry about."

"Good. You gave them the tour of our fallen trees?"

"Complete with the agonizingly true story of how we're out of pocket with lawyers and repairs."

"Hey, Franklin, my love, they should hear that. We are out of pocket. Plenty. We'll never get those big, beautiful trees back. Not in this lifetime."

I shook my head.

"And we'll never get Miss Aria back, either."

"You're right, Izz."

We lost something irreplaceable when our trees fell—and it was far more than just the trees. We lost our faith in the law. We no longer believed the law would deliver justice because some laws were written specifically to legalize injustice.

If I sound like a broken record—well, that's just too damn bad. Keep in mind, we pursued the injustice against us the way we'd been taught our entire lives. First, we hoped to "reason" with those who had wronged us. Failing that, we filed a lawsuit. Our lawyer said it wouldn't make any difference because the law was on the side of the lawless—aka, the developers. Naturally, the developers didn't see themselves as lawless. If called into court, they'd sit there with their lawyers and quote city ordinances and settled law designed to make litigants like us lose.

Our choice was to accept the reality of the law—you know, suck it up, grin and bear it—or privately redefine reality so that, once again, the law and justice were synonyms.

That's what we decided to do. Call it a new—If private—reality.

In our new reality, owners and employees of Serrene Homes would pay for the injustices visited upon us. And they'd keep paying until our new reality burst in the harsh light of real-world law enforcement.

C'est dommage, I thought.

Isabel and I had spent long evenings wondering what's next after our lawyer told us that our lawsuit was probably hopeless. A dead end.

Then Jacob jumped the Hemlock Hill fence to steal my wine, and a whole new set of possibilities opened up. We'd already killed one kid—and maybe the police would figure it all out and come knocking at our door. But now we're aiming our vengeance at the people who truly deserve our anger. One down, two to go.

What was it my mom used to say? *In for a dime, in for a dollar.*

Isabel—who'd spent a whole decade in London—invariably corrected me. "It's in for a penny, in for a pound."

"But we're not in England," I'd point out.

"Clearly," she pointed out. "If we were, the developer would never have been permitted to cut our tree roots."

"Oh, to be in England," I said in grand poetic style. "Nevertheless, Mick Walther is still on the hook for what he did to us," I said. "I aim to make him pay."

"Go get'em." Isabel hugged me, kissed me, smiled, and then walked toward her office. "You be careful, okay? I gotta get back to work. Oh, by the way, you missed your episode of *Law and Order*."

"Reruns, my love, reruns." I said.

I really love that woman. We're both in for a dollar...or a pound.

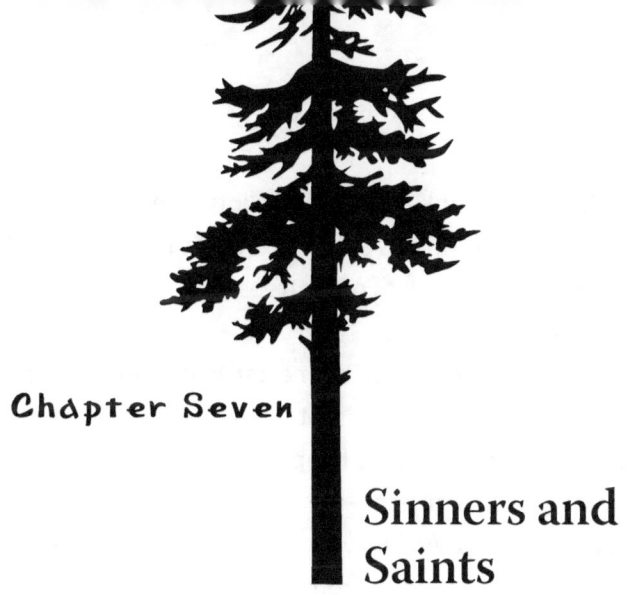

Chapter Seven

Sinners and Saints

Jimmy Brautigan
February 1, 2019

"Do you believe him?" Olson asked as they backed slowly out of the driveway—three dogs barking from the fence line.

"About what? About being royally pissed that a developer can cut the roots of his trees? Kill his dog? About the law not being on his side when he's the one who's lost his dog, five huge trees, part of his house, a custom shed, and peace of mind? About not trusting the cops after they stopped by to intimidate him 'cause he threatened to do a dance on a city planner's desk?"

"Mick Walther said Hannigan threatened him with a gun," Steve said.

"After talking to Hannigan, I'm not inclined to believe Mick Walther. How would you feel if someone did to you what Serrene did to him?"

It was a rhetorical question. They had both felt their sympathies rise as they spoke with Frank Hannigan.

"You think the local police wanted to intimidate him?"

"What do you think, Steve? Does 'dancing on the desk' sound like a serious threat to you?"

"Not really."

"So, like it or not, Frank Hannigan has lots to be mad about. I find it interesting that Serrene Homes seemed...I don't know...so indifferent to the death of his dog...or the loss of his trees."

"Yeah," Steve agreed.

"Or crushing the roof above the master bedroom. Or destroying his shed. Christ almighty, Steve, the first thing Serrene mentioned was a threat which Hannigan says never happened."

Jimmy rather liked Hannigan—the suspect, the man under the microscope. It was Brautigan's tendency to get close to the people he was investigating, and that drove his lieutenant crazy. Frequently, his lieutenant would have a sit down and ask him whose side he was on. As far as the lieutenant was concerned, everyone was a potential suspect—but Jimmy felt just the opposite.

"You're a cop, for Christ's sake," his lieutenant would say. "You're a detective whose job is to detect...and enforce the law. You're not supposed to get in up to your eyeballs in somebody's troubles. Just enforce the law."

"Jesus, lieutenant," Jimmy would say. "They're not suspects until they act like suspects. Or until we have real proof. Until then, they're just citizens like you and me—but I'm not so sure about you."

Early on, Jimmy would find himself arguing with his lieutenant, but then he realized he couldn't win the argument—even when his lieutenant was wrong. Which was most of the time. As they drove away, Jimmy could feel how wronged, how betrayed Hannigan felt, after a lifetime of being civic-minded.

"You think he's got a burr in his saddle?"

"A burr? Maybe. More like a stick up his ass—shoved up there hard by a developer who probably should have taken greater care."

"Let's stop by Snoquamish City Hall and find out what's up with that missing boy," Olson suggested. "Don't you wonder if there's a connection?"

"Connection?"

"Sure, we went to question Hannigan because he may have had a beef with Serrene Homes. Right? That's why we went there. At the same time, a kid who lives in the subdivision built by Serrene Homes disappears. This kid just happened to live in the house right behind Hannigan's property—and if what Hannigan says is true, he's also the kid who the Snoquamish police know was probably stealing wine from Hannigan. This kid vanishes...without a trace. No ransom request. No body. No clues. Just gone. A month after a kid who lives in Hemlock Hill disappears, a woman who works for Serrene Homes, the company that built Hemlock Hill—and who happens to be the wife of one of the principal owners—is murdered. You think that's just a coincidence?"

"Alright, Steve, what are you saying?"

"I think there's a common denominator, don't you?"

Jimmy always made a face—Steve called it Jimmy's "What-the-hell-is-going-on?" face—whenever he was trying to figure out what the hell was going on.

"You're making that face, Jimmy," Steve said.

"Yeah, I know. We've gotta see Jack Stahl. He's handling the boy's disappearance for the Snoquamish PD."

"The kid's still missing," said Detective Jack Stahl, tapping on the plastic lid of his Starbucks latte. "I'm not real optimistic."

"Okay," Jimmy nodded. "You've ruled out him being a runaway...?"

Stahl shook his head. "He didn't run away. No way. According to the happily-married parents, everything was just fine. Jacob's got three younger sisters who swear their brother would never run away. Has a girlfriend who says the same thing."

Jack pulled a labeled manila folder from beneath a pile of folders sitting on his desk.

"Here," he said, handing the file to Jimmy. "We transcribe all our interviews. This is the interview with Jacob's family."

Jimmy opened the folder.

"You can see his dad did most of the talking. Dad's a big defense attorney with a Seattle law firm—he calls damn near every day wanting to know if we've made any headway. I've gotten tired of telling him we really haven't. But I don't think he's gotten tired of calling us incompetent."

"Is it true that Jacob's a wine thief? That's what Hannigan thinks," Olson asked.

"Alleged wine thief," Jack admitted. "His fingerprints were all over Hannigan's backyard shed—inside and out. We found at least eight bottles of wine with Jacob's fingerprints all over them. So, he'd definitely been in the shed—and yeah, it looks like he was probably Hannigan's wine thief. As you may know, Hannigan never called us when he discovered any of his wine was missing."

"Did you ask him why?" Steve asked.

Jack shook his head. "He said the Snoquamish police have an excellent reputation for doing nothing at all. Said he didn't want to waste his time."

"Did you ever tell Jacob's dad about the evidence you found?" Jimmy asked.

"Yeah. It wasn't a happy conversation. His dad kept insisting that we'd be better off spending time on the disappearance/kidnapping angle than worrying about petty theft. He also made vague threats about a lawsuit if his son's wine-thieving ever made it into the newspapers. Says the police better not besmirch his son's reputation. Especially since his son isn't around to defend himself. That's it. That's where we are."

"So nobody knows where he is...or even when he left?" Steve asked.

"Apparently, Jacob was the alpha child—did almost whatever he wanted. Staying out late on a Friday night was apparently no big deal," Jack said. "I suppose the Forrest Method of parenting is the opposite of helicopter parenting."

"Yeah," said Jimmy, "it's called no parenting." Jimmy continued scanning the interview. "What did Jacob's mother have to say?"

"Practically nothing. Jacob's mother could barely talk—she was constantly breaking down and sobbing. Maybe we should go back and talk with her now that some time has passed."

Jimmy ran his finger along one of the pages of the transcribed interview.

"According to this statement, one of Jacob's sisters says she remembers her brother being home just before midnight that Friday night."

"That would be Camille. Read a little further down. She said her brother came in soaking wet, shivering, and mad as hell. He slammed his bedroom door, and that's the last anyone remembers seeing him."

"So how would a kid get soaking wet on a rainy Friday night in the middle of December if he was out in a car with his friends?" Jimmy asked.

"That's just it," Jack said, a quizzical look on his face. "His car was still parked in the driveway. His sister is pretty sure it never moved that night."

"Was Jacob the kind of kid to take a long walk on a rainy night?" Steve asked.

"Not according to his dad."

"Who else did you talk with?"

"We questioned Jacob's girlfriend, Jasmine, too—she's a senior at Eastsound. She's positive he's not a runaway, either. In fact, she and Jacob had a date to see some new movie on Saturday, the day after he disappeared."

"So Jacob wasn't with her on Friday night?"

"Not according to Jasmine."

"And Jacob was a no show on Saturday?"

Jack nodded.

"Do you have any suspects at all?"

"We asked around Snoquamish Catholic to see if anyone had a grudge against Jacob. Talked to teachers and to a whole bunch of students. Apparently Jacob is something of a pain in the ass."

"Really? At a Catholic school?" Jimmy asked with mock surprise.

"Imagine that."

"Come on, Jimmy. You've never heard of redemption?" Steve loved needling his partner—the product of a Catholic school education.

"A pain in the ass who wasn't thrown into the open arms of the public schools?"

"Nope," Jack said plopping himself into the chair behind his desk. It took a moment for him to tap his way to the screen he wanted. "Here we go," he said, looking closely at his computer screen. "We've got almost three dozen statements. About fifteen from teachers and coaches, and the rest from his classmates. Want me to read you a few of Jacob Forrest's greatest hits?"

"Entertain us, Jack," Jimmy said. "Start with his classmates."

"One kid said Jacob was 'an arrogant prick. Always talking about himself and how the rest of humanity sucks. No one likes Jacob more than Jacob.' Nice talk for a Catholic school kid, right?"

"Teenagers are teenagers everywhere," Jimmy said. "Some are alphas. Some are arrogant pricks. What else?"

Jack continued. "One senior girl said, 'Jacob took me to a basketball game and left—just disappeared—without telling me before the game was over. I had to find my own way home. He's good at disappearing.'"

"Another stellar recommendation."

"Hey, should I be writing any of this down?" Steve asked. "Or is all of this in your files?"

"If you ask something we haven't asked, I'll let you know," Stahl said. "Everything's been by the book, and all the interviews and other pieces of information have been transcribed and logged in right here." He patted the computer.

"Grades?" Jimmy asked as he scribbled something in his journal.

"Jacob is a B student. Most of his teachers feel he could be an A student, but," Stahl tapped his keyboard again and scrolled. "Let me quote his Government teacher: 'Jacob is hoping he can get by on his size, football prowess, and good looks.' She goes on to say, 'Jacob is a smart kid who will go far if he majors in schmoozing at university.'"

Jack, long and lanky, had been an NCAA Division One defensive safety until a broken collarbone brought his collegiate football career to a premature end. He scrolled the screen a bit further. "His coaches say he's been recruited by a couple of universities...let me jump in with a comment his football coach made...'His indifferent attitude toward almost anything makes it unlikely that he'll play for a Division One university.'"

"So," said Jimmy, "smart but lazy."

"Seems like," said Jack.

Steve and Jimmy were like an old married couple. They looked at each other to find out who was going to ask the question that brought them there.

"We just left Frank Hannigan's house," Jimmy said. "He's got a real hard-on for this police department. I wouldn't be overstating things to say he hates your guts, and if he never sees another Snoquamish policeman, it'll be too soon."

"Well, let me say that we are not universally loved."

"We decided to drop by because Steve thinks there might be some connection between Jacob's disappearance and the murder we're working on."

"The Walther murder?" Jack asked, looking at Olson.

"It's been bugging me for some time, Jack. The common denominator is Hemlock Hill, the Serrene Homes subdivision. First, a resident of a Serrene Homes' subdivision—your kid, Jacob Forrest—disappears. Then Kelsey Walther, who worked for Serrene Homes, is found bludgeoned to death right next to her truck that has Serrene Homes painted all over it. Okay? This Frank Hannigan hates Serrene Homes and he's decided to tell anyone from the Hemlock Hill side of the fence to go to hell."

"You looked at Hannigan, right?" asked Jimmy.

"First one we looked at," Stahl said. "Our search dogs started at the Forrest house and tracked Jacob's scent in damn near a straight line from his Hemlock Hill neighborhood, across the fence, and right into Hannigan's shed. The kid left prints all over the door frame and inside the shed as well. Found his prints on Hannigan's wine bottles, too."

"Let me guess. He didn't want the chardonnay?" Steve chimed in.

Stahl just shrugged his shoulders. "Who knows? We're sure he'd been in the shed. There's absolutely no question about that. And he probably was the one who picked the lock to get in. Probably took a few bottles of wine, too, at some point. At least that's what Hannigan suggested to Jacob's father. But the day we were there, the wine rack was full—even if his fingerprints were on a slew of bottles—so if he came over the night he went missing, it looks like he didn't take anything."

"So where did the search dogs end up?"

"Right there in the middle of the yard. The scent went cold smack dab in the middle of the yard."

"The middle of the yard?"

"Yeah. Like he was abducted by aliens or something. The dogs scoured Hannigan's backyard looking to see if the scent went off in some other direction. If you believe the dogs, it looks like Jacob simply went back the way he came. We don't know. We don't even know for sure if he was in Hannigan's yard the night he disappeared."

"If he was in Hannigan's yard, trying to get into the shed, that could explain how he got soaked," Steve offered.

"True. But it seems he ended back at home soaked and pissed and empty-handed. At least his sister didn't see any wine. And if he didn't get any wine, why are his fingerprints all over the shed—outside and inside—and on a whole bunch of bottles of wine?"

"And what do you have on Hannigan?"

"Other than he's got a bad attitude?"

Jimmy might have debated that description, but Jack was a long-time friend. He let it slide. "Yeah, other than that?" he said.

"Nothing. He's retired. Taught English at Eastsound High before he took a job as a national consultant for a textbook company. We talked to his neighbors. He tends to keep to himself, but they all say he's been with

Isabel for more than a decade and both he and Isabel are neighbors you can rely on. In fact, they installed a stand-by generator to run the well house when there's a power outage. There are three families on that well. No power, no water. So, Frank Hannigan is a hero. We phoned a number of his former colleagues. Same story. They say he's a good guy—with a whacky sense of humor. None of them thinks he could be involved in anything like this."

"Like what?"

"I don't know...like kidnapping or murder."

"And his wife?"

"Same for Isabel. Born and raised right here in the Northwest and no one has anything but good words for her. She's an accountant and works from her home office. When we asked her if anyone would vouch for her, she gave us her complete client list and the names of family members and friends without missing a beat. The ones we called are right there on the record. I'll print it out for you."

The printer began spewing out more than forty pages of information that his detectives had gathered.

"Nobody has said anything even vaguely critical of her. For Christ's sake, all her animals are rescued animals and she works *pro bono* as the accountant for *Kirkland Kitty*, one of the local animal rescue groups. *Pro bono*. Ask anyone. She's a saint."

"A saint?"

"Oh, yeah. One more item that I hadn't seen until I did my online search. Back in 2010, Isabel rescued a human being. Went way above and beyond. This woman, whom she met through a mutual friend, showed up on her doorstep because this woman's husband decided she made a great punching bag. This woman had two dogs and no place to go. She'd gone to a shelter—left her dogs in the car—but her husband tracked her down. She ended up at Isabel's home pretty badly bruised. Isabel took her and her dogs in, called the cops—yeah, she called us—and that SOB husband of hers spent the next 18 months in county lockup."

"Sounds like a saint to me," Steve admitted.

"A saint that rescues people as well as dogs and cats," Jack said, shaking his head. "I just don't see her as a bad guy." He shrugged his shoulders, "She may be mighty pissed off about what happened because of the Hemlock Hill development, but she's got a great track record."

Jimmy turned to Steve. "So much for a common denominator."

"Before we go, could we drop in on the city planner? The one who asked you guys to pay Hannigan a visit."

"I wish you could. That's no longer possible," said Jack. "Her office used to be just down the hall—actually, it still is. But she's not. The woman you'd like to talk to is Amelia Artaud. I think it's French because she always insisted on not pronouncing the "d"—sounded like Are-toe. Miss Artaud is no longer with our City Planning Department, probably because she never seemed to be able to answer her phone. Even worse, she didn't seem to know anything about anything..."

Jack stopped himself mid-sentence.

"Sorry. I should learn to keep my mouth shut. She's now working somewhere in Montana." Jack paused, "If you ever cross paths with her, don't tell her I said that."

"If I ever see her while I'm touring Montana, you may rely on my discretion," Jimmy said, his finger to his lips, "until the day I can use your careless comment as blackmail, Jack."

As Jimmy and Steve stood up, Jimmy asked, "Would you object if I had another run at the Forrests? Something just feels strange."

"Be my guest. Just send me a copy of whatever you get, okay? Maybe I can get Jacob's dad to start calling you every day rather than me."

Jimmy and Steve and Jack weren't exactly nowhere in their investigations, but they were closer to nowhere than somewhere. No body, no hard evidence in Jacob Forrest's inexplicable disappearance. No video, no murder weapon, and no motive in the parking lot murder of Kelsey Walther.

On the way back to the department, Jimmy called his daughter, Amanda. She was hosting his birthday dinner this year...for last year. The party was tomorrow night. She practiced family medicine at a large HMO, a fact that gave him a great deal of pleasure.

He loved getting together with his children. They were all bright, all professionals, and all of them loved sparring verbally with their dad. Whenever he gathered together with his son and daughters, he'd point out what he'd pointed out too many times before. "I've bored hundreds, maybe thousands, of suspects to death by bragging about you kids. I tell them I've got a landscape architect, an accountant, a computer geek, and a doctor. When I start listing all the things you're really good at, they usually blurt out a confession just so they don't have to listen to me anymore."

"Really, Dad?" his daughter Rebecca would say in *faux* surprise. "We've never heard that before."

"Not ever," Amanda would say confirming what her sister said.

"Yep. First time ever," Benjamin would agree.

"Okay. I guess I'm getting old," Jimmy would say laughingly.

"Ancient," Becky would chime.

"Senile," pronounced Amanda the doctor.

"Version 1.0," Benjamin would conclude.

At some point, his oldest daughter, Michelle, would come to his rescue and scold all the others for picking on their "poor, defenseless father."

Amanda picked up the phone on the second rIng. "Hi, Dad."

"Just checking in," Jimmy said. "I'll be at your place at five. Sharp. What should I bring?"

"Just your handsome self," Amanda assured him. "It is your birthday, you know."

"We could do a two-fer," Jimmy said. "Celebrate 62 and 63 together. After all, it's already 2019."

"So you want to be 63 when you've only been 62 for thirty-nine days?"

"Tomorrow it will be forty days, not thirty-nine. Being 62 for forty days is quite long enough. Can't we go for 63, too?"

"Sorry, Dad, one birthday at a time," Amanda said. "What kind of cake would you like?"

"Chocolate. With chocolate icing."

Small talk, Steve thought to himself as he listened to his partner. *The stuff of life. Chit-chat. The reason we can get out of bed every morning.*

When Jimmy hung up, Steve commented. "I envy you, Jimmy. You've got great kids. You know that, don't you?"

"You're right, Steve, I just wish Felicia were still alive—she's the reason I've got great kids."

They drove on in silence.

Jimmy spoke up, quietly, almost as if he were speaking in church. "I can't imagine what I'd do if one of my children disappeared without a trace. How does a parent survive that?"

February 4, 2019

The following Monday, Jimmy and Steve were ushered into Harold Grosvenor Forrest's Seattle law office. They were told he'd join them momentarily. It had been more than a month since his son, Jacob, had disappeared.

"Kind of a long commute from Snoquamish," Jimmy said to Steve as they moved to peer west out of the 40th floor window. "Seattle always looks beautiful from high above."

They watched as the Bremerton ferry slipped into its dock. Just beyond, the waters of Puget Sound glittered brightly beneath a flawless blue winter sky. Not even the hint of a cloud. The majestic Olympic Mountains rose purple further west.

"On a clear day, you can see forever, can't you?" Jimmy said.

"Sure feels that way," Steve agreed.

Harold Forrest walked in and joined them at the window.

"Perfect winter day, isn't it, Detectives?" Harold said, a trace of sadness in his voice. He introduced himself and shook hands with the detectives before moving behind his desk. He invited Jimmy and Steve to sit. "So, how can I help the Eastlake Police?"

"Thanks for seeing us," Jimmy said. "This is about your son and the case we're working on. Tell, Mr. Forrest what you've told me, Steve."

Steve took out his notes and perused them for just a moment before tucking them back in his suit coat pocket.

"Here's the thing, Mr. Forrest. Your son's disappearance in December of last year and the death of Kelsey Walther last week have a common denominator—Serrene Homes. You live in Hemlock Hill built by Serrene, and Kelsey was an employee and the wife of one of Serrene's owners. Maybe it's a reach. A coincidence." Steve struggled for what to say next.

Jimmy jumped in with a quiet comment. "Mr. Forrest, we know your son was in the shed in Comstock and Hannigan's backyard. We don't know when exactly—and perhaps you don't know when either—but it's certain that he was in the shed, that he handled wine in the shed, and probably that he picked the lock to gain access to the shed. We're not interested if your son took any wine—we're just trying to figure out how he could disappear into thin air last December. Your daughter, Camille, told the Snoquamish police that Jacob had come home soaking wet and angry at 11:30 that Friday night. Your wife said she found his wet clothes in the hamper the next morning. But his bed hadn't been slept in. And his car was still in the driveway. Apparently, he still had his wallet and cellphone. The car keys were found on his dresser. Do we have the facts straight?"

Harold nodded, his fingers rubbing his temples.

"Yeah," Harold said. "Those are the facts—the few damn facts that we have."

"And no one in your household saw Jacob go back out that night?"

"No."

"Do you have home surveillance?" Steve asked. "You're in a brand new development."

"We do now. A little too late," Harold said quietly. "If we'd had it back in December, we'd at least know what time Jacob left—and maybe which way he was headed."

"And no one knows what he was doing before he came in from the wet—nor do they know why he apparently went back out?"

"No. You probably know the Snoquamish police searched with dogs to see if they could pick up his trail, but they kept running between our house and the shed. All trace of him was lost in the middle of the yard, as if he'd evaporated."

"We understand that Frank Hannigan and you had a brief—let us say unhappy?—encounter on his front deck the next day," Steve said. "Saturday morning...the morning after your son's disappearance."

"Do you have any idea what it's like to not know what's happened to one of your children?" Harold asked. "I was going out of my mind. Jacob wasn't answering his phone. His car was parked in the driveway. We called all his friends." His voice hovered between sadness and anger.

"Nothing. We came up with nothing. And when I went out looking for Jacob, this asshole accuses my son of stealing wine from his shed."

Harold shook his head. It was a fearful, tangible memory.

Steve spoke up. "I don't have children, Mr. Forrest, but Jimmy does. I'm sure he knows exactly how you feel."

"Just so you know," Jimmy said, "we've spoken to Mr. Hannigan, and he's expressed regret at having spoken to you the way he did. He's a parent, too. I think he understands how most parents would feel if one of their children went missing. Unfortunately, you met Mr. Hannigan when you were both in a bad place. You probably don't know anything of the grievance he and his wife carry around. They hate Serrene Homes—and consequently, they want nothing to do with Hemlock Hill. After talking with him, I must say, his feelings are understandable. There seems to be a lot of pain everywhere."

"Is Hannigan a suspect?" Harold Forrest asked.

Steve shook his head. "Not really. I'm afraid things are at a standstill, Mr. Forrest," Steve said. "I know we're not assigned to your son's disappearance, but I still have this gnawing feeling that there's a link between him and Kelsey Walther. We just can't see the whole puzzle yet. I know that's cold comfort."

Harold Forrest stood up and came around his desk to shake hands again with the detectives and offer his thanks.

"I'm expected in court in half an hour. But I want to thank you for coming," he said. "I mean that. The pain doesn't go away. Not for me. Not for his mother. It's an unbearable silence."

"If anything changes, if we get any information, you'll find out at the same time as Detective Stahl. He suggested we come see you," Jimmy lied.

Harold Forrest turned and looked out the window at Puget Sound.

"Do you ever wonder how anything can ever go wrong on such a perfect day?"

Chapter Eight

Big Brother

Frank Hannigan
March 2019

I need to say something here. It upsets me when friends or even casual acquaintances toss off what's happened to Isabel and me with innocuous comments.

It's terrible the law's not on your side. But what can you do? You did everything you could, now you just have to let it go.

I found arguing with them a fruitless expenditure of breath. Well-intentioned people can be so maddening. It's always easy to counsel someone to *Let it go* when they're not the ones holding on.

See, I can let things go when it's a natural disaster. I remember what my former brother-in-law said when the angry Susquehanna River, swollen from the rains of Hurricane Agnes, flooded the first two floors of his home and undermined its foundation.

"It's nobody' fault, Frank," Don said as he stood next to his lop-sided and collapsing two-story home. "I suppose I could blame Mother Nature, but what's the point? We'll rebuild and just get on with our lives."

Don was right. The loss of his home was nobody's fault. And when no one is at fault, the best anyone can do is "let it go" and "get on with their lives." I understand. I haven't spent my life looking for culprits—or looking for people to blame when misfortune happens.

And let's be clear, accidents do happen. But just because something is an accident doesn't absolve the party that caused the accident from responsibility.

I often reflect on one humorous moment during my teaching career. I was watching two students in the hallway throwing a textbook at one another. Back and forth. Back and forth. They were goofing around, laughing, and having a great time playing "Pitch the Textbook" until the student standing in the middle of the hallway decided to throw a screaming textbook fastball. The student expected to catch the book stepped aside and the book smashed through a fairly large window. The sound of broken glass echoed throughout the corridor.

When they saw me watching them, they turned away and started moving quickly down the hall. That's when I called out to them.

"Hey, guys, hold on."

They knew I was a teacher, and as they turned, they gave me that sheepish look that said, *We weren't doing anything.*

"Whose textbook was that?"

The taller boy spoke up. "I don't know, it was just leaning against the wall in the 200 Wing."

"And now it's sitting outside a broken window in the 200 Wing," I pointed out.

Trapped somewhere between arrogant defiance and frightened submission, neither of them offered a response.

"Okay, here's what's going to happen. The three of us are going out to get that textbook. Then we're going to the office so you two can arrange to pay for that broken window."

The word *pay* got their full and complete attention.

"Pay?" they both said in comic unison.

"Yeah, you know what 'pay' means. You broke the window...you own the window...you pay for the window."

"But it was an accident."

"Yeah. It was an accident. I know neither one of you wanted it to happen. I was watching, remember?"

"If it was an accident, why should we be expected to pay?" the taller boy asked. He was clearly exasperated by my expectations.

Sometimes the teenage mind reaches curious conclusions. I changed direction.

"You drive to school?" I asked the taller boy.

"Yeah."

"Where do you park?"

"In the upper lot, why?"

"Let's say I'm leaving the parking lot this afternoon, and while you are backing out, my car hits your car, okay?"

"Okay," he replied, unsure of where I was going.

"Should I pay to repair your car? After all, it was an accident. I never meant to hit your car. It just happened."

"Yeah, but you caused the accident," he said with conviction, as if he'd seized on a thoroughly unique line of argumentation. "It's your fault. You'd have to pay."

"Really?"

"Yeah," both boys agreed.

"You're absolutely right. And whose fault it is that the window is broken?"

The shorter student finally spoke up. "Ken threw the book."

"And you ducked," Ken—I hadn't known his name until that moment—immediately replied. "So it's your fault."

Ken and Gil were each about to award full responsibility to the other when I put an end to their squabble.

"You both did it."

I turned first to Mr. Tallboy. "Ken, my boy, you threw the book. And you..." I turned to Ken's shorter companion.

"His name is Gil," Ken growled.

"Thank you, Ken. And you, Gil. You ducked. Cause and effect. You both pay. Now let's go."

I've always liked that story—probably because it's both funny and true.

Imagine if Serrene Homes had said, *Your beautiful trees have fallen because we accidently cut their roots. Those fallen trees killed your beloved dog, caused damage to your home and to your shed, and we are at fault. We are sorry. Let us make you whole—or as whole as we possibly can.*

I would have said thank you. And that would have been the end of it. A fair-minded company accepting responsibility and reaching a financial accommodation with two civic-minded people. That would have been ideal.

But Serrene Homes wanted to pull a Ken and Gil.

Golly, gee, Frank and Isabel. It was all an accident. Gosh, we shouldn't be held responsible if it's an accident...even if we are the ones who caused the accident. Besides, the law says we can cause accidents just like the one we caused.

That's bullshit. Can I say it any more clearly than that?

And to the people who surrender with a milquetoast shrug and a *What can you do?*—as if we should plead helplessness in the face of the unfair legalities—I've got an answer.

Plenty. We can do plenty. Serrene Homes will wish they'd come with an apology, some compensation for the loss of our dog and our trees, and a fistful of cash for our repairs, instead of their in-your-face "screw you."

This whole business—killing an armed and dangerous teenager and then Mrs. Serrene Homes—we didn't start any of this. Isabel and I were content to live our lives and raise our dogs and cats. Happy to be good neighbors and good citizens.

Just so you know, those two teenage boys that I had to deal with when I was teaching, Ken and Gil, they did the right thing. Sure, they were reluctant and it took some prodding—no one likes to be out-of-pocket for a problem they've caused—but they did the right thing. They took responsibility. Taking responsibility is something we all expect of decent people. That's all we can ask of anyone. Just do the right thing.

So, let's be clear, neither Isabel nor I ever intended for any of this to happen—but it's happening because someone else started it. And it's going to keep happening. Two down—one actually—and two to go. It'll end when justice has been served—when equilibrium has been restored—when we've gotten our dead dog, smashed shed, shattered roof, and five trees' worth.

The key to planning a murder—one where you don't get caught—hinges on careful observation. Watch your intended victim. Carefully. Probably over a few weeks, maybe even months. Take copious notes and begin plotting out your victim's days. Sooner or later, patterns will emerge.

I'm retired, so stalking an intended victim is just another of the many perks of unobligated time. I'm certain that my experience is not unique—being retired with nothing but time on my hands—but the simple truth is that most working folk don't have the luxury of plotting and planning a murder because their jobs interfere. Can't you hear them saying, "I'd kill the SOB, but who's got the time? I have to work."

Well, I don't have to work. I've got the time. Time is my friend. Time is what I needed if I wanted to discover the personal patterns of my intended victim.

Patterns are the key, and as most of you know, people are pattern creatures. Creatures of habit. Consider your own life—your own habits, your own patterns. What time do you get out of bed? Do you eat breakfast? Stop at Starbucks? Drive the same route to and from the office? What TV shows do you watch? Do you watch the eleven o'clock news? What time do you tuck in? If you wrote it all down, you'd discover that your life was one grand and glorious pattern. Okay, maybe not grand and glorious. But chances are, your life overflows with predictability, interrupted occasionally by your annual vacation or dinner out.

Breaking the pattern is the exception, never the rule. Once you know what someone's pattern is, it's relatively easy to show up precisely where they are or where they'll be. That knowledge certainly facilitates dispatching them to the hereafter.

My current assignment—self-imposed, naturally—was to figure out the patterns of Mick Walther, husband of the now deceased Kelsey Walther, and one of Serrene Homes' principal owners. Their website referred to the owners as "principals," and that made me chuckle. As a former teacher, I realized that principals could be especially unpopular—just like the principal I planned to kill.

My biggest problem was that I didn't have the needed skills to kill someone. I know you're thinking, *My God, you've already killed two people,* but that's not true. Yes, I killed Kelsey, but her death was simply a matter of opportunity. I was going to say luck, but luck and murder shouldn't occupy the same sentence. And Isabel shot Jacob defending me. Jacob made his own death possible due to the late hour, the darkness, the bad weather, and his own stupidity. I'm grateful that Isabel is a good shot. If the situation had been reversed, who knows?

I've never shot Isabel's .45 caliber pistol, and if I have my way, I never will. I had no idea what shooting a pistol felt like or sounded like, and I couldn't have imagined anything like the way things actually occurred when Jacob lay dead in our backyard. The truth is this. When Isabel shot Jacob, she couldn't miss. Even better, she didn't miss. If this were another time or place, I might be able to brag to my two brothers—both former Marines—that my wife qualified as a sharpshooter. But this is neither the time nor the place.

I'm not sure what kind of evidence the police found when they brought their team of dogs and officers to search our property. From the back deck I watched as the dogs ran between our shed and the old fence that Jacob had hopped over to get onto our property. The dogs sniffed their way from Hemlock Hill practically up to our bedroom window, but they never went into the woods. Apparently, Jacob's scent trail never took the dogs in that direction. I'm glad I hadn't invited Jacob into our house, because then there would have been all kinds of questions.

I know the crime scene unit found Jacob's fingerprints—on the door of our shed and on bottles of wine—but evidence like that didn't implicate me or Isabel. The investigators could see that the shed's door lock had been picked. That's something I would never have noticed. It helps when you know what you're looking for.

I laughed to myself when several of the investigators wondered why Jacob's prints were on bottles of wine that were still in the shed.

"Who knows? Maybe he's picky—only came for certain varietals. His father's a rich attorney. No one wants to drink merlot."

The search only proved that my early suspicions were correct—Jacob was our wine thief. None of it pointed at us. We lived here. He was the trespasser.

I approached one of the investigators and asked if he could tell me what they'd found.

"Afraid not, Mr. Hannigan. You can ask Detective Stahl after we're done. Off the record, your shed lock was picked, and we're pretty sure the missing boy's been inside your shed. But I think you already suspected that."

More than a month later, and still no one knew where the missing boy was. Jacob's parents put up posters all over town—Safeway, QFC, Starbucks, local restaurants. I saw a few posters taped to light poles. His parents appeared on both local and national television appealing for information.

On one of the early broadcasts, a few of Jacob's teachers commented on this sad state of affairs, and it appeared there were two schools of thought about what happened. Either Jacob was kidnapped—no one knew who or why or how, and there was no ransom demand—or he was murdered. If true, no one knew why. One rumor surfaced that one of his father's unhappy clients may have done it, but that idea faded quickly.

Where could Jacob Forrest—a good football player, an above average but lackluster student, and something of a narcissistic jerk—where could he be?

Running away and suicide were dismissed immediately—by everyone. I can't remember the exact language, but one teacher intimated that Jacob was far too arrogant to commit suicide—or "too Catholic," Isabel would say.

His parents keep hoping someone will call with news. The reward for his safe return is now north of $100,000, a reward that no one will ever collect.

As for Kelsey, when I bashed her head in the QFC parking lot, it was just luck that I wasn't being filmed or that no one saw me. The lousy weather helped me, too.

I'd figured out her pattern in just a few days. She kept late hours and she was forever grocery shopping late at night. She always went to the same QFC, and she had the strange habit of parking out in the hinterlands. She parked far away even when it was raining. Maybe she didn't want anyone parking near her perfectly-coiffured truck—maybe she liked the exercise. I don't know. But it made it easy for me to flatten her tire. Et cetera.

Oh, yeah. Isabel talked me out of delivering flowers to Serrene Homes after Kelsey's funeral. I bought the flowers at Safeway and put them in a lovely cobalt blue vase belted with a gold ribbon.

Isabel grabbed the vase and placed it on the shelf next to Miss Aria's ashes. "Now Miss Aria has the flowers she finally deserves. Serrene Homes never sent us flowers when they killed our dog, did they?"

I just shook my head.

"If you're determined to get caught, Frank, just walk into the police station. Alright?" she asked.

"Sorry." That's all I could think to say.

I was sorry for their indifference to our pain—pain that they caused—and sorry that we had to return it.

The next two murders won't happen that easily. We can't always depend on the weather and a woman choosing to get her exercise by walking across a wide parking lot...or on a brazen teenager acting recklessly in the middle of the night in our backyard.

So far, we've had luck. Now we needed stealth.

Stealth requires planning. Here are my ten rules for successfully surveilling a person you intend to dispatch. These rules will allow you to discern and understand a person's patterns over a fairly short period of time.

FRANK'S TEN RULES...OR...
from FRIENDLY FOLK to FELONY FOLK

* Don't trust your memory. Write everything down. Day of the week. Times. Places. Routes. Restaurants. Companions. Weather at that time. It'll be a pain at first, but as the pattern emerges, you'll be able to formulate a plan. Don't try to remember anything.

* There are cameras everywhere. Always act as if you are on camera. Never skulk.

* Dress conservatively. Nothing bright or distinctive. Nothing that shouts, "Hey, look at me!" What you really want is a cloak of invisibility. But I think Harry Potter has the only one. Don't wear the same clothes two days in a row. Get yourself a closet full of dull clothes. No hoodies. Hoodies make you look suspicious...like a hoodlum. No clothes with logos. No alligators. No swooshes. Have a variety of dark, dull hats—no team logos. Keep a daily diary of what you wear...every day.

* Plan to wear disguises. Subtle disguises. They can include a variety of hats, wigs, moustaches. You can change

any visible skin by using lighter or darker foundations. Consider buying a cane. Consider doing a lot of surveillance on rainy days—with your umbrella up. Make sure it's a black umbrella. [Avoid things like eye-patches that make you look like a pirate. Avoid sunglasses at night. AVOID standing out.] Record your disguises in your diary. Consider giving each disguise a name. "Today I'm Perry the retired teacher. Yesterday I was Whitey the retired newspaper editor." Choose career identities that you understand. People ask questions. You'll need answers.

* Find/Use a car that has NO GPS built in. That's critical. Technology is both the gift and the curse. Don't let your tech tattle on you. I'll use Isabel's Kia.

* Get tech savvy. Use GPS trackers. You'll know where they are—or where their vehicle is, anyway—every minute of every day. On days when you aren't physically following, write down when your person moves and where your person is. Use burner phones.

* Obey the law. Yes, obey the law. No jaywalking. No speeding. No illegal parking. No arguments in public. Walk away from any possible argument.

* No drinking on the job. Yes, it will be boring, but drink lots of water, tea—and coffee, too, if you must. Remember, coffee and tea will make you pee. Always a useful rhyme.

* Plan on long days.

* REMEMBER: Night is better than day. Quiet is better than noisy. Dead is better than injured. (Them, not you.)

If I succeed in not getting caught, perhaps I'll publish Frank's Ten Rules in a book, *How to Get Away with Murder, A Successful Murderer's Perspective.* I'll have to use a *nom de plume,* of course. And I don't think I'll be able to collect royalties.

Chapter Nine

Slowly I Turn

Jimmy Brautigan
March 2019

There is something unsettling about not being able to solve a problem.

Especially when the whole world expects you to solve it—and even you expect you to solve it. Jimmy's mom used to caution her children not to get "all discombobulated," but Jimmy Brautigan was feeling particularly discombobulated after sifting through the meagre evidence for the Kelsey Walther murder for the umpteenth time. Jimmy was sitting at his desk, sipping his Monday morning latte, alternately looking through one stack of papers or another and staring into space.

Steve arrived and asked Jimmy if he was alright.

"Yeah." Jimmy said.

He dropped his chin onto his chest. "No. No, I'm not alright. This whole Kelsey Walther case seems to be one dead end. If I read just her file, I'd want to meet her. Every damn person in the whole friggin' western world thought she was a sweetheart. We've talked to unhappy homeowners—all of whom she managed to make happy. We've talked to grumpy vendors who break out into a smile whenever we mention her name. We talked to Serrene employees, we talked to all the outside people she had to deal with, we talked to the people in her neighborhood, we talked to the mailman, and to the UPS and FedEx guys…"

"The FedEx guy was a girl," Steve said.

"They're all guys, Steve. In my vocabulary, *guy* is gender neutral. It's a new world." Jimmy gestured at all the papers on his desk. "I looked through all this—I spent five hours poring over all of it yesterday, on a Sunday—and from the glowing recommendations and praise joyously spilling from everyone's lips, Kelsey Walther should be alive. But she's dead. Dead. Her head bashed in on a rainy January night…in a goddamn QFC parking lot. None of it makes sense."

Jimmy took another sip of coffee. "I know we're missing something, Steve. I just don't know what it is."

Eastlake didn't have many murders, and the few that it did have had been solved in a matter of weeks if not days. Steve knew this case was bugging Jimmy more than most.

"Well, let's go over everything, item by item. I'll read to you, you read to me, and we'll see if we can create a spark."

It was a long and mostly unproductive morning. Just before lunch, Jimmy pulled out the small green note he'd found on the front passenger seat of Kelsey's truck—the one he once described as a Post-it note—right next to the undisturbed purse and the undisturbed groceries.

"Have we figured this out?" Jimmy asked.

Jimmy handed the note to Steve.

Steve looked at it. "It appears to be ballpoint pen. Printed in blocky letters with a back slant." He read it aloud. "The most dangerous game? Is it a question?"

"No prints on the paper—not even Kelsey's—which is strange," mused Jimmy. "None. We can suppose whoever wrote it didn't want to be identi-fied. No handwriting that we could identify. It isn't Kelsey's or anyone else at Serrene Homes. Just the phrase: *the most dangerous game.*"

"It's a short story," came a voice from behind them. Their newest de-tective colleague, Caroline, was just arriving at her desk. She plopped her purse in her bottom desk drawer and pushed it closed with her knee. She walked over to Jimmy and Steve.

"*The Most Dangerous Game* is the title of a short story. I'm a proud graduate of Holy Names Academy and Miss Monzollilo told us that *The Most Dangerous Game* was the 'archetypal short story.' Maybe it was, maybe it wasn't...but it was a good story."

Jimmy and Steve traded glances.

"Well," said Jimmy, "I'm game. Tell me what it's about."

Caroline smiled at Jimmy's pun. She turned and looked at Steve.

"Yeah, I'm game, too," Steve said as he stretched out his legs in front of himself and leaned back in his chair. "Do you remember the story?"

Caroline retold the story about a shipwrecked man who is hunted by the wealthy owner of Ship-Trap Island. The wealthy man thinks of the ship-wrecked man as his game. But the hunted man turns the table, and kills the hunter.

"The title has a double meaning," Caroline pointed out. "The original hunter was playing a dangerous game by hunting an innocent man. One could say that killing is a dangerous game. But...at some point, the hunter became the hunted, because man"—and here she paused and smiled sweetly—"and woman, too"—she pointed at herself—"is the most dangerous game to hunt. See, a story title with a *double entendre*."

"Why aren't you teaching English instead of shooting at bad guys?" Jimmy asked.

"That, Jimmy Brautigan, is a sexist question."

"Sorry, I didn't mean it that way. Hell, I can't remember what I had for breakfast, and here you are remembering a short story you read...well...a couple of years ago."

"When I was in ninth grade."

"That's a couple of years, right?"

She gave Jimmy a baleful look.

"So this story is about a man who hunts down other men? For sport?

Caroline nodded. "Yeah. Gruesome, isn't it?"

"And this was required reading...in the ninth grade...at Holy Names Academy? A Catholic school?"

"I don't know if it was required reading for everyone...but it was required in my class. A story about a man who makes a game out of tracking down and killing other men."

"Hey, Jimmy, wasn't Frank Hannigan a high school English teacher?" Steve asked.

There was the spark. The moment when nothing turns into something.

"Grab your coat, Steve, we're going to ride out to Snoquamish to see if Frank remembers *The Most Dangerous Game* as well as Caroline does. We'll grab lunch on the way." Jimmy couldn't help but smile.

Despite Seattle's vaunted reputation as Rain City, USA, this was one of those lovely Chamber of Commerce days—when the temperature outside was cool but not cold—60 degrees—and it was gloriously sunny. Jimmy and Steve could see puffy cumuli pushing up against the Cascades as they drove to the home of Frank and Isabel.

They drove in silence until Steve broached a topic that had been taboo for a while. "You have a chance to talk with your daughter about your plans? You made any decision, yet?" Steve asked as they exited the interstate and drove north.

"About what?"

"Come on, Jimmy. Don't start playing coy after we've been together for twenty years.

"Twenty-one years."

"Twenty-one years...aaahhh...and one week. We worked our first case on St. Patrick's day...twenty-one years ago."

Jimmy laughed. "I remember. The Minnie Mouse bandit. Jesus. That was twenty-one years ago? Feels like another lifetime."

"It was, Jimmy. But come on, you've been talking about pulling the ripcord, bailing out, for the past five years, maybe more. Ever since Felicia died."

"My daughter, the doctor, thinks I should stop chasing bad guys for a living. But that's nothing new. She's thought that since I joined the police force 31 years ago."

"So? Are you ready to start sipping Scotch and watching television?"

"Didn't I say I'd let you know when I made that decision?"

"Yeah."

"Have you heard me say anything?"

"No."

"There's your answer."

"Okay. Okay. Message received."

They lapsed into silence, the quiet interrupted by the occasional broadcast from headquarters.

"Nice day," said Steve to no one in particular.

"So far," said Jimmy as he pulled down Frank and Isabel's unpaved lane. "Day's still young."

They knew that Frank was retired and that Isabel was likely working from home. She made trips to clients about three times a month, but that was it.

"No more commuter rat-race for me," Isabel had once told Jimmy on the phone. "That's why IBM created the computer—get us out of our cars and into cyberspace. Next time you want to see me, we can Skype or use my GoToMeeting account."

"I prefer face-to-face," said Jimmy.

"Skype *is* face-to-face, Detective. Unless I decide to turn off my camera."

"I like to be there...in person...with all my senses gathering information."

Steve's comment intruded on Jimmy's reveries. "Trees are all in bud," said Steve, as they pulled into the driveway. "And the grass already needs to be mowed."

As they walked up onto the front deck, the din of barking dogs grew louder and louder. They knocked on the door. Frank had said that ringing the doorbell was of little use, and that a hard steady knock would more likely be heard over the dogs.

Frank answered the door.

"Come on in," he said. "None of these guys will eat you. They're just enthusiastic. Come on over and get comfortable. I was working at the dining room table. You want some coffee?"

Jimmy could see that Frank had a laptop open and a small pile of papers neatly stacked beside it.

"I'll take a cup, thanks," said Jimmy.

"Me, too," said Steve.

"Cream?"

"No," they said in unison.

"You guys are brave. Black coffee drinkers in a latte universe."

"I get lattes sometimes," said Jimmy, "but I'm in a black coffee mood."

Frank brought two black coffees to the table. He'd used two of his favorite mugs. He handed his Irish Diplomacy mug to Jimmy.

Jimmy read it out loud. "Telling someone to go to hell in such a way that they look forward to making the trip." He couldn't help but laugh.

He gave Steve his Shakespearean Curses mug. Steve inspected his mug, noting that every inch was covered with Renaissance jibes. Holding up the mug, he began reading aloud.

"O gull, o dolt, as ignorant as dirt." He gave the mug a quarter turn. "Lump of foul deformity." Another quarter turn. "Beetle-headed, flap-eared knave." He turned and looked at Frank. "Are you trying to send us a message, here?"

Frank laughed as he seated himself behind his computer and held up his mug for the detectives to see. "Got this mug from my daughter on Father's Day."

They laughed as they read it. *Great Job, Dad. I Turned Out Awesome.*

"The mugs I gave you are my favorites. Isabel got both of those mugs for me at one time or another. They're just fun. That's all." Frank raised his coffee as if to make a toast. "Here's to a beautiful day, gentlemen. What brings you here?"

After sips, Jimmy jumped right in.

"The most dangerous game."

Frank cocked his head to one side and grinned. "Alright. *The Most Dangerous Game.* It's a short story by Richard Connell. Published, I believe in the 1920s. Probably the only short story Connell ever had anthologized—he was mostly a screen writer. It's a story I taught in the ninth grade at Eastsound High and a story that has appeared in every ninth-grade anthology I have ever sold. How am I doing?"

"He seems to know the story," Steve remarked.

Jimmy reached into an envelope and pulled out the piece of light green paper—about the size of a Post-it—and showed it to Frank.

"What do you make of this?" he asked.

Frank could read the words carefully printed in all caps, in a block letter style—THE MOST DANGEROUS GAME. There was no hint of any handwriting style.

"It's the name of the short story, alright. But if it is, it should only have capital letters at the beginning of every word and be bracketed by quotation marks or italicized. As written, it's just a phrase. So what is it, exactly?"

"This piece of paper was found in Kelsey Walther's truck the night she was killed in Eastlake," Jimmy said.

"Okay," said Frank. He took another sip of coffee.

"We're trying to figure out where it came from. It's not Kelsey's handwriting. We've looked throughout Kelsey's home to see if she had green Post-its or green paper. Her husband helped us look. We looked at all the paper she had at the Serrene Homes office, too. No green paper."

"Isn't it a Post-it?" asked Frank.

"No. There's no stickum on the back. It's just a carefully cut piece of paper."

"Okay," Frank said again. "So it's not a Post-it."

"Why would this note show up on the front passenger seat in Kelsey's truck the night she was murdered?" Jimmy asked.

"I have no idea, Detective."

"You know the short story, though," Steve pointed out.

"Of course, I know it. I bet I taught it a hundred times. Every high school English teacher knows that short story—and every book salesman selling literature books knows it, too. And if you were paying attention as a ninth-grader, I'll bet you read that short story, too. It's universally known. And loved."

"That may be, Frank, but who would put this note on the seat of a truck with a murdered woman lying in the rain ten feet away? Whoever killed her didn't steal anything. From what we can tell, she wasn't robbed. She had over one hundred dollars in her purse. The groceries were all undisturbed on the front seat...and then there's this piece of paper."

Frank raised his hands in a gesture of helplessness.

"Your guess is as good as mine. I'm not a detective—except in the literary sense. I used to tell my students that a good story or poem was full of clues. Find the clues and you'll discover the meaning." Frank rubbed his chin. "So, you think that piece of paper is a clue?" He sipped his coffee.

Steve had been taking notes during the conversation. He looked over at Jimmy and closed up his notebook...and immediately re-opened it.

"One last question," Steve said. "Do you own a gun?"

"No, I don't. Never have. But Isabel owns one. A .45 caliber pistol. She keeps it locked up in the bedroom."

"Has she used it lately?"

"Only at the gun range in Fastlake. I don't go with her. I don't like guns. Accidents happen. Isabel lived alone here for over a decade—well before I arrived and back when Snoquamish was rural, if anyone can remember back that far—and her dad got her the gun for her birthday. He asked her what she wanted for her birthday, and she said, 'Get me a pistol.'"

"So, the pistol's been fired recently?"

"Maybe two weeks ago. She's gone shooting a few Wednesday

evenings with her friend AJ. Too many bad things going on. Cops show up on our front deck and suggest we are terrorists. Developers make false accusations about us threatening to shoot at them. Someone breaks into our shed and steals our wine. A kid from Hemlock Hill disappears. As I said, too many bad things. Then two months ago, Isabel gets out of bed and says, 'Maybe it's time I limber the Kimber.'"

"She owns a Kimber?" Steve asked scribbling in his notebook.

"So I'm told. I'd never heard of Kimber. I'm not terribly familiar with brand names where firearms are concerned. Winchester and Smith and Weston. That's it."

"That's Wesson, Mr. Hannigan. Double S. No T."

"I rest my case," Frank said, smiling at Detective Olson. "Gotta tell you, though, my Marine Corps brothers were impressed when Isabel told them that she owned a Kimber .45…and that she knew how to use it. They suggested I keep my head down."

Frank got up from the table. "How's the coffee? Need a warm-up?"

Isabel appeared from the hallway and walked to the coffee-maker.

"Don't get up, Frank. I'll do that, if anyone wants a fresh cup," she said.

"Hello, Mrs. Comstock," Jimmy said. "Frank tells me you own a gun."

"He did, did he? Did he tell you he's never shot my Kimber even though I invite him to accompany me to the range every time I go?"

"Something like that. Can we see the gun?"

"Detective," Frank said as he resumed his seat, "I think that's "*May we see the gun?*"

"Please excuse my husband, gentlemen, he's never stopped being an English teacher."

"So I see, Mrs. Comstock," Jimmy acknowledged with a smile. "Alright then. May we see the gun?"

Isabel looked at Frank and gave him a *Why not?* look. "I'll get it from the gun safe. It's in the bedroom."

Everyone waited, quietly drinking coffee while Isabel disappeared for a few minutes. She returned and handed the pistol to Detective Brautigan.

"As you can see, it's not loaded. I have three clips that I keep in the safe. Nothing is ever out of the safe—unless I go target shooting."

"She's a good shot, too. She should show you the targets she brings home. Anything bad ever happens here, I'll be right behind her."

Steve and Jimmy both chuckled at Frank's remark.

"Nice gun. Hear it was a birthday present."

"My late father gave it to me on my thirty-fifth birthday. Got it registered and took classes in gun safety...one conducted by a female FBI trainer."

Jimmy handed the pistol to Steve.

"Here's our problem, Isabel...Frank. The local police—Eastlake and Snoquamish—have two unsolved...situations. One's definitely a murder, and the other is a disappearance. The common denominator is Serrene Homes. They built the Hemlock Hill subdivision—and you two had an ongoing disagreement with them and even considered a lawsuit. And the missing young man, Jacob Forrest, lived in the Hemlock Hill subdivision, and is someone you thought might be stealing wine from you. In fact, the local police found this boy's prints all over wine bottles in your shed. And the only clue points to someone who knows the short story, 'The Most Dangerous Game.'"

Frank listened attentively, drained the last of his coffee, while Isabel finished pouring her own fresh cup.

"Really? If you're sure it's a clue, maybe you should be out looking for a ninth-grader to arrest. Most of them would know that story."

Jimmy ignored Frank's remark. "Do you see how unusual it is to have someone from Hemlock Hill disappear a month before someone associated with the company that built Hemlock Hill—Serrene Homes—turns up dead?"

"Why is that unusual?" Isabel asked. "I'll bet two people drop dead in Seattle on any given day—sometimes in the same building—and no one goes looking for a connection."

"If they were both murdered you'd bet we'd be looking for a connection," Steve assured her.

"Yes. *If* they were both murdered. But only Mrs. Walther has been murdered. As of this moment, no one knows what's happened to Jacob Forrest. Or do they? Has he turned up?" Isabel asked.

"No. No clue. But his fingerprints were all over the inside of your shed and on about a dozen wine bottles that clearly were never taken," Jimmy said.

"Which proves he was in our shed," Frank said. "Probably proves he stole our wine, too."

"But, Frank, some of the bottles we fingerprinted had your prints on top of his prints. How could that be the case?" asked Jimmy.

"I have no idea. But let's be clear. Only one set of fingerprints belong on the wine bottles out there—whether they're on top of or underneath someone else's. I live here. When I go out there to get a bottle of wine, I pull out a bottle, look at it, then decide if that's the wine we're in the mood for. If not, I put it back. I never dust the bottle for prints. I'm guessing Jacob pulled out lots of our bottles looking to see what kind of wine it was—just like me. He probably put some bottles back, too. There's some pretty expensive wine in our shed."

"So, Jacob is a wine connoisseur?" Steve asked in a slightly teasing tone.

"You got me. All I know is someone managed to steal about a case and a half of our wine last year between August and December. So we began locking the shed. Wouldn't you know it, someone began picking the lock. That's all I can tell you."

"And you never called the police, right?"

"No, we didn't," Isabel chimed in. "Seemed like a waste of time. The Snoquamish police have different priorities than we do. They're interested in protecting the moneyed interests—like the developers—and we're interested in protecting our lives and our property. They'd take a report about stolen wine to make us feel better, and then it would vanish into some black hole. After all, where are they gonna look? Nobody's gonna fence our wine. If Jacob was our thief, I bet he sold it to his high school buddies. Probably at a discount. No, talking to the Snoquamish police would have been a waste of our time and theirs."

"That's pretty cynical," Steve remarked.

"We have every right to be cynical," Isabel countered. "If your needs were as manifestly ignored as ours were when our dog was killed, you'd be cynical, too."

Everyone fell silent for a moment. Isabel's comment put a string of exclamation points on the obvious schism between law enforcement and themselves.

Frank broke the silence. "Anyone ever tell Jacob's father that his son's prints were all over our wine bottles?"

"As a matter of fact, yes. But whether Jacob was a thief or not, Mr. Hannigan, his father is still struggling with his son's disappearance." Steve's tone was subdued but slightly unfriendly.

Jimmy changed the trajectory of the conversation.

"So how do you plan to protect your wine if they can just pick the lock to your shed?"

"I don't know," said Frank. "I hate to say it, but maybe I won't have to worry in the future."

"Why would you hate to say that?" Jimmy asked.

"For one thing, no wine has gone missing since Jacob disappeared."

"How does that make you feel?"

"It's hard to say. The jury's still out. We'll see if any more wine goes missing."

Jimmy pushed back from the table and stood up.

"Just for the record, you have no idea where Jacob is or what happened to him," Jimmy asked.

"Well," Frank began, "if I'd caught Jacob stealing my wine, I'd have photographed him with my cellphone then run like hell back into the house, called 911, and sent the incriminating pictures to the police. But it takes me forever to take a picture with my phone, and I can't run very fast."

Jimmy leaned forward. "You haven't answered my question."

Frank paused and stared at Jimmy. His voice became low and subdued. "Your question doesn't deserve an answer, at least not from me. When the Snoquamish police decided to ignore our plight, I stopped being Frankie Good, Civic-Minded Citizen—and Isabel stopped being Izzy Good, Civic-Minded Citizen, too. We're done with that. We don't plan to be bad citizens, just indifferent ones. You need our help? Sorry, we're not interested. You'll have to look elsewhere. The police have got to realize one important thing: life isn't a *quid pro quo* if there isn't a *quid* to go along with the *quo*."

"I didn't mean to upset you," Jimmy said. "I understand you have an ax to grind with the Snoquamish police, but you'd be wrong to put all police in that 'Rotten Apple' basket. We're just trying to figure out what happened to Kelsey Walther, and we're at a dead end."

"A dead end? You know, Detective, that's just what our lawyer told us when we tried to sue Serrene Homes. 'It's a dead end.' Those were his exact words. We understand what it means to be at a dead end, don't we, Izz? Despite the dead end of our dog and trees, plus a smashed shed, unreimbursed losses, legal bills, and sleepless nights, we were told we'd just have to live with those dead ends. There's nothing we could do. So we understand. Now you're at a dead end, and you'd like our help."

Jimmy nodded.

Frank pushed back from the dining table and turned to look out the bay window at his backyard.

"That's a damn shame, Detectives. But sorry, we've got nothing for you. Not with Kelsey. Not with Jacob. You'll just have to live with it."

Jimmy could hear bitterness and sorrow in Frank's voice. He looked at Steve, and Steve shut his notebook and slipped his pen in his pocket. Frank's tone pretty much said, "We're done."

Frank turned back toward the detectives and pushed his chair under the table before walking into the family room.

"Now, if you don't mind, there's a Barclay's Premier League game on at noon. Tottenham is playing Liverpool. If you'd like to watch the game with me, I've got chips and beer. If not, you'll have to excuse me. It's one of the benefits of being retired."

"Sounds like that's our exit cue," said Jimmy walking toward Frank. "You have to know we're on your side, Frank. I can understand how you feel—I bet I'd feel the same way if what happened to you happened to me. But we're just trying to do our jobs as well as we can, and we need your help to rule you out."

Frank picked up the remote and turned the TV on as he sat down on the sofa. He made no attempt to reply to Detective Brautigan.

"Thanks for showing us your pistol, Mrs. Comstock," Steve said as he handed the pistol back to her. Isabel and their three dogs accompanied them to the door.

As they backed out of the driveway, Steve asked, "Well, did we find out anything?"

"Not sure. Why wouldn't he answer the question about Jacob? He was pretty square with us until I asked him that direct question."

"It's pretty clear that police don't score high on his trust quotient."

"I don't think they score at all."

Chapter Ten

The Most
Dangerous Game

Frank Hannigan
Spring 2019

Richard Connell's classic short story, *The Most Dangerous Game*, is often compared to things like Cole Porter's classic tune, *I've Got You Under My Skin*. They're both classics, both standards. For decades, every ninth grader read the story of Sanger Rainsford, the story's protagonist, being hunted through the jungles of Ship-Trap Island. The villain, General Zaroff, tracks his big game, Rainsford. However, it seems that the endangered game also proves to be "the most dangerous game" when Rainsford kills Zaroff.

As I set out to surveil Mick Walther, that particular short story was much on my mind. Perhaps I was concerned about one of the main ideas in the story: Just when one thinks that he is in the clear, the tables get turned.

About the same time as I began keeping minute-by-minute tabs on Mick, I'd begun going to the gun range with Isabel, now that we possessed a 9mm pistol—the one Jacob had threatened to shoot me with.

It was probably his father's gun, but there was no way we could return the gun to his father without drawing additional attention to ourselves. I'd considered wiping the gun of all fingerprints and taking the gun outside—leaving it tucked next to one of the huge remaining stumps that populated our backyard. Then, when I begin mowing the yard and trimming the bushes, I could "discover" the pistol. We'd then call the Snoquamish police and they could take possession of the gun.

I may be wrong, but I'd lay even money that Jacob's father had registered the gun—the ownership would be traced back to him—and the gun could be returned.

That was one possibility.

Isabel's sense of reality prevailed. "After all that's happened here with the police, and knowing what you know about Jacob's disappearance," Isabel wondered, "would you actually pick up a gun you discovered in the dirt? Or would you simply leave it where it was?"

"It never occurred to me there were two options."

"And when the police recover the pistol, will they think it's strange that there are NO prints on the gun? Not the son's prints? Not even the father's prints?"

Isabel specialized in minutiae and details. The "what if's" that seldom occurred to me always loomed large in her imagination.

"Besides, you might need a gun in your dealings with Mick Walther. If that possibility ever arises, you can't use my gun. The police know I own one—they've handled it. We need Jacob's 9mm. When we don't need it anymore, we'll figure out the best way to make it disappear. We could bury the gun in Jacob's grave or throw it into Lake Washington. No one will find it there."

I'd also suggested that Isabel and I write another letter to Serrene Homes.

"We already have a cease and desist from their lawyer after the monthly letters we sent. So, no. On top of which, if the principal owner ends up dead with our brand new letter sitting on his desk, the police might well decide that we had motive."

"We do have motive," I protested.

"Yes, we do. But we don't have to give the police proof that we have motive."

"You're right. Sorry. No letter."

We kept the gun, and we didn't send a letter.

I probably shouldn't have left the first message—*the most dangerous game*—but I just couldn't resist. A story that well-known couldn't really point to anyone in particular, although Isabel rightly observed, "It brought them to our door, didn't it?"

As for Mick's coming demise, I'd already written the message that I intended to leave next to Mick when I'd finished with him. For Mick, I'd selected George Bernard Shaw's humorous epitaph, *I knew if I hung around long enough something like this would happen.* It was either that or the enigmatic quote from "Bartleby, the Scrivener," a Herman Melville short story. Whenever asked to do anything by his employer, Bartleby would simply aver, "I would prefer not to."

Ultimately, I decided to reserve Melville for my last victim because Bartleby's quote embodied exactly how I feel about what I'm doing. I actually would prefer not to. I'd rather the laws and the legal establishment give us justice. But since they don't...or won't...or can't, I'll just have to do what I would prefer not to.

A month after Kelsey's funeral, I began my surveillance. I waited a full month because any traumatic event—a life-altering trauma like the death of a child or spouse, or the loss of a job—upsets a person's daily schedule. What was once predictable becomes erratic and arbitrary. Norms break down. The usual disappears, at least until those grieving can restore some measure of emotional equilibrium.

I waited a month.

"Do you think it's too early to follow him around?" I asked Isabel.

"Maybe," she said. "For the first two weeks, follow him every other day. You'll always be able to track him with the GPS, once you've attached it to his truck."

I'd gotten a GPS tracker with a magnetic case—one that I could attach to a metal surface like the inside of a vehicle's wheel well. It would stay hidden. I was amazed to find I could actually buy a GPS tracking device online, but I also realized I'd better not do that. I needed to purchase my tracker with cash—no traceable credit card purchase—in a town that was nowhere near my home. I ended up buying it in Corvallis, Oregon. Not only was I anonymous when I bought the GPS, Oregon doesn't have any sales tax.

The only down side to the GPS was that I'd need to replace the batteries every two weeks—provided Mick didn't find my planted tracker before that. If he did, I was sure all hell would break loose and the death of his wife and the GPS tracking device would be inevitably linked...and I really didn't want that.

I don't know if you're curious to know what Mick Walther did every day. Fortunately, the answer is "not much." I could only surmise when his morning routine began by consulting my watch when his bedroom lamp turned on.

In order to be where I could observe that, I morphed into my early morning identity—one that wouldn't draw suspicion from people in the neighborhood. I became Old Bobby Jameson, a once-upon-a-time postman in burgundy sweatpants, dark blue sweatshirt, and black cross-trainers. With white socks, of course. I carried an aluminum cane and limped as if I had a bad right knee. Occasionally a jogger would zoom by—some would bid me good morning, while others just plowed ahead without comment. I remember my jogging days.

I'd walk around the block listening to an ancient cassette player, and as I passed Mick Walther's home, I'd make note if the bedroom light was on or off. It took me eight to ten minutes to make one circuit—depending on the severity of my fake limp—so if the light was off on circuit A and on for circuit B, I could estimate Mick's usual rising time. I went as Old Bobby three times one week, but I stopped when one of the joggers stopped and asked me if I was new to the neighborhood.

I never directly answered her question. Instead, I launched into my "lot of memories in this neighborhood, young lady," soliloquy, talking about my fictional first girlfriend, Adele, and about the time a bicyclist hit my dog while I was delivering papers. "Happened just down the street there. The bicyclist ended up in the hospital," I'd say and laugh—by that time, my conversational jogger was on her way. If necessary, I was prepared to create a whole life story.

If any of the current residents remembered seeing Old Bobby, they'd remember a harmless old man, a man in his dotage, a man with a limp, out to get his exercise, and walking with his cane to help his bad knee.

Mick got up around 6:30.

Mick left his house close to 7:15 every morning. I found it interesting that he'd begun driving his dead wife's truck. It goes without saying, Mick wasn't as careful or fastidious with that truck as she was. Who could be?

She was one-in-a-million.

Mick stopped at Starbucks every morning—well, almost every morning. He went there often enough that I knew I could win a bet if I laid odds that he'd walk into Starbucks about 7:35.

He'd arrive at the office somewhere between 7:45 and 8:00 every morning. Occasionally he'd go to a job site before he went to the office, but that was not typical. I expect he paid his foremen well, and it was their job to be on site at 7:00 a.m. when work began.

I kept the times of all Mick's movements in my handwritten Observation Record. If anyone picked up my Observation Record, I'm betting it would look like anybody's calendar. Anybody's. Except I moved months around and did my record keeping with three different colored pens. If someone felt like snooping in my sloppily-written observation journal, they'd be hard-pressed to figure out what I was up to—which is precisely what I wanted.

Knowing my kids, they'd wonder why I did anything by hand. *There's an app for that*, they'd say. And they'd be right. But I'm not using any apps—except my GPS app—because when police decide to sweep people up, the first things they sweep up are someone's phone, computer, and tablet. *Follow the tech trail* seems to be the newest mantra.

I do keep records electronically, but they're all on my thumb drive which I've squirreled away in my snowy owl puppet that snuggles into a niche in my bookcase in my office. It sits between the 9th Grade volume of Prentice Hall Literature—the book that has "The Most Dangerous Game"—and the 12th Grade British Literature volume—the book that has the George Bernard Shaw quotation. Only Isabel knows where the thumb drive is.

I can already hear my kids saying, *Thumb drive? That's so 20th century.* Absolutely. That's me. Mr. Stuck-in-the-Last-Century. When anyone asks, I tell them *I'm a 20th century kinda guy.*

If they ask me what that means, I tell them it means I come from an era when people actually spent time talking to one another, instead of staring at their cellphone screens all day long. People talked. Face-to-face. I know it sounds like fiction, but I'm prepared to give sworn testimony.

I tell them it means that I don't belong to Facebook or Instagram or whatever social media site is now putting everyone's lives under the microscope.

I admit, I felt grave reluctance about attaching the GPS tracker to Mick's vehicle, so I decided to use the tracker as a backup, something that would simply validate the patterns that I'd already established via personal observation. I figured it would take a month to establish Mick's travel and dining patterns, but surprisingly, in less than two weeks, I had a bead on one of his after-work rendezvous points.

After work, he loved going to an Irish pub named Finnegan's. I don't know if he'd made that a habit before the death of his wife, but he was driving to the pub three times a week when I began recording his movements. For two weeks in a row, he went there every Tuesday, Wednesday, and Friday. According to my notes, he'd get to the parking lot about 7:00 p.m., hop out, and walk to the pub.

I don't know who he met—if anyone. I don't know if he went to have a meal, shoot some pool, watch some sporting event, or rendezvous with a girlfriend. I surmised that he was meeting some of the people he worked with, or the folks who worked at his various jobs sites. I didn't know, and I really didn't care. Who he spent time with inside made no difference to me.

Once I was tempted to go inside and see if he was alone. Curiosity will do that. However, I decided going inside would be unwise. Someone would invariably see me—or I'd be caught on some closed-circuit surveillance camera. I may be paranoid, but invisibility has never been my strong suit. If I've learned one lesson from crime stories on television, the camera's eye never forgets. Avoid it.

The latest he ever left the pub, while I was watching him, was 10:15 p.m. He was home by 10:40 every night—if I could trust my trusty GPS. I never followed him home at night. That was way too creepy—even for me.

So...on TWF, Mick visits Irish pub from 7:00 p.m. to 10:00 p.m. That seemed to be a predictable window of opportunity—a pattern I could rely on.

I noticed Mick parked his truck in just about the same place every time he decided to patronize the pub. To test my two-week-old Tuesday, Wednesday, Friday theory—recorded in my surveillance journal as WTF, just for my personal amusement—I decided to drive to the parking lot structure on Tuesday of the third week. I parked one row over from where I expected Mick to park, and while I waited, I turned on the GPS App on my burner cellphone. About 7:05, my phone beeped to inform me that his white Dodge pickup was on the move. I watched as the big blue dot moved along my cellphone screen, assuring me that Mick Walther was headed my way. In less than fifteen minutes, his white pickup rolled into the predicted spot. He hopped out and headed into Finnegan's.

Patterns. You gotta love'em.

To further test my pattern conclusion, I parked two blocks away from the parking structure on Tuesday of the fourth week. On the day I finally decided to send Mick to join his lovely wife, Kelsey, in the afterlife, I didn't want my vehicle spotted driving in or out of the parking lot. The police would be certain to review CCTV footage and I'd be blocks away. As I said, the only way to be invisible is to be invisible—to human eyes and digital eyes.

I thought, *Mick's reckoning is in the offing.* I chortled at the bad pun. *The word "offing" is a double entendre. Kind of like "the most dangerous game." How appropriate.*

Chapter Eleven

Epitaph

Jimmy Brautigan
June 5, 2019

Jimmy hated it when his phone rang late at night. Since Felicia's death, few things got him out of bed except his job.

Usually when the phone rang at this time of the night, it was the job calling.

Jimmy attempted to rouse himself into a reasonably conscious state.

"Whoever this is, it's very late," Jimmy said.

"Jimmy, it's Steve."

"Yeah, I know. Your voice sounds vaguely familiar."

"Sorry to call so late."

"You sound wide awake, Steve."

"I'd better be. I'm here in the parking garage at Bella Square. And you'll never guess who's slumped in a white Dodge pickup with a 9mm hole in his head."

"Hang on, Steve." Jimmy swung his legs over the side of the bed and looked at his alarm clock. The dial glowed 1:30 a.m. "Where'd you say you were?"

"Bella Square. I got a call maybe 30 minutes ago from the lieutenant, who got a call from one of the patrol cars that checks out the parking structure every night."

"So who's dead?"

"Who owned a white Dodge pickup?"

Christ, it's 1:30 in the morning. What's with the twenty questions routine?

Suddenly Jimmy's drowsiness evaporated like summer rain on a hot pavement. He was wide awake. "Kelsey Walther did. But she's dead."

"And who drives her truck now?"

"I'm guessing Mick Walther."

Steve didn't say anything on his end.

"Jesus, Steve. Are you telling me Mick Walther is dead?"

"Yep. The face on the dead man in the truck matches the face on his driver's license—except for the bullet hole. Looks like a 9mm. Someone shot him in the cab of his truck. The crime scene folks are still arriving, and I thought you might want to come on down and join in."

"I'll be there in twenty," Jimmy said.

At moments like this, Jimmy's brain shifted into high gear. Kelsey's killer still eluded them, and now her husband, Mick, is murdered.

Jimmy wondered. *Is this the break we've been looking for?* His Catholic-school-self scolded him. *How the hell can you call another dead body "the break we've been looking for?"* Then his detective-self stepped back in. *Don't give me that crap, you know what I mean.*

Steve's growing peevishness hadn't been lost on Jimmy. *Steve hated anything unfinished.* Just yesterday, Steve had started listing their recent successes—all the nagging mysteries that they'd brought to a successful close.

"We solved that string of Gates's Point burglaries, and we finally caught the two little shits who'd decided that their graffiti should grace the walls of the Eastlake Art Museum."

"Don't forget the guy we caught passing all those counterfeit twenties," Jimmy pointed out.

"But damn, we don't seem to be making any progress on this whole

Kelsey Walther murder. This should be easier, shouldn't it? We should have something by now, shouldn't we?" Steve said, clearly upset.

Jimmy had no information or suggestions to drag Steve from his doldrums.

Maybe that's about to change, Jimmy thought.

When Jimmy arrived, the parking structure was alive with flashing lights, and the crime scene was bathed in a glaring sheet of light from the lights set up around the Dodge pickup. Crime scene investigators looked otherworldly as they worked the scene in white-hooded uniforms, white masks, white shoe covers, and blue latex gloves.

Jimmy saw Steve standing about thirty yards away, scribbling in his notebook. As he walked toward his partner, he thought, *It appears that the Walthers like to die late at night in remote parking lots. At least it's not cold and raining.*

Jimmy put his hand on Steve's shoulder. "Hi-ho, Stevarino. Okay, what do we have?"

"Another late night, I'm guessing."

"I wish you were wrong. I was actually sleeping peacefully when you rang. Fill me in on what we know so far."

Steve read directly from his notes. "Mick Walther. Dead. One shot through the right side of his forehead. Exit wound at the back of the skull with a 9mm bullet found in the roof of the truck's cab."

"A suicide, maybe?"

"Probably not. We didn't find a gun in the cab."

"Okay. Not a suicide."

"The Medical Examiner places time of death at about 10:30 to 11:00. It's a warm night. Right now there are no witnesses."

He looked up from his notes. "Well, no witnesses, yet. We'll be collecting all the CCTV and surveillance footage from Bella Square when the world wakes up in the morning."

Steve returned to his notes. "Medical Examiner seems to think he'd just had a meal, and we'll know more after the autopsy—probably know which restaurant, too. I asked the ME to see if we could get those results ASAP, and he says he'll do the autopsy tonight over in Seattle."

He closed his notes. "If you ask me, someone has a real big grudge against Serrene Homes."

"Or the Walthers."

"I'm supposing we can take Mick Walther off our list of possible suspects in his wife's murder?" Steve asked sarcastically. "Oh, yeah. We found this on the front seat, passenger side."

Steve pulled out a small plastic evidence bag that contained one small, green piece of blood-spattered paper. He held it out to Jimmy.

Jimmy squinted at the message written on the paper. It was the same block lettering used for the Kelsey Walther message. Jimmy read it out loud. "I knew if I hung around long enough, something like this would happen." Then he looked at his partner.

"Any ideas?"

"I googled the sentence on my tablet," Steve said, "and guess what popped up?"

"I never make guesses at 2:30 in the morning," Jimmy said in a teasing tone. "And look at you. Using our department's latest and greatest technology to further our investigation. You may end up in the 21st century after all."

"No, thank you. I'll only go there as a visitor—but I did find out something interesting. Let me see..." Steve opened his notebook. "That sentence is the epitaph of George Bernard Shaw, Irish playwright and critic."

"A fact that a former high school English teacher would probably be familiar with?" Jimmy asked.

Steve nodded.

"The sentence is written on the same kind of green paper, Jimmy. No stickum...and no fingerprints."

"Any prints on the truck that don't belong to Mr. Walther?"

"Too soon to know, but I'll bet you dinner at the best restaurant in Seattle that Frank Hannigan is involved in this."

"Either that or someone is trying to frame him. Remind me. What did you say was the time of death?"

"Best guess is sometime between 10:30 and 11:00."

"And whoever did it used a 9mm?"

"Yep. One shot to the head...or so it appears."

"What kind of gun did Mrs. Comstock have?"

"A Kimber .45."

Jimmy scratched his head and looked at the crime scene investigators moving around like ghosts. "Is that her only gun?"

"The only one she's ever registered."

"Well, despite the hour, I think it's time to call on Hannigan and Comstock again. I don't think we should wait until morning either."

"It is morning," Steve replied. "In case you haven't noticed."

"Not according to my internal clock. It's dark, and it's late, and I'm damn tired of getting out of bed because people can't murder someone at a decent hour. So, whatta ya say? You up for getting verbally abused by two people at zero-dark-hundred?"

"Not really, but we've got to go where the clues take us."

"I think I better call Stahl, too. We're working his side of the street."

Along the way, Jimmy phoned Stahl—woke him out of a sound sleep—and explained what was going on...and why he thought he and Steve needed to interview Hannigan immediately. Jack said he'd meet them at Hannigan's place.

It was a few minutes past three in the morning when Jimmy and Steve turned left down Hannigan's unpaved lane. Stahl's Snoquamish police car was parked on the ivy on the south side of the road, and Jack was leaning against the car, shielding his eyes from the approaching headlights. They pulled in behind Jack's cruiser.

"Glad to see you dressed for the occasion," Jimmy said as he climbed out of their car. He walked over and shook hands with Jack. "It would appear, however, that you are a little conflicted."

Jimmy was referring to Jack's choice of outwear: University of Washington sweatpants and a Washington State University sweatshirt. The two schools were archrivals.

"That's what happens when you have one child attending the UW and the other at WSU. I'm only conflicted about the cost of tuition. But here I am. What's up?"

"We found this piece of paper in Mick Walther's truck." Jimmy handed the plastic evidence envelope to Jack. "Turns out it's a literary quotation—from George Bernard Shaw. I'm guessing whoever left it is taunting us. Playing a game of 'catch me if you can.'"

"You think Hannigan left the note? That he killed Mick Walther?"

"That's what we're here to find out. He's an ex-English teacher, and—if all of our facts are right—he's not Serrene Homes' biggest fan."

"That's pretty slim evidence," Jack warned.

Steve stepped out of the car. "When slim is all you've got, you go with slim. It may be slim, but it's reasonable—or at least it seems reasonable at 3:15 in the morning."

"Okay," said Jack. "Let's go knock on his door."

The first knock woke the dogs. Suddenly the darkness was alive with the sounds of three dogs barking.

Frank thought he might have heard the knocking, but he was certain he heard the dogs. He motioned for Isabel to stay in bed, and he threw on his robe and walked to the front door. He had to move all the dogs out of the way. He opened the front door and looked through the locked storm door. He saw three men standing on his front deck. Fortunately, he recognized each of them.

He opened the storm door, and the barking dogs streamed into the night before returning to the deck to sniff the strangers.

"Gentlemen, you're either too late for cocktails or too early for breakfast. I can only assume this isn't a social call, so why don't you step inside so we can talk." Frank held open the storm door with one hand and took off his glasses with the other to rub his eyes.

As they filed in, Jimmy jumped in immediately. "You have any idea why we're here, Frank?"

Frank just shook his head. "Nope. Apparently whatever it is couldn't wait until the sun came up. And I've got two different police departments in my living room simultaneously. So something big is afoot. Yes?"

"Yes," said Jack Stahl.

"Well, however big it is, nothing's ever too big for the kitchen table. Why don't all of you sit? I'll make coffee."

Frank noticed for the first time that each of the detectives was about the same height—six feet tall, maybe a bit taller. Frank described himself as a "squatty five-feet-eight-inches."

As they pulled out their chairs to sit, the coffee machine began whirring to life.

"Mick Walther is dead," Jimmy said.

Frank couldn't be sure if he heard an accusatory tone or not.

"Dead?" Frank replied. "When? Where? How?

"The Eastlake police found him murdered in his truck tonight. He was parked in the Bella Square parking structure."

"You said he was murdered?"

"Shot in the head," Steve said.

"And why did that bring you here in the wee small hours of the morning?"

"Because," Jimmy said pulling out the evidence envelope, "we found this in the cab of his truck. It's a note just like the one we found in Kelsey's truck."

"Does it say *the most dangerous game*?"

"No. It's different. It's the same color paper—except for the blood spatter. This time it says*, I knew if I hung around long enough, something like this would happen."*

Frank laughed. "May I see that?"

Standing at the coffeemaker, Frank reached out and looked at the small green note through the plastic envelope. Frank laughed again.

"Is that funny?" Jimmy asked.

"No...well, yes, actually, it is funny. It's George Bernard Shaw's epitaph. Or almost. Whoever wrote that came very close to quoting the original quotation.

"Really? How does the original go?"

"The correct version of that quotation is: *I knew if I waited around long enough something like this would happen.* I can't imagine Shaw ever using the word 'hung' the way someone did there. The correct word is 'waited.'"

"Are you sure?"

"Absolutely. Anyone who teaches Brit Lit for a dozen years—and teaches kids George Bernard Shaw—and demands fidelity and precision from students when they quote anything in their research papers, that person would be expected to know a counterfeit version of the Shaw quotation. And this version is a counterfeit. Only slightly incorrect, but incorrect. By the way, gentlemen, there was no 'slightly incorrect' in my classroom when it came to research papers."

Frank laughed as he said that, and added, "One more thing. There shouldn't be a comma in the quotation either."

The coffeemaker finished its second cup just as Isabel arrived. She walked to her husband who was putting the cream back in the refrigerator.

"I made you a cup of coffee, Izz. It's early and I thought you might need one. I sure do."

For a moment, everyone fell silent—as if the night had returned.

"We're sorry to wake everyone up in the middle of the night," Jack said, "but something important—something tragic…"

"Mick Walther is dead," Frank said. "No sense in saying it any other way. He was shot? Is that right? In Eastlake? Right? And they found this note"—Frank handed Isabel the note entered in as evidence—"which is a famous Shaw quotation. It's misquoted, but close."

Isabel turned and looked at the three detectives seated around the table. "And you think…what? That we had anything to do with Mick Walther's death? We may have wished him ill—and we won't mourn his passing—but that's as far as it goes. As you gentlemen know, we don't always get what we want."

Steve jumped in. "Just a few questions. Okay?"

Isabel looked at Frank and Frank returned her look. They stood next to one another, sipping coffee, when Frank said, "Ask away."

"Where were you at 10:30 last night?" Steve asked, his notebook open.

"Right here," Frank said. "At home. Unless we're going to the theatre or the symphony, we're homebodies."

Isabel agreed. "We were both right here, at home, with our dogs, our cats, and our DVR. In fact, I don't believe either of us left the house at all yesterday."

Each one alibied the other.

"Do you own any other guns? Other than your .45 Kimber?" Steve asked.

"No. Don't need to," Isabel assured them. "My dad had several guns in his collection when he passed away in 2017, but those guns are at my brother's home. I can't even tell you what kinds of guns they are."

"And you've never owned a gun, Mr. Hannigan?" Jimmy asked.

"Well, I had a BB gun when I was kid," Frank remarked, "but that's all. Don't like guns."

The three detectives seem to have run out of questions. Except for the living room and kitchen lights, they were cocooned in darkness. There was no TV or radio droning in the background, and the silence dominated the room until Jimmy spoke up.

"Well, Frank and Isabel, we expect to come back with a search warrant tomorrow morning."

Neither Frank nor Isabel said a word.

"Is there anything you want to tell us?" Jimmy asked.

"Yes," Isabel said. "I'd like to go back to bed. Please be quiet as you leave." Isabel walked down the dark hallway and disappeared. Frank looked at the detectives at the table.

"How about you, Frank?"

"Gentlemen, I'm afraid there's nothing to tell. I never realized that being an English teacher could bring the police to my door...but what time can we expect you?"

"I'll call you when we're on our way," said Jack. "We'll have a Snoquamish cruiser parked at the top of your lane. If you need to go somewhere before we arrive, you'll have to let them know."

"Okay," Frank said yawning. "We're under house arrest. Got it. Is there anything else?"

Jack turned to Jimmy and Steve. "You guys get what you needed?"

They nodded and walked to the door.

"I'll have fresh coffee for you in the morning," Frank said. "Goodnight."

They were back at their cars in a few minutes.

"What do you think?" Jack asked.

"Not sure," said Steve. At least they didn't start screaming at us."

Jimmy gave a wry smile.

"Yeah, Steve," Jimmy commented. "I was thinking the same thing. They didn't seem upset at all. The whole interview felt weird. They're too calm. Shit, if someone knocked on my door at three in the morning, there'd be hell to pay. But what do they do? Invite us in for coffee."

"What did you want them to do?" Jack responded.

"I'm not sure," Jimmy replied. "Just not what they did. They invited us in for coffee with absolutely no objection. And Frank knew the Shaw quote right off the top of his head. He knew the *exact* quote. Knew it well enough to tell us we had an incorrect version of Shaw's epitaph."

"So?" Jack asked.

"Don't you see? Someone's screwing with our minds." Jimmy's face was set and determined. "Those two pieces of paper were left deliberately at the crime scenes. Whoever killed Kelsey and Mick knew we'd find those slips of paper. Whoever left them wanted us to find those slips of paper. Take *the most dangerous game.* It's a story title with a double meaning and the title is ironic. The story ends in death—for the bad guy. And now we have a famous Shaw quotation —an epitaph, for Christ's sake. You don't get closer to death than that. Someone is screwing with our heads. We have to find out who."

"Well, until we do, we're going to get that search warrant and take a look around tomorrow," Jack said. "What should we specify in the search warrant?"

"Well, we've got to have a look at their phones and computers," Jimmy said. "If they're doing this, there's got to be some information in their technology that we're not seeing. I'll bet their phones have a built-in GPS. Maybe their cars, too. We can check that out. And we're looking for anything with blood on it. I don't think you can shoot a guy in the forehead and get away without blood on you. And we're looking for the gun. Hell, we've got the motive—all we need now is proof."

"I thought you liked this guy, Jimmy," Steve said.

"Frank? Yeah, I do like him. And if he's our guy, he's the most likeable killer I've ever come across."

The search warrant turned up nothing. Between eight and noon, eight investigators swept through their automobiles, their home, their garage, their shed, and the wooded area of their property, and found nothing. No gun. No bloody clothes.

Closets were emptied, dog beds unzipped and inspected. Someone even went under the house into the crawl space.

Their technology—phones, tablets, and computers—was being checked out at the lab, but it appeared that might be a dead end, too.

As Frank stood out in the front yard with Jack, he remarked that it felt like his house was getting a colonoscopy. That's when one of the investigators, a short, balding man that Jack called Sparks, asked Jack if they could inspect the small wooden structure just west of the property.

"I don't know," Jack said. "Let me ask our host. How about it, Frank? Can we inspect that building?"

"You want to inspect the well house?" Frank asked. "Well, that building doesn't sit on our property. That's my neighbor's property. I doubt if it's technically covered under the warrant. However, if you want to have a look-see, I'll be happy to walk over there with you. This well serves three households—including ours—so I suppose I can take you over there.

"Sounds like a plan," Jack replied. "Be back in a second."

Jack disappeared into Frank and Isabel's home and emerged with another of the crime scene investigators.

"Frank has given us his permission to look at the well house. I want you and Sparks to go over there with Frank and take a look. See what you can find."

They took a look. They found nothing.

The investigators looked closely at Frank's 2014 Toyota Prius V—it had an internal GPS system that synched up with a satellite for its computerized map feature, but all it proved was that Frank made a lot of trips to pet stores, Italian restaurants, and wineries. Isabel and Frank's other car held no interest for the investigators. A 2003 KIA, Frank overheard one of the investigators say, "Forget it, you guys. This car is a technological dead-end."

While all this was happening, Frank and Isabel did their best to stay out of the way. The thin cloud cover burned off, and the day turned sunny and warm. As the investigators moved quickly here and there, Frank and Isabel sat quietly on their front deck sipping coffee laced with Baileys. The dogs, alternately curious and confused, finally joined them on the deck.

Chapter Twelve

The Snowy Owl

Frank Hannigan
June 5, 2019

I walked into the darkened bedroom, looked at the illuminated face on my phone and noted it was 3:55 a.m. I knew Isabel would be awake. Sleeping has never been her strong suit.

"They've gone," I said. "Detective Stahl said there's a police cruiser parked at the end of the lane—probably to keep us from fleeing the country."

"As if we'd ever leave the dogs and cats," she said from the darkness.

"They'll be back later this morning with a search warrant," I said yawning. I felt suddenly weary.

"They won't find anything," Isabel said, her certainty filling the darkness.

"No, they won't. Not here anyway. Let's hope they don't get too curious."

"They wouldn't have gotten curious if you hadn't left your calling card at the murder scene," Isabel said. I detected a trace of disapproval in her voice.

"Sorry," I said. "I gave into temptation."

"I love that you are an English teacher at heart. And that the incredible words uttered by important authors come trippingly off your tongue. I love that. But I need to ask, why George Bernard Shaw?"

I looked at my lovely wife Isabel in the dim light of our bedroom. She loved language as much as I did, and, together, we have always encouraged one another in our mutual love of language. I like to think we nurture and caress one another with words.

"I've always thought Shaw's epitaph was both insightful and comic," I said. "Maybe it's unwise to leave comic commentary at a murder scene, but it just felt right. Besides, Shaw has so many wonderful things to say about the human condition."

Isabel took my last remark as her cue to ask, "Like what?" She never missed her cue.

I took a deep breath, slipped under the covers, and rolled over to face Isabel before answering.

"I suspect that if anyone else knew what we were doing, they'd tell us what a terrible mistake we're making. They'd assure us that there's absolutely nothing we can do—as if there were, in fact, absolutely nothing we could do. You know what they mean when they say there's nothing we can do, don't you? They're saying that *they* would do nothing. They're advising us to grin and bear it. They'd suffer the obligatory slings and arrows of outrageous fortune. Well, if they can do that, good for them."

I could feel the tears welling up. Isabel reached over and touched my face. I took another deep breath and continued.

"Sorry, Isabel, I won't be like those people. *We* won't be like those people. The do-nothings. The suck-it-ups. If we're making a mistake, so be it. Let me quote George Bernard Shaw when he said, 'A life spent making mistakes is more honorable than a life spent doing nothing.'"

We lay facing one another in silence.

"Miss Aria's death deserves more than nothing. More than the shrug we got from the developer and city hall. More than a quiet and civil acquiescence. That goes for our trees and our shed, too."

"You're right," Isabel said. "But you realize, of course, you wasted a perfectly elegant epitaph on a Neanderthal. You wasted a George Bernard Shaw on a Mick Walther. If it had been left to me, I should have gone for an Ogden Nash."

I love it when laughter erupts in the darkness. How could I not love this woman?

Isabel and I were enjoying the warm sunshine with Detective Stahl on the steps of our front deck while his crime scene crew scoured our home and our lives. Wolfie and Jackson were wrestling over a five-foot fallen branch in the front yard. Luigi lay at my feet.

"We told you there was nothing to find," I said to Detective Stahl. "We wouldn't lie to you."

I smiled at him.

Jack smiled back at me, one hand stuffed in his pants pocket, jiggling coins—probably a nervous habit—and the other holding his suit jacket over his right shoulder. I think I heard him chuckle. It was clear that the crime scene crew was getting ready to leave, walking back and forth, and returning equipment to their trucks parked in our driveway.

"We're just here to do our jobs," Jack replied.

"We hear that a lot, Detective," Isabel said. "'We're just doing our jobs.' That must be the universal excuse for disrupting or shattering innocent people's lives, wouldn't you say, Frank?"

"Oh, yeah," I agreed. "The developers were just doing their jobs. You were just doing yours. It would have been nice if the Snoquamish police had figured out how to do their jobs when our tree roots had been cut."

That comment put a damper on the conversation.

"I'm sorry, Jack. Police visitations seem to have become the norm here at the Comstock-Hannigan household. And at all hours of the night and day."

"I am sorry about last night, Frank. That wasn't my call."

"And yet..." Isabel remarked.

"And yet" was one of Isabel's favorite tag lines. For instance, I might tell Isabel I didn't mean to do something, or that I didn't mean to forget something, and she'd turn to me with her beautiful smile and say, "And yet..." It always made both of us laugh.

"When can we expect to get out computers back, Detective?" Isabel asked. "That's my livelihood you've got stashed in your truck. I'm an accountant with clients who expect me to get their work done."

"We'll try to have your technology back to you by the end of the day," Jack replied.

"I've never liked the word 'try,' Detective. My clients always want to know when they can expect something from me. They don't want to know when I might 'try' to get it to them. They want to know when. I'd like to know when, too."

"Understood," Jack said nodding to himself. "I'll guarantee you'll have your business computer...and all your phones...by tonight. You've got my word. If that doesn't happen, you call me at this number." He circled one of the phone numbers on his business card to emphasize his point and handed the card to Isabel.

Isabel didn't miss a beat. "And with your kind permission, Detective, I'm sending Frank up to the store right now to get us a pair of cheap, pre-paid phones. That's alright, isn't it? We can't live without phones. Unfortunately for us all, this is no longer the 20th century."

Detective Stahl had to laugh. "You sound just like Jimmy Brautigan."

Five minutes later, everyone was gone. The dogs had run along the fence line, barking at the police vehicles, as they departed.

I went inside and opened a bottle of wine. It was a bit early, but I felt we had something to celebrate.

"So, our plan worked?" Isabel asked as I handed her a glass of chilled rose'.

"So far, so good," I said. "You've been exactly right about everything you said they'd do. You predicted they'd show up here after Mick's death.

Probably in the dead of night. Oops! No pun intended."

"And yet..."

We laughed.

"Here's to your clairvoyance."

Isabel and I raised our glasses and took a sip.

"I'm not really clairvoyant, you know?"

"You're not?" I asked in a teasing tone.

"No, my love. I just knew where the police would come if you decided to leave your former English teacher's calling card. George Bernard Shaw? Their arrival was as easy to predict as the rising of the sun."

I took a long sip of my wine. Isabel was right, of course.

"What would you do without me, my love?" Isabel asked

The truth is, I didn't know. My wife's attention to detail, her ability to plan, her ability to anticipate contingencies, those were her gifts, not mine. More than once she warned me against being too impulsive.

Early on, when I was first beginning to surveil Mick, she asked me, "So...once you've got Mick's patterns figured out, once you can properly and regularly anticipate where he'll be and when, then what do you plan to do?"

"I'll walk over and shoot him," I said. It all seemed pretty simple to me.

"And then what?"

"What do you mean, 'and then what?' Then he's dead, that's what."

"And you, Mr. Hannigan, will be captured. You've got to grasp the concept of *quid pro quo*. This isn't the Hatfield and McCoys—where the killing continues in an endless stream of cause-and-effect. When you've achieved your justice—when Mick Walther has been sent to the hereafter—then that must be the end of it. To do that—to achieve your justice without repercussion—you need a plan. Do you have a plan?"

"Not really," I said. "I haven't really thought that far ahead."

But Isabel had. Thank goodness.

She'd also anticipated the possible problems our cellphones could cause. Apparently, cellphones like ours have an internal GPS that literally can tell someone—like the police—where you've been. Isabel forbade me from turning off my phone or from carrying my phone whenever I went out to watch Mick Walther's movements. You can probably tell I have a love-hate relationship with modern technology.

"If the police ask to see your cellphone, just hand it over. Your phone—the one you wisely left at home while you were out and about on the evening of June 4th will tell them you were here at home with me, probably watching *The Equalizer*, when Mick died. See?"

Isabel patted me on the cheek. "Your phone and I will be your alibi."

I hoped that was true.

"They've taken all our technology—at least for the rest of the day. You were spot on about getting burner phones. If we hadn't, we'd never be able to talk to one another while I was out and about doing what I was doing. And I'm glad you thought about the GPS in the Prius. Hell, if I'd been driving that car over to Mick's—or to the Bella Square parking lot—they'd know a lot more than we'd want them to. Like the guy said, your Kia doesn't have a lick of technology that helps them out."

"Aren't you glad we still have my 'old' car?" Isabel asked in a mocking tone.

"I will never again call your Kia 'old,'" I said. "I shall venerate The Blueberry"—that's the nickname Isabel had long ago bestowed on her beloved automobile—"until the end of days."

"Everything's at Mom's?" Isabel asked.

"Yep. Everything."

Isabel's mom, Dorothy, moved into an adult living community a few years ago, but the house where her mom had lived for twenty years had never been sold. When Dorothy moved out, our niece and nephew moved in, taking advantage of a rent-free offer made by their grandmother. Who can resist rent-free? Three months ago, Jennifer married, and naturally, she decided she didn't want to live there anymore. Go figure.

About a month later, our nephew Sam accepted a great job offer, and he probably would have stayed—as I said, who can resist "rent-free?"—but the commute was a killer. So Dorothy's house currently stands empty.

"I stashed everything—the GPS locator, my clothes, the plastic seat covers from the car, everything but the gun—in large plastic bags and stuck them in the garbage bins in the garage just as you suggested. Then I showered—scrubbed hard until the skin practically came off—and came home. I remembered to put the towels and wash cloths in Mom's washer with bleach before I left. Your idea—that I keep a change of clothes—that was perfect. There really was a lot of blood involved."

"I'm glad I thought of that," Isabel said. She hadn't seen me until I arrived home freshly showered.

"Jesus, when I shot him, his head burst like a melon. I'm glad I was wearing glasses and had a ski mask on. I had blood all over me. I knew he was dead. I got out of his truck in two seconds. I pulled out the garbage bag I had in my pocket, grabbed the GPS tracker from the wheel-well, and began throwing everything in the bag. GPS first. Ski mask. Gloves. Sweatshirt. I kept to the side street as much as I could because I was worried I'd be naked by the time I reached the car."

"Did he say anything to you? Before you shot him?"

"No. And I didn't say anything, either. All I did was leave my Shaw quote on the floor on the passenger side."

Isabel and I would often talk about how killers, in the movies we've seen, always feel obliged to talk to their victims before killing them. Sometimes we'd just sit there and yell at the TV screen, "Are you gonna shoot them or talk them to death? You're wasting valuable time. Just pull the trigger!"

We agreed in advance that I wasn't inviting Mick Walther to dinner.

"Just shut up and shoot," Isabel advised.

That's what I did.

"Where's the gun?" Isabel asked.

"I put it in the box with all my old albums in your mom's garage."

"What? In with your 33 1/3 platters in the old wooden crate?"

"Yep. The gun's underneath a whole stack of albums." I broke into a broad grin. "I put the Beatle's *Revolver* album on top. I knew all those vintage albums would come in handy someday."

"You're incorrigible," Isabel said.

"Isabel, my love, I try never to be incorrigible," I said.

"And yet..." she replied.

We're done with all of this, at least for a while. Killing someone—even the someones who deserved it for their sins of omission and commission—has taken a predictably hefty emotional toll on both of us. We're hoping that if we put all of this out of our minds for a few months, we'll be able to sleep at night. Well, one of us, anyway.

Tomorrow, I'll return to my mother-in-law's home and do the laundry at my leisure. Wash and bleach all the incriminating bloodied clothing. The laundered clothes will go to Goodwill. As for the plastic bags, they'll end up in some commercial dumpster when I make a trip to eastern Washington next week. Empty plastic bags hold little fascination or interest for anyone.

I won't leave anything at my mother-in-law's home. That would just be inviting trouble. Everything goes except the pistol—the 9mm pistol can stay right where it is.

I keep wondering if the Serrene Homes folks will get the message—that Kelsey and Mick's murders are a signal that developers can't simply disenfranchise those on the boundaries of the property they're developing. But I doubt it.

Sure, that's pessimistic, but that's reality. Money and profit will always blind developers and city planners to the misery they might cause others. It costs too much to care.

Like the two notes I left—containing the title of Richard Connell's short story and Shaw's epitaph—I wish I could send a simple clear note to

Serrene Homes. It would tie up everything in a nice, neat package. I know what it would say.

> Consider how you hurt people. If you hadn't cut down trees that were not yours to cut down, or if you'd only found a way to be contrite about it and compensated the victims of your thoughtlessness, Kelsey and Mick would be alive today. They're dead because neither they nor you ever considered how people are hurt by your thoughtlessness. But...
>
> *   You did destroy those trees;
> and,
> *   You didn't find a way to show your contrition.
>
> That's why Kelsey and Mick paid the price for all of you. Perhaps you should all think about the future of Serrene Homes as well as your own future. Perhaps you should consider not hurting people.

Isabel said a note like that would definitely bring the police to our door. And a note like that—a note I will never deliver—was actually on a thumb drive that was buried in my Snowy Owl Puppet in the back office. Until last night.

I worried that the crime scene investigators would be exceedingly thorough, inspecting even the innards of a child's puppet. They're professional investigators, after all. Since an investigator's entire life revolves around conducting investigations—and since the people they investigate are seldom as clever as they think they are—I guessed the interior of my Snowy Owl would doubtless be subjected to inspection as well. Investigators turn the expression "every nook and cranny" into a literal experience. In this case, it's nooks, crannies, and an owl's butt.

However, when the crime scene investigators left with all our technology, they left without that thumb drive and my backup comput-er. I'd buried them under a bunch of leaves and twigs inside our now, half-destroyed, wooden doghouse that forlornly sits beneath one of our giant spruce trees. An errant limb from our crashing fir—the one that de-stroyed our shed—dealt the doghouse a glancing blow. The crime scene guys thought it was "cute" that we decided to keep our fractured dog-house in our backyard.

"It reminds me of what I've lost," I told them. They just nodded and continued their fruitless search. No one looked inside the doghouse. Thank goodness.

So, for the next few months, there will be no notes, no cryptic quota-tions, no surveillance, no nothing. Nothing that has anything to do with our search for justice. Isabel and I will be laying low, drinking bottles of wine from our shed that Jacob had deemed unworthy of stealing, and do-ing our best to ignore the Hemlock Hill folk who must still be wondering what happened to Jacob Forrest.

It's June. I'm keenly aware that he would have been graduating from high school right about now. I read in our local newspaper that Snoquamish Catholic's student body president wanted to have a Jacob Forrest memorial service, but Jacob's dad refused. A memorial service would acknowledge the death of his son—and even after more than six months, he is unwilling to let go.

Isabel and I are both sorry that Jacob made the decisions he made.

While I can't speak for Isabel, I'm not particularly proud of myself either, but then I believe we've only been given bad options. We could do nothing and absorb the hurt. Or we could do something illegal, because there are no legal remedies available.

One thing was clear: We could not do nothing.

So there you are.

There is only one individual remaining on our list—Amelia Artaud—the city planner who sent the police to our door because I got upset when she failed to return any of my nineteen phone calls. The city planner who was as instrumental in permitting the successes of the developers as she was in permitting the failures of the city to protect its extant inhabitants and ecosystem.

She's our next and last. I don't yet know what any of Amelia's patterns might be. I wonder if her local newspaper published articles about Kelsey and Mick Walther. If it did, how could she miss it? The local Seattle media went crazy after Mick's death.

Would Amelia feel anything at all if she saw that both of them have been murdered—two people with whom she must have had regular contact when the Hemlock Hill subdivision was being planned? I can't say. City planners work with all kinds of developers, and I'm betting that Mick Walther was just another developer to Amelia. She'd view his unfortunate death and that of his wife as remote, unconnected events. Certainly no connection to her.

She'd be wrong.

I'm relying on her inability to ferret any connection between their deaths and her own impending doom.

I wonder if Ms. Artaud's patterns will be as easy to decipher as Kelsey and Mick's. From what I've been able to discreetly find out, after she left the Snoquamish city planner's office—I don't know if she resigned or was fired—she moved to Bozeman, a city in south central Montana. Isabel suggested that Amelia went to Montana to get out of the rat race. I said she went there because incompetent city planners aren't as obvious in Montana as they are here. Isabel said I shouldn't slight Montana that way.

The real problem with pursuing the last person on our list is that I can't just roll out of bed, climb into my car, and watch her movements. We looked at a map—no online searches—and Bozeman is around 670 to 680 miles from our home—a straight, unwavering drive along I-90—but still, almost seven hundred miles east and a whole time zone away.

"I don't know why you're worried, Frank," Isabel said. "At 70 mph, you'll get there in under ten hours. Bozeman's not the end of the earth."

"No," I said, "but you can see it from there."

Going to Bozeman to complete our plan is going to be a challenge because it may be a big city by Montana standards, but it's small by metropolitan ones. It has close to 50,000 people. About the same size as Snoquamish. I'm hoping a city boy like me won't stick out like a sore thumb. I'm hoping I won't be the stranger that came to town. People usually notice strangers. I worried about losing the unassailable advantage of being anonymous.

The voice in my head cautioned me: *Goodbye, anonymity.*

As I said, patterns are the key. I'll bet that's exactly what the police say, too, when they're knee-deep in a perplexing, head-scratching who-done-it? They're looking for patterns.

Fortunately for us, and unfortunately for the police, our patterns are about to return to our heretofore, non-criminal normal. We'll return to the life we had before our trees fell, and before our beautiful Flat-Coated Retriever, our shed, and our home fell victim to Serrene Homes' carelessness. Isabel and Frank, a lady accountant and a retired English teacher, living their quiet, unassuming life on an unpaved, dead-end road with their three dogs, three cats, and thirty one-hundred-foot-tall trees. That will be enough.

For now.

Chapter Thirteen

No Stone Unturned

Jimmy Brautigan
June 5, 2019

Jimmy Brautigan and his fellow investigators—Steve, Caroline, and Ben—were all gathered together in the conference room. Kelsey Walther's picture was still on the wall under the "Why?", and now her husband's picture hung right beside hers—with a scribbled caption "Revenge?"

Jimmy's friend, Jack, Chief of Detectives for the Snoquamish police, had run a by-the-book search of the Comstock-Hannigan property. Eight investigators had searched everywhere for more than four hours looking for something that resembled a clue to the deaths of Kelsey and Mick. They'd even swabbed Frank Hannigan's skin for GSR—gun-shot residue— despite Frank's assertion that he'd never, in his whole life, shot a gun bigger than a BB gun.

The simple fact that Frank gracefully submitted to the GSR test should have absolved Frank of any connection to the previous night's shooting, but something just felt "off" to Jimmy. And that "off" feeling—the one that began when Frank blithely invited them in for coffee at three o'clock in the morning, without ever raising his voice, without complaining about the hour, without acting like a goddamn normal human being who's been rudely roused out of a sound sleep at that time in the morning—simply reinforced Jimmy's suspicion that Frank was somehow involved in the two deaths.

"Have you seen today's headlines in *The Chronicle*?" Steve asked Jimmy. A copy of today's edition sat next to his coffee on the table. He shoved it towards Jimmy.

"How could I miss it?"

"The Serrene Homes Killer?

"Can you blame them?" Jimmy asked. "Two murders in Eastlake this year—the only two—and they're husband and wife. Killed months apart, but they both worked for Serrene Homes."

Jimmy shoved the paper back toward Steve.

"Why does it feel that we have less than when we began this whole investigation?" Jimmy asked.

"Probably because we are running out of leads," Steve said. "We're running out of places to go and people to question."

"Alright," Jimmy said, pushing himself out of his chair and moving to the pictures of the murdered couple, "let's just retrace our steps. Would you step us through that, Caroline."

"Sure." Caroline booted up her tablet and began reading the summary that all of them had heard too many times before.

Who: Kelsey Walther. Age 44. Serrene Homes employee since 2005.

Date: January 30, 2019 at 23:00 – 23:30

Place: The Eastlake QFC parking lot

Weather: Cloudy, rainy, and cold. [32°F]

Details: Body found face down by the right rear tire of her white, Dodge pickup truck. Bludgeoned to death. One blow, with an unknown object. Probably metal. Truck's tire had been flattened. Probably deliberately. Otherwise truck was spotless, inside and out. Only out-of-place item was a green slip of paper—three inches by two inches—with the words "the most dangerous game" printed in block letters in black ink...probably a ballpoint pen. No prints on the paper. No prints on the truck. No murder weapon found. No DNA evidence except for the victim's DNA, her husband's DNA, and that of two employees who had ridden in her truck. No CCTV.

Motive: Unknown. No robbery. No car theft. No sexual assault. Everyone liked Kelsey. Reportedly.

Possible: Unknown person or persons disliked Kelsey or Serrene Homes. Most likely the latter.

Suspects: Frank Hannigan (?) Snoquamish, WA

"I have a question mark after Hannigan's name. Is he still a suspect? Do you want me to keep him as a suspect?" Caroline asked. "Doesn't look like much has changed—even after Mick's death."

"I know," Jimmy said. "Believe me. And yes, he's still a suspect."

"Is Frank's wife a suspect, too?" Ben asked. "A co-conspirator?"

"One thing at a time," Jimmy cautioned.

Jimmy turned and faced his colleagues. As the lead on this investigation, he'd already decided what needed to be done today. His uneasiness with Frank Hannigan hadn't abated one bit, and he couldn't shake the feeling that the Walthers had something in common with Jacob Forrest.

Just do your job, Jimmy, he told himself.

"Okay, Caroline, now read the Mick Walther summary."

Who: Mick Walther. Age 47. Owner Serrene Homes since 2005.

Date: June 4, 2019 at 22:30 – 23:00

Place: Bella Square parking structure: Level 2

Weather: Partly cloudy, warm [62°F]

Details: Body found behind the steering wheel of his white,

Dodge, pickup truck. (Same truck once registered to Kelsey Walther.) One shot in right temple with a 9mm pistol. Green slip of paper found on the floor of passenger side with the sentence: "I knew if I hung around long enough, something like this would happen." Apparently, the George Bernard Shaw epitaph. (BUT: an incorrect rendition.) Like the note found in Kelsey's vehicle (same truck), it was printed in block letters in black ink...probably a ballpoint pen. No prints on the paper. No prints on the truck. No murder weapon found. No DNA evidence except for the victim's DNA. No CCTV. **NOTE:** The note left behind indicates that the murders of Kelsey and Mick are closely related. Possibly the same perpetrator.

Motive: Unknown. No robbery. Mick could be difficult, but he was generally liked. In November 2015, Mick had accused Frank Hannigan of threatening to shoot "at him." Frank Hannigan denies he ever said that. Hannigan does not own a gun. Never has.

Possible: Unhappy homeowners among "the usual suspects." Perpetrator probably did not like Serrene Homes or people who ran Serrene Homes.

Suspects: Frank Hannigan (?) Snoquamish, WA

"Two peas in a pod," Steve commented. "Seems like it anyway. Except for the murder weapon."

Jimmy agreed.

"Sure looks like it. Jesus." The frustration in his voice was clear. "Someone murdered a husband and wife. Months apart, but that's probably just a matter of timing and opportunity."

"We even have the same suspect," Steve said. "Except we have not one iota of proof, and he has a solid alibi for both murders."

The group discussion encompassed the possible involvement of competitors—other developers who might not be terribly fond of Mick—but there was no proof of that either. Besides, Kelsey appeared to be universally loved even if her husband was occasionally a hard-ass. Why would someone murder them both?

Jimmy took charge. "Ben and Caroline, I want you to re-interview everyone at Serrene Homes. Start with Millie. She's the office manager. And be gentle. They've already lost two people this year—they're all grieving. Listen, find out who the other principals are. I'm worried that they may be in danger. They have to be warned. If our killer is getting revenge against Serrene Homes, there are a whole slew of other targets."

"That could include employees and homeowners. Like the folks who live at Hemlock Hill," Steve said.

"And Ben, get whatever CCTV you can from the Serrene Homes office. Maybe someone was tracking Mick's comings and goings at the office parking lot; if so, we might get a look at the cars that make regular appearances, and cars that simply don't belong. Steve and I will do the same for any CCTV around Finnegan's and Bella Square. We'll have their security people send you what they've got.

"Steve, you and I are going to begin our day at Finnegan's and then we're going back to Seattle to see Harold Forrest again. Okay? Jack texted me this morning, said that he'd love it if I could be 'another face' for Mr. Forrest to talk with. But I also think you may have been right all along—Jacob's disappearance and the Walthers' deaths are somehow linked."

What Jimmy and Steve discovered at Finnegan's didn't surprise them. Finnegan's is an Irish pub, the kind with a cadre of regulars who love patronizing their favorite watering hole—sometimes several times a week. Like most pubs, Finnegan's was a place to meet friends, share a ploughman's lunch, toss back a Guinness over jokes and impossible tales, or watch a football game or soccer match.

Mick and his wife regularly hobnobbed after work with friends and colleagues at Finnegan's, and Mick had continued going there after Kelsey's death. Not only did his friends provide much needed solace and comfort, they were experts at diverting Mick's morose tendencies into happier thoughts.

Jimmy and Steve interviewed a lot of the regulars to see if anyone remembered anything that might shed light on Mick's murder. No one at Finnegan's could recall any kind of problem between either Mick or Kelsey and anyone else who came there. Quite the opposite. That's because the regular patrons were always striking up conversations with strangers, and as the owner proudly said, "No one's a stranger for very long when they come here."

That comment solidified Jimmy's doubt that Finnegan's would be a good place to "stake out" an intended victim. Nevertheless, Jimmy asked if they could get a copy of credit card receipts dating back to the beginning of the year—before Kelsey's death in January. It was a *pro forma* request. Finnegan's felt like the latest dead end. If Finnegan's somehow fit into Mick or Kelsey's murders, Jimmy and Steve just didn't see it.

As they drove to Seattle, Jimmy remembered why he loved the Pacific Northwest. Seattle was wearing her best face on this perfect spring day.

Crossing the SR 520 floating bridge, Jimmy and Steve looked south to see Mt. Rainier rising into the cloudless blue sky like a giant mound of ice cream. At least eighty miles away, it looked like you could reach out and take a scoop with your hand. The waters of Lake Washington reflected the bright sunshine and blue sky. It was a perfect day.

Jimmy exited near the University of Washington Arboretum. It wasn't the quickest route downtown.

"Why are we exiting here?" Steve asked.

"It's time to stop and smell the roses," Jimmy said. "Well, actually, it's too soon for roses. Today, it's time for the dogwood, and I just want to take a peek."

Jimmy had planted a dogwood in their front yard in memory of Felicia, and this morning he'd noticed that it was in full bloom. Seeing the tree awash in flowers reminded him of better days, when their love was in full bloom.

Before the spring had actually arrived, the azaleas had bloomed—azaleas that Felicia had lovingly planted. And now the dogwoods were center stage. Jimmy's wife had always loved flowers—every spring she'd plant the flower boxes in the kitchen windows, and insisted on a half-dozen hanging baskets outside to add color. Felicia didn't much care for the muted, neutral colors that the Home Owners Association favored—even demanded.

His wife used to call the head of their HOA, "The Leader of the Bland. I bet he knew Henry Ford," she'd always say, putting on her most officious face. "You can paint your house any color you want, as long as it's beige, beiger, or beigest."

Jimmy and Felicia painted their house beige—but Felicia undermined the HOA's penchant for the drab with riotous color every spring and summer. She used to tell Jimmy she was the founding member of the "Flower Resistance."

"I remember how beautiful your home was every spring," Steve remarked.

"That was all Felicia. She loved flowers, and they loved her back. I just happened to be the beneficiary. She always said spring was her favorite time of the year."

Ten minutes later, they drove into the thicket of tall buildings that is downtown Seattle. They took the elevator to Harold Forrest's law offices on the 40th floor of the Columbia Tower. A legal aide ushered Jimmy and Steve into Mr. Forrest's office—the corner office that faced west, toward Puget Sound and the Olympics and south, toward Seahawks stadium.

Steve walked to the windows and gave a low whistle. "Still have to say it. Helluva view."

Jimmy joined Steve at the window and watched a ferry slip soundlessly out into Elliott Bay. "You almost feel like God from up here," he said to Steve.

"Yes, you do," Harold Forrest said as he walked into his office and joined Steve and Jimmy at the window. "I have to remind myself that I'm not God. Not even close. If I were, I'd know exactly where my son is."

Without any of the usual niceties, Mr. Forrest turned and sat on the edge of his desk.

"I didn't go into work until late yesterday. I saw a bunch of Snoquamish police at Hannigan's place. That have anything to do with Mick Walther's death?"

Jimmy looked at Steve. "We're just at the beginning of that investigation."

"Okay. Okay," Mr. Forrest said. "You don't want to talk about it."

"That's true, we don't want to talk about that, but we are curious about Frank Hannigan."

"And his wife," Steve pointed out.

"Curious?" Mr. Forrest was happy just to let the question hang in the air.

Steve pulled out his omnipresent notebook. "Remember the last time we were here? We were attempting to see if there's a common denominator for Ms. Walther's murder and your son's disappearance. And now Mick's been murdered. We're still trying to connect the dots," he said. "So give me a moment to go through the chronology with you, okay? First, your son disappeared last December."

"It was either Friday night, December 14 or Saturday morning December 15," Mr. Forrest said with precision. "His mother and I last saw him on Friday, the 14th. What happened after that is still unknown."

"Alright. Your son disappeared last December. Since his disappearance, there's been nothing."

"That's an understatement. There's been a whole lot of nothing. Less than nothing, actually," Mr. Forrest commented, with obvious bitterness.

"Then, in late January, Kelsey Walther is murdered in the Eastlake QFC parking lot, and her husband Mick is murdered just two days ago in the Bella Square parking structure. She was bludgeoned, he was shot."

Steve turned the page. "What they all have in common is not just Serrene Homes, but also Hemlock Hill. Your son lived there, and Kelsey and Mick owned the company that built Hemlock Hill. It strikes me that it would have to be the most far-fetched coincidence when three people associated with Hemlock Hill have either disappeared or been murdered over the last six or seven months. So there is one question we need to ask. Who hates Hemlock Hill enough to murder two people?"

Steve looked at Mr. Forrest.

"Or maybe three."

Mr. Forrest stood up and walked to the window. He gazed across Elliott Bay and Puget Sound at the Olympic Mountains, rising purple in the distance. "I never get tired of the view. Never. But I'd give it all up just to know what's happened to Jacob."

Jimmy stood up and joined him. "We know that Frank Hannigan thought the person stealing wine from his shed was probably a teenage boy. I don't believe he knew your son, Jacob, but he told the police that he and his wife were convinced that the thief or thieves were teenagers—probably boys. We also know there was no love lost between Frank and Serrene Homes."

"But that's as far as we ever get, Mr. Forrest," Steve said. "We have Hemlock Hill as the common denominator...but then we have nothing. By all accounts, Frank and Isabel are terrific people. We've spoken with Isabel's clients and with some of Frank's former colleagues and we always get rave reviews. The only black marks come from the Snoquamish police interview notes. The police first interviewed Hannigan in November 2015 about threats he allegedly made, and then they interviewed him last December, the day after your run-in with Frank Hannigan."

"Plus his alibis are solid. He doesn't own a gun and he doesn't appear to be a physically aggressive person. The sharpest thing he owns is his tongue."

Mr. Forrest shot Jimmy a knowing look. He turned and walked behind his desk "I know my son was no saint. I don't know if he ever stole or attempted to steal wine from Hannigan's shed—but even if he did—even if he did, you don't kill someone over something like that." His voice cracked. "There are some things you simply don't get over."

Jimmy and Steve knew they simply had to let Mr. Forrest talk.

"You know, Jacob's SATs weren't terrific, but he was headed to college. He'd already started applying to universities. I was hoping he'd apply to Stanford—that's my alma mater—and his mother was hoping for Cornell. All those plans..." Mr. Forrest's voice drifted off.

"We're sorry, Mr. Forrest, about Jacob," said Jimmy. "I cannot imagine anything worse than what you've endured. But here's the thing. We're concerned for the safety of anyone who lives in Hemlock Hill or works for Serrene Homes. Your son, and the Walthers—all they had in common was Hemlock Hill."

"I appreciate your concern, but I don't think you need to worry about me or my family. In a previous life, I was Army. I own a gun, and I know how to use it. And don't worry, it's registered and locked up in a gun safe in the back of the closet in the master bedroom."

"Army? Where'd you serve?"

"Iran and Afghanistan. A total of three tours."

"What was your MOS?"

"I was Army Intelligence. Trying to find the bad guys—keep the good guys safe."

"That sounds familiar," Steve chimed in. "I was in ROTC until I screwed up my knee playing soccer. The Army told me, 'Thanks, but no thanks.' I'm one of those guys who *almost* went into the Army. At least they paid for two years of college."

They both looked at Jimmy.

"Military? Me? No. No military here. I was born in 1958, just a tad too late for Vietnam. I entered the academy in 1980 right out of college. Been a cop now for three decades."

"What kind of gun do you have?" Steve asked.

"A Beretta 92 9mm. I got myself a .22 a decade ago when a client made threats against me. Kept it in my office. When I finally got around to taking lessons and going to the firing range, it was maybe eight years later. The instructor took one look at my pistol and said I'd be better off with a baseball bat. He recommended a 9mm. So I bought one just before we moved to Hemlock Hill. I've shot it maybe three or four times at the range. The last time I had it out was months ago—probably last September—when I had the gun safe installed in the house."

"A 9mm?" Jimmy knew the world was filled with 9mm pistols, and Mick Walther was killed with a 9mm bullet.

What are the odds? Jimmy thought.

Still, Jimmy was curious. "Any chance we can see it?"

"Sure. Swing by the house any time and I'll show it to you."

Everyone lapsed into silent reverie. They seemed to have reached the end of their conversational string.

"So that's why we came by, today, Mr. Forrest. As Steve said, Hemlock Hill seems to hold the key to whatever's happening, but the only suspects seem to be a damn decent fellow and his damn decent wife, who feel they've been betrayed by the legal system. I should add, these are damn decent folks who have no record of any kind—speeding tickets excluded. Plus they have alibis for both murders.

"Can you let your HOA folks know about our concerns for their safety?" Steve asked. "We don't want anyone to panic, but I expect you'd want due diligence from us."

"Of course. I'm on the HOA board. I'll send out a memo to everyone tonight."

"We wish we had better news," Steve added.

"I've given up hoping for better news," Mr. Forrest said. "Any news would be better than living without knowing."

Investigations move in spurts. Find a clue, track it to its source. That's the way detectives work. No clues, no tracking.

The next morning, a text message from Mr. Forrest to Jimmy moved the investigation in a slightly different direction. The message was lawyerly: brief and to the point.

9mm Beretta not in gun safe.

Looked everywhere.

Called police at 8 pm last night to report gun missing.

Call me.

Jimmy shared the text with Steve, and the two of them made the call.

A receptionist answered. "Mr. Forrest's office. This is Shana. How may I help you?"

"Shana, this is Detectives Brautigan and Olson. Is Mr. Forrest available?" Jimmy felt a quiet urgency.

"Yes, he is. Please hold."

"Harold Forrest."

"Mr. Forrest. This is Jimmy Brautigan. I'm here on speaker with my partner, Steve, and we're calling you because I just now read your text."

"Thanks for calling, Detective."

Jimmy and Steve waited for a moment. The ball was in Mr. Forrest's court, but Jimmy's curiosity grew by the second.

"You say you couldn't find your gun?" Jimmy asked.

"That's right. I locked it away last September and I haven't given it a thought since then. When I opened the safe last night—after talking with you in my office yesterday—it wasn't there."

"Who has access to the safe?" Steve asked.

"Anyone who lives in my home, I suppose. But I'm the only one who has ever opened the safe. At least, I think that's true. I opened it a few times last September to see if I knew the combination. I don't know if my daughters know the combination. I'm not even sure if my wife knows it."

"Did you ever write the combination down?"

"I keep it on my computer with my file of passwords."

A lot of people are pretty cavalier with passwords, Jimmy thought. *Until they get hacked.*

"I have an idea," Jimmy said. "I'm going to call my friend, Jack Stahl, and ask him if he'll send a crime scene unit to see if there are any fingerprints on the safe other than yours. So, whatever you do, don't touch the safe again. Just leave it alone, okay?"

The crime scene crew found Jacob's fingerprints all over the safe—and he'd been missing for more than six months. The only other prints belonged to Mr. Forrest. The Forrests moved into their new home in early August and the safe was installed in September. Sometime during those three months—September to December—Jacob had become quite familiar with the safe.

Jack phoned Jimmy.

"Jacob's prints are everywhere on the safe, Jimmy. Outside. Inside. Everywhere. So, when he disappeared in December, do you think he had that gun?"

"Sounds likely," Jimmy acknowledged. "But why would he need a gun?"

Jimmy hated it when the questions piled up higher than the answers.

Chapter Fourteen

I Would Prefer Not To

Frank Hannigan
September 2019

Two down and one to go.

I know that sounds cold and callous, but I've hardened my heart and steeled my will. The idea of acquiescing to injustice or endorsing the "nothing-to-be-done" acolytes stirs a bitter potion deep in my soul.

Whenever I consider relenting—saying, "It is enough"—voices erupt in my head. *What if it had been you in the bedroom and not Miss Aria? What if it had been Isabel? A flood of what ifs.*

I hear morbidly idiotic comments, *She was just a dog. They were only trees. It was only a shed. Insurance will cover most of it.*

Their answers to our trauma—to our loss of the home we'd come to love, to our nightmare-inducing loss of any sense of safety, to our loss of faith in those entrusted with keeping us safe—was a hermetically-sealed silence. An all-embracing silence. Silence from Serrene Homes; silence from Amelia Artaud. A cold, callous silence.

From deep within, a voice quietly replies, *I will show them the true meaning of silence.*

And so I have. Two down and one to go.

Isabel and I know that our third quest for justice will not come easily. Fortunately, I suffer from ETS—English Teachers' Syndrome. A whole literary cast of characters from classic novels and plays rally round to encourage and advise me. When I fret about finishing my task, Lady Macbeth summons me to "Screw your courage to the sticking place, and we'll not fail."

Lady Macbeth understands that there are two down, one to go. So do I. So does Isabel.

Bozeman, Montana sits just 80 miles north of Yellowstone National Park. I love Yellowstone.

Old Faithful, Yellowstone Falls, Mammoth Hot Springs, bubbling paint pots, geyser basins, and steaming fumaroles always ignite my imagination. Yellowstone feels prehistoric, even otherworldly. I can't imagine how the first humans felt when they found themselves wandering amid Yellowstone's unique thermal-filled geography.

It's best to visit after Labor Day has come and gone, when school is back in session, and the deluge of summer tourists trekking and tracking through the park has dwindled to a trickle.

When I was a textbook consultant, I visited Yellowstone every chance I could. Fortunately for me, both the Bozeman and Livingston school districts purchased my literature program. That multiplied my opportunities to visit Yellowstone. I visited the park when I was selling the books to the selection committees—during the winter in late February—and I visited again when I trained the teachers to use the books they'd purchased—in late August. Consult a map, and you'll see that Bozeman and Livingston sit on Yellowstone's northern doorstep.

I can't remember when I last visited Yellowstone, but I'm guessing I hadn't returned in at least a decade. I've been retired for five years now, and my final consulting trips in Montana were to Butte and Hardin, two Montana cities just far enough away from Yellowstone to make a visit inconvenient.

When I worked in Montana for the last time, I toured the wind-swept battlefield of the Little Bighorn—probably for the fifth or sixth time—and several of the teachers from the Hardin school district tagged along. They were wonderful guides. Like me, they wondered what it would be like to be systematically dispossessed of one's ancestral home. We talked about how the Sioux might have felt when they realized that the deck was stacked against them. Like me, these teachers remembered being fans of the US 7th Cavalry's General George Armstrong Custer.

That was a lifetime ago. As we drove back to the high school, we concluded that Custer got what was coming to him. That sentiment rings true in the current circumstances, too.

It was serendipitous that Amelia Artaud became a city planner for Bozeman. If she still worked for the City of Snoquamish, and turned up dead like Kelsey and Mick, I'm certain police would be at my door before her body was cold.

Amelia would be our last—the grand finale—but her distance posed problems we hadn't yet encountered. We would need a more comprehensive plan than any we'd devised for either of the Walthers. And before we could plan, we had to determine her patterns. The question we needed to address was: Is it possible to determine her patterns remotely?

After considerable discussion, Isabel and I settled on a three-stage plan.

Stage One: Go to Bozeman and attach the GPS tracker to Amelia Artaud's car.

Stage Two: Go to Bozeman and remove the GPS tracker.

Stage Three: Analyze Amelia's movement data and construct a plan to accomplish her exit from this mortal coil.

Each stage would be fleshed out in minute detail, and the results—or lack of results—in that stage would determine our next move.

I'm glad I married someone with a gift for minutiae because Isabel considered many contingencies that had escaped me entirely. To address those contingencies, Stage One had tons of misdirection built in—as the name of the stage will quickly reveal. She called it: Frank's National Parks Photo Vacation. I'd be visiting three national parks—the Olympic National Park, Mt. Rainier, and finally Yellowstone—ostensibly to enjoy myself while honing my photographic skills using my spanking-brand-new digital camera.

"Just tell anyone willing to listen that I told you I needed quiet time to meet my September deadlines," Isabel said. "Tell them I encouraged you to do your thing while I stayed here to do my thing. My thing has absolute deadlines."

Just after Labor Day, Stage One began.

I left home as Frank Hannigan, amateur, and perhaps inept, photographer, going on his first ever photo-taking excursion to the Olympic National Park. I frequently consulted the camera's manual because this damn thing had all the bells and whistles, and I'd been pretty much an Instamatic guy my whole life. What amazed me were the number of people willing to offer me advice about taking pictures with my camera. Far more people than I ever realized are still in love with "real" cameras—each advisor quietly denigrating the cellphone revolution.

One very frustrated man who helped me adjust my depth of field exclaimed, "Those damn cellphones have undermined and hijacked great photography."

Naturally, I agreed with him.

As I clumsily adjusted my camera at every photographic vantage point, I'd proclaim, "I'm a novice at this." And the semi-professionals who understood "real" digital cameras—and apparently they are everywhere in our national parks—were only too happy to help me.

A few days later I traveled to Mt. Rainier and replicated my previous experience. This novice photographer received advice and instruction from a whole cadre of digital camera aficionados.

I also added another layer of information for my cover story. While I was at Paradise—the tourist center in Mt. Rainier National Park—I asked one gentleman if he would photograph me taking a picture of one of Mt. Rainier's meadows.

"I'm going to send this to my wife with the caption, 'A novice no longer.' She's at home working, while I'm up here learning to be a photographer. I'm retired, and she tells me I need a hobby."

The gentleman was only too happy to take my photo, and I gave him my email address so he could forward the picture. Now I had proof I was at Mt. Rainier, and I had a witness to me being there—along with his email address. He also knew why I was there—or thought he knew.

Then I drove toward Yellowstone National Park. I say "toward" because my real destination was Bozeman. I drove through Bozeman, and stopped for the night in Livingston, Montana.

During each of these trips to various national parks, I drove my Prius—the one with a built-in GPS and great gas mileage. Isabel and I weren't worried about anonymity on these trips. We wanted anyone curious about my trips to know where I was and when I was there. My credit cards would vouch for my trips' itineraries.

Unlike the first two trips to parks in Washington State, the trip to Yellowstone was the critical piece of our plan. The four-day plan was simple.

Day One: Drive to Livingston, MT, (through Bozeman). Stay the night.

Day Two: Take pictures at dawn in the Gallatin National Forest—just a few miles east of Bozeman. *Be a photographer*. Eat breakfast in Bozeman at a restaurant close to city hall. Discover where Amelia Artaud's car is parked and plant the GPS (I have Amelia Artaud's picture from a social media site.) Stay the night in Livingston.

Day Three: Visit Yellowstone. Take lots of pictures. Stay the night in Livingston.

Day Four: Drive home.

Things went even better than I hoped. True, it's a long drive but it's all interstate. I checked into my Livingston hotel, and I told the hotel clerk I was meeting some friends in Bozeman the next morning. I asked where I could meet my friends and have breakfast. She suggested the Western Café on Main Street.

The next morning, I drove off in the pre-dawn twilight to take pictures in the Gallatin National Forest. I took pictures galore. In fact, I couldn't turn in any direction without blurting out, "My God, that's a picture." The experience of standing in the middle of such majestic beauty almost derailed my purpose that day. Almost.

Sometime around mid-morning, I returned to my car, and transformed myself into "The Old Geezer" before driving the few remaining miles to Bozeman.

As I entered the Western Café for breakfast, I stared at my reflection in the glass doors. I thought my gray beard looked very professorial. Not too long, not too short. I'd deliberately donned my disguise to defeat the omnipresent eyes of CCTV. Any digital eyes recording my presence in Bozeman would reveal a bearded, limping old man, using an aluminum cane, and wearing a Colorado Rockies ball cap. Someone who was not me.

The role I played was one I enjoyed—an out-of-town geezer thinking about making a move to Big Sky Country. That's precisely the conversation I had over breakfast with my waitress, Barbara.

"Barbara," I said—using people's names generally puts them at ease and makes them more talkative and more congenial—"do you think I'd like it here in Bozeman?"

"Course you would," she said. "Once people come here, they never leave. They might die here, but...Montana gets under their skin. I love it here."

We traded some light-hearted banter as she refilled my coffee. As I paid the bill, I asked Barbara for directions to city hall. She walked out the front door with me and pointed the way.

"One block west—you're facing west. Then three blocks north. It'll be on your left. You can't miss it, she said, waving good-bye. "I hope you move here. You'll love it."

I don't think she ever asked my name. I wonder what name I would have given myself.

I hung around city hall for the rest of the morning—grateful that the weather was partly cloudy and warm. I'd brought John Irving's novel, *A Prayer for Owen Meany*, so passersby would simply see an old man lounging and reading. Around noon, Amelia and an older gentleman—a colleague, perhaps—went to lunch in Amelia's blue Honda Civic. She drove, so I assumed it was her car. I couldn't follow them, so I stayed where I was. When they returned to city hall, I scribbled Amelia's license number on my hand.

Once she disappeared into the building, I walked as quickly as "The Old Geezer" could to her car and attached the GPS tracker.

Mission accomplished.

I returned to my car and drove back to Livingston. The next day I drove south to enjoy the fascinating phenomenon named Yellowstone. I took a slew of pictures, just in case someone wanted proof that Yellowstone was indeed my destination.

On the morning of Day Four, I drove home.

"How'd everything go?" Isabel asked as I drove back to Snoquamish.

"Flawlessly," I said. "The GPS will let me know where she goes and when, and I'll be 670 miles away. I'll monitor her for about two weeks, and then I'll drive back to Bozeman and retrieve the GPS. By then we should know how to proceed."

Amelia was a homebody. That's not a criticism, just an observation. The GPS that I attached to her vehicle outlined almost the very same path each and every day. There were slight deviations on occasion, but the one certainty was that when her day concluded, she went home. I could anticipate her being home from 7 p.m. until 7 a.m. That was her pattern.

If she had a broad social network with lots of friends who convened for dinner and conversation a couple of evenings each week at a local bar or restaurant—like Mick Walther—the GPS would have said so. But the GPS told a different story.

If she did, indeed, have a multitude of friends, the GPS testified that she made no attempt to visit them. At least not during the two weeks that my GPS tracked her travels. Isabel suggested that it could be that her friends flocked to her door—or that she walked to their homes. Could be, but that seemed unlikely, too.

All the evidence declared Amelia to be a certifiable homebody.

I gathered all this data, all this intelligence, remotely. Sure, I had to drive to Bozeman to place the GPS inside the wheel well of her car, but that proved to be the easy part. Amelia, herself, had inadvertently made it easy to install the GPS tracker by parking her car in the city hall parking lot. It only took a few seconds to plant the GPS, an operation I'd rehearsed dozens of times on various cars.

Two weeks—actually, sixteen days—of data were all we really needed.

Now for Phase Two. On my return trip to Bozeman—this time in the GPS-free Blueberry—I easily retrieved my GPS tracker because Amelia's car was exactly where I'd hoped it would be—in the city hall lot. In her spot. "The Old Geezer"—that is, me—easily retrieved the GPS.

Two weeks of data helped me know where she lived, so I drove by her home to evaluate her neighborhood. She lived in a modest-sized, light-beige home—a rambler—with a matching, scraggily brown lawn. *They sure could use some rain*, I thought. She had a two car garage, and I laughed when I wondered if her garage was as stuffed as my own with random collections of foodstuffs, wine bottles, tools, insecticides, bird-feed, hot tub paraphernalia, old books, and a lifetime of assorted detritus that I readily confess I should toss, but find too dear to part with.

I returned to Interstate-90 and headed west on my long drive home. I napped occasionally at the rest stops, but not before I was in Washington.

So now, both the who—Amelia Artaud—and the how—Jacob's 9mm pistol—were done. All that remained, now that we had a sense of her patterns, would be the where and when.

After carefully studying the data, Isabel and I decided the deed were best done at Amelia's home. The data strongly suggested that she would be home almost every night—except for nights when she had clearly remained at city hall. Town council meeting perhaps?

That's when we seized on the idea of a Halloween murder. This year, Halloween was a Thursday—a week night, and more importantly, a school night—but the Bozeman town council was promoting Halloween trick-or-treating on Friday evening. That made sense.

That meant that Friday evening's streets would be filled with costumed kids and teenagers—adults tended to go to parties—and who would notice one more ghastly Halloweener?

On what other day can someone wander around in ghoulish garb—maybe even bloody clothes—and draw, not gasps, but laughter? Halloween night normalizes the unusual or bizarre. I was relying on that.

Phase Three, my final trip to Montana, was much like Phase Two—a fast "cash only" trip. One day over, do what I needed to do on Trick-or-Treating night, and return immediately. No hotels. Sleep in the car if necessary. If anyone ever asked, I never made this trip. I wouldn't have Yellowstone to alibi me.

The media furor about *The Serrene Homes Killer* had quieted down—although still without resolution. The possibility of a serial killer targeting the residents of Hemlock Hill made brief headlines, but that fear had only a short shelf-life. I continued being passively un-neighborly, ignoring my Hemlock Hill neighbors. I didn't wave to them, and after Mick's death, and Harold Forrest's memo that the police were concerned for their safety, they stopped waving to me. Or so it seemed.

That was fine by me. No one was stealing my wine anymore.

Detectives Brautigan and Olson had called only once since mid-June. Perhaps their investigation had stalled. I didn't know, but I decided to sequester my curiosity, too.

For three months, Isabel and I returned to the life that had been our bedrock, our psychological anchor before November 2015—a time when we could comfortably sit outdoors on our back deck in the shelter of our towering firs and hemlocks, sipping wine, watching and listening to the twittering birds, and enjoying our dogs lounging and playing in the grass that always needed mowing. Then Serrene Homes, in concert with Amelia Artaud, decided they could pull up our anchor and set us adrift. Without consequences to them.

There are always consequences.

Before I left, Isabel made one request.

"No notes, Frank. I know you've been conjuring something clever, but I'm asking you to avoid leaving a note."

"Okay," I agreed, reluctantly. "Herman Melville will be disappointed," I said. "But okay, no note."

I'd been considering leaving the famous line from the short story, "Bartleby, The Scrivener." In Melville's masterpiece, a Wall Street lawyer hires a clerk named Bartleby who soon refuses to do any work his employer requests. Bartleby's only response is "I would prefer not to." I'd chosen that quotation because it embodied my own current feelings. I would have preferred an apology and compensation. I would have preferred justice through the courts. But since I cannot have what I prefer, I will do what I would prefer not to.

Leaving a note on Amelia Artaud that declares, "I would prefer not to," would be the perfect denouement to the story we were writing.

Nevertheless, Isabel's point was well taken. The absence of a note might indicate a different killer. Leaving a note, however, would definitely make the death of Amelia Artaud an investigative hat trick.

"Promise me, Frank. I love Melville as much as anyone, but I don't want any more late night visitations from the police because you were an English teacher."

"I promise, my love. Cross my heart."

She kissed me warmly and sent me on my way.

I timed my arrival in Bozeman for Friday at dusk. It was a typical Halloween night. Already there were tons of tiny princesses and Draculas, as well as a whole panoply of costumed ghosts, ghouls, and goblins walking up and down sidewalks with their treat bags. Scores of parents hovered at a distance, watching as their children ran back to them, squealing with delight and eager to show their parents the loot they'd just landed.

My own Frankenstein costume rested in the back seat of the Blueberry. Isabel thought it would be wonderful to have a Frankenstein named Frank.

From years of experience—and from the city council announcement—I knew that city-sanctioned trick-or-treating would end at nine o'clock. And as all seasoned trick-or-treaters know, the best treats require an early evening foray. As nine o'clock approached, trick-or-treaters would discover the time was none o'clock.

Sorry, all out. You should have come earlier.

Wish we had more candy, but we don't.

I had parked on the street near a baseball park about a half mile from Amelia's home, donned my costume, and emerged from my car in the darkness. Just so no one would find my presence "different," I carried a large plastic bag with plenty of goodies I'd purchased back home. Kids and teenagers carrying bags of candy posed no threat. I hoped others saw me as a chubby teenager.

No one who sees me will be able tell that I'm not a teenager. With candy. With a really cool Frankenstein costume.

As I walked the distance to Amelia's house, I heard a few comments like, "Look. There's Frankenstein."

"Man, you're ugly," someone shouted.

I arrived at Amelia's front door in the dark just before nine o'clock.

By now, most trick-or-treaters were home—the streets were practically empty. I wasn't sure if Amelia had been giving out candy, but her porch light was on—typically a signal to trick-or-treaters that candy was available. Beneath my costume, I had a foam pillow, and behind the foam pillow, I held Jacob's pistol. I could do that because Frankenstein's right arm was a fake. His left arm was mine—complete with scars penciled on my gloved left hand—but the right arm was simply a sleeve stuffed with newspapers.

I rang the doorbell.

My breath quickened and I could feel the nervousness ball up in the pit of my stomach. Isabel and I had decided that if no one answered the door, I would return to the car and drive home. And maybe that would be the end of it.

Amelia answered the door.

"Trick-or-treat," I said in a slightly soprano voice.

"Oh," she said. "Frankenstein? Right? Great costume."

When she turned round to get some candy from a bowl she had in her foyer, I shot her. Once in the side, and the second in the back of the head. The foam pillow had muffled the sound just as I'd hoped. Then I turned round, turned off her porch light, and closed her front door making sure it was locked from the inside. I shouted "Thank you" as I walked out to the street.

Step by step. Moment by moment. Isabel and I recited that mantra whenever we engaged in a planning session.

"Don't get ahead of yourself," she'd say. "Step by step. Moment by moment."

I walked back to my car wondering if Amelia was actually dead. These kinds of interior monologues are disconcerting, and they proved especially disconcerting when I realized I was talking out loud to myself in the darkness. Fortunately for me, the streets were fairly deserted. Standing outside the Blueberry, I pulled off the top of my costume—which included a *papier mâché* head—and slipped it into a large plastic bag. The same for the bottom.

As I drove off, it occurred to me that I'd be arriving home on November 2, All Soul's Day—another irony for an English teacher to consider.

It took me all night to get home from Montana. Even without construction and using as much interstate as possible, it took me thirteen hours. I stopped only for gas. I had a backseat full of protein bars and licorice to munch on as I drove. Two thermoses, filled with coffee, would hopefully keep me awake.

Whenever I did gas up, I played the imaginary invalid. I wore a fake moustache, a tan hat with a chin-strap, and used a cane as I limped around the car. My left arm was in a sling as if I had a broken arm. I thought it was a nice touch.

I was gassing up outside Coeur d'Alene when the guy at the next island over took pity on me, and he pumped my gas for me.

"Hey, old-timer," he said while putting the nozzle into my car, "you ought to have one of those disabled placards that hang from your rearview."

"Yeah, I suppose I should," I said.

My wish was that anyone who saw me would remember an old geezer with a broken arm who had a tough time walking. They might remember my moustache, but they'd never see my hair. For the trip, I wore a black t-shirt, dark trousers, and black shoes.

I'd driven the Blueberry even though it used twice as much gas. As I said, it was an all cash trip.

I arrived at my mother-in-law's home around ten o'clock on Saturday morning. I took all my bloody clothes and tossed them with bleach in the washing machine. I put all the plastic bags in one huge plastic bag, and dropped them into a dumpster in the garage. I dismantled my Frankenstein costume, planning to bury the pieces under the pile of lawn clippings near Jacob's grave. The gun went back into the wooden crate with my old albums. The Beatles' *Revolver* album still sat atop like a twisted joke.

I swabbed with alcohol, showered at least three times, soaked in a tub forever—or what seemed like forever.

Then I drove home.

Isabel opened the front door, and the dogs streamed out, surrounding the car, barking, and wagging their tails.

Normally, the dogs can rescue me from my emotional doldrums, but not today. I rolled down my car window.

"Done," I called out to Isabel.

"And how does that make you feel?" she asked as she walked toward the car.

"How does it make me feel?" It took a moment to find the words that described how I felt. "Awful...sad...confused..."

I sat in the car with my hands on the wheel. I felt empty. Perhaps it was just the thirteen-hundred-mile roundtrip with nothing but coffee propping me up—perhaps it was something more.

Isabel opened the car door, and I climbed out. She hugged me. We looked at one another, tears in our eyes.

I offered Isabel a wan smile. My sense of sadness was unshakeable.

Mission accomplished, I thought. And then the tears came.

Isabel took my arm and walked with me into the house where the dogs all gathered round to welcome me home.

Chapter Fifteen

A Simple Question

Jimmy Brautigan
November 5, 2019

Dusk was falling when Jimmy Brautigan stood at Frank Hannigan's front door, shifting his weight from one foot to the other, trying to ignore the fact that he should have worn an overcoat. Frank answered the door, pushing the barking dogs aside to get there.

"Come in, Detective. You look cold."

Jimmy thanked Frank and came in.

"Let's go warm up in the family room," Frank said. "Follow me. The fire makes the family room toasty."

A fire flickered in a raised gas fireplace that cast its delicious warmth from four feet above the floor. Beautiful bookcases flanked the fireplace. Jimmy stood directly in front, watching the flames dance, and enjoying the heat radiating into the room.

As he rubbed his hands together and warmed himself before the fire, he commented, "I don't believe I've ever seen a raised fireplace like this."

"Isabel wanted a fireplace she could see from the kitchen while she cooks."

"It's beautiful, Frank. What kind of stone is that around the fireplace?"

"It's granite, Detective," Isabel said as she walked into the family room. "Did I hear my name?"

"I was telling Detective Brautigan here about our fireplace."

"Did you tell him we've remodeled using granite as a theme throughout the house?" Isabel asked. "Can I get you a cup of coffee, Detective?"

"No, thanks, Mrs. Comstock. I'm already over my caffeine limit. I'm hoping to sleep tonight. "

"Then, maybe a Scotch?" Frank asked in a mischievous tone.

"Don't tempt me," Jimmy said.

"My dad used to say he could resist anything except temptation."

Jimmy laughed. "I think I would have liked your dad. Is he still with us?"

"No," Frank said. "Passed away in 1999."

Frank sat back on an unreclined recliner while Jimmy continued his efforts to quell the early November chill.

"What kind of Scotch?" Jimmy asked as he turned to look at Frank.

"I'll let my Scotch aficionado tell you what's available," Frank said nodding in Isabel's direction. "I learned long ago that my wife consumes only the finest Scotch. She is not a cheap drunk, Detective."

Isabel moved to the granite-topped cabinet that stood between the family room and the kitchen. "I'm a purist. Only single malt Scotches," she said. "The Balvenie..."

"The Balvenie," Jimmy interrupted. "Wow. How old?"

"Seventeen years, I think."

Isabel reached for a crystal decanter on the black granite lazy Susan, and held it up. She wore a seductive *Want Any?* look on her face.

"Sure, why not," Jimmy replied as he got comfortable on one end of the loveseat. "Neat, if I may."

As Isabel poured Jimmy's amber liquid from the crystal decanter into a crystal glass, she asked the question that had to be asked.

"What brings you to our door today, Detective?" Isabel handed the detective his glass of Scotch.

"You're going to enjoy that," Frank said. "Isabel has exquisite taste."

Jimmy took a sip and sat back heavily in the loveseat's embrace.

"Incredible Scotch on a comfortable sofa," he said as he put his head back. "Don't let me fall asleep."

"Glad you like it. The Scotch is seventeen years old, but the loveseat is less than a year old. By the way, it's a loveseat, Detective, not a sofa."

"I stand corrected," Jimmy said, taking another sip. "Perhaps I should say, 'I sit corrected.'"

Jimmy seemed to be formulating exactly how to say what he was about to say. "Do you remember Amelia Artaud?"

"Amelia Artaud? Yes, I remember Amelia Artaud." Frank said.

"I do, too," said Isabel. "Not fondly, sad to say."

"I think we both remember her only too well. She's the Snoquamish city planner who didn't respond to my nineteen phone messages back in 2015. I made every one of those calls the day we discovered the roots to our trees had been cut—by the people working for Serrene Homes."

Isabel could see Frank's anger rise in the retelling.

"When we knew the developers were about to begin clear-cutting the property south of us," Isabel said sitting down, "I went to ask Amelia what the timeline for construction was. We met for about an hour, and I thought we had a fairly good meeting about the green buffer that would be maintained between our property and Hemlock Hill. So, when bulldozers tore up the entire green buffer and slashed our tree roots, I was beside myself. I asked Frank to call her. I thought she'd at least pick up. But she didn't. My husband left nineteen messages, and she never had the decency to call him back. Not once. Instead of doing her job and protecting the good citizens of Snoquamish, she felt it appropriate to dispatch a pair of Snoquamish policemen to our home. They seemed as disinterested as she was in the destruction of our trees."

There was no subtlety in either Isabel or Frank's response. None. Four years down the road, and their ire remained branding-iron hot.

"Did you ever go to City Hall to talk with her, Frank?"

"No," Frank said, doing his best to calm down. "I didn't see the point. It's funny, Detective. I've never met the woman, and I have this visceral hatred for her."

"Never met her?"

"I don't think so."

Isabel shook her head. "No. No, you're mistaken, Frank. I believe we both met her at one of the public hearings for Hemlock Hill. The night we addressed the issue of the stub road that was going to come to the edge of our property. I remember her being at that meeting."

"Well, that only proves she's entirely forgettable," Frank said.

Isabel turned toward the detective.

"We got them to agree to a twenty-foot green buffer. If they'd let that green buffer alone, if they hadn't bulldozed where they had no need to bulldoze—where no homes were going to go—we'd still have our trees."

"Do you remember what she looks like?"

"Vaguely," Isabel remarked. "Why?"

Jimmy reached into his inside suit jacket pocket and pulled out a folded piece of paper.

"This was emailed to me today, Frank."

Jimmy handed the piece of paper to Frank. Isabel walked over and looked over Frank's shoulder. Frank read the short news story aloud.

Bozeman Daily Sentinel

Tuesday, November 5, 2019

City Planner Found Murdered; No Suspects

The body of Amelia Artaud, age 50, Bozeman City Planner, was found shot to death in her home in NE Bozeman early Monday morning. The police have released few details. Ms. Artaud had worked for the City Planner's office since January 2019. She had previously worked for the city of Snoquamish in King County, Washington.

"This is from today's newspaper?"

"Yep. That's today. Got it from Bill Lawford, Bozeman's Chief of Police."

"Well, it makes sense that we didn't see it on our local news. After all, Montana's a whole world away." Frank began handing the paper back to Jimmy.

"You can keep that," Jimmy said.

"No thanks. Look, Detective. I think I can speak for both Isabel and me when I say we're sorry to hear of Ms. Artaud's death. That's a shame. However, you realize Ms. Artaud wasn't high on our list of people we'd like to invite to dinner. She steadfastly ignored us in our time of need. And we've never had any contact with her since. Not in person, nor over the phone."

"Did she have a family?" Isabel asked.

"Not that I'm aware of," Jimmy commented. "The article doesn't mention any family members."

"Here." Frank handed the newspaper article back to Brautigan. "I don't need any reminders of Ms. Artaud—alive or dead."

"You know, murders in Bozeman, Montana, are even rarer than murders in Eastlake, despite Montana's wild-west image. I looked up the crime stats for Bozeman before coming over here. Bozeman has one murder every three years," Jimmy said.

"Or one-third of a murder every year," Isabel drolly remarked.

"You didn't come just to tell us that Amelia Artaud has been murdered, did you?" Frank asked.

"Or to quote crime statistics," Isabel added.

"No. Along with the newspaper article, I received this information. Bill Lawford emailed all of it to the Eastlake department earlier today. I thought you might find the information...well, interesting." Jimmy handed Frank a second piece of paper.

Frank reviewed the page with the heading LAB SUMMARY. It contained information from NIBIN—the National Integrated Ballistic Information

Network. The summary detailed one very interesting conclusion. It was underlined. Frank read it aloud.

The 9mm slugs found at the murder scene—the residence of Amelia Artaud in Bozeman, MT—on Monday, 4 November 2019, are an exact match for the single slug recovered at the scene of Mick Walther's murder in Eastlake, Washington, on Wednesday, 5 June 2019. <u>Conclusion: The same gun killed both Amelia Artaud and Mick Walther.</u>

"You're right, Detective. That is very interesting," Frank said. "But I still don't know why you've ended up at our door, yet again."

Jimmy Brautigan watched Frank and chuckled to himself. "Look, Frank, it's no secret that you disliked Serrene Homes and the Hemlock Hill development."

Frank looked down at his folded hands and quietly said, "I don't dislike Serrene Homes. I loathe them, Detective. I despise them. I could recite an entire thesaurus of words expressing far more than just a simple 'dislike.'"

Jimmy could hear the depth of Frank's pain.

"We know you were unsuccessful in bringing suit against them for the loss of your trees and all the damage that came with the Hemlock Hill development. And Serrene Homes didn't do themselves any favors when they ignored the fact that they were responsible for the death of your dog."

"Miss Aria," Isabel said softly.

"I'm really sorry about your dog. I told my lieutenant that, and he thought I'd gone around the bend. I think he believes that dogs don't have much value."

"Well, you can tell your lieutenant that I don't think lieutenants have much value either. In fact, in my book, dogs are worth ten times whatever a lieutenant is worth."

"Touché," said Isabel.

"But taken altogether, you both have a truckload of motive."

"Motive?" Frank asked. "Come on, Detective. We all have motives for doing all kinds of ugly and sordid things. Things that we would never actually do. We're hardly the first people to hate developers for destroying our quality of life—and, doubtless, we won't be the last. Isabel and I aren't outliers because we hate developers. Hating developers is the norm. You'll have to do better than that."

"Fair enough," Jimmy said. "So let me ask this. Where were you this past Friday night, November 1st, the day after Halloween?"

"He was right here, Detective," Isabel said. "I'd tell you we were both here warding off rabid trick-or-treaters, except we didn't have any trick-or-treaters. With Hemlock Hill right behind us, we stayed at home with our porch light off, hoping to avoid any Halloween hijinks—like people breaking into our shed and stealing wine."

"That's right," Frank agreed. "We want no tricks from them, and they get no treats from us. We simply want to be left alone. It helps that our front door is 100 feet from the street. Our long driveway discourages many people from coming to our front door."

"Except the police, Frank," Isabel said with a mock smile. "Let me cut to the chase, Detective. You're here because you think that Frank and I have something to do with Amelia Artaud's death, aren't you? Did the murderer leave another tell-tale English teacher's quotation? Is that why you've come knocking?"

Jimmy wanted to duck the question. "I just came by to..."

Isabel interrupted him. "That's a yes or no question, Detective. They don't come any easier than that. Has another note been left behind that has led you straight to our door?"

Jimmy grimaced, the reluctant witness on the witness stand. "No. If there was a note, I don't know anything about it."

"But you still think we had something to do with the murder?"

"Yes."

"Because the bullet from Mick Walther's murder and the bullets from Amelia Artaud's murder match." It was a statement, more than a question.

Jimmy looked up at Isabel and nodded. "Yes."

There was a moment of silence. Everyone seemed to be waiting for someone to say something.

Jimmy rose from the loveseat. "The Scotch was superb," he said. "Thank you. I probably shouldn't have come."

"Don't you want to know the answer to your question, Detective?" Isabel asked him. She was quite in earnest.

"Only if I can have a bit more Scotch while I listen to your answer," Jimmy said with a self-deprecating laugh. Somehow he felt as if he'd lost control of the interview.

Isabel walked to Jimmy with the crystal decanter, and poured him another drink. Jimmy resumed his seat.

Isabel cradled the decanter in both hands.

"Whatever happened to Amelia Artaud," she said, "is not our fault. Period."

Frank jumped in. "No. Not period. Exclamation point."

"First, we don't own a 9mm pistol. Never have," Isabel pronounced with conviction. "Never. Whoever killed Mick and Amelia was in possession of a 9mm pistol."

"And second?" Jimmy asked.

Isabel pounced on his question. "There is no second."

"How about credit card receipts? We know that one of you drove to Montana. In mid-September." There was something sad but smug in Jimmy's voice.

"Well," Frank began, "then you know that one of us also visited the Olympic National Park, Mt. Rainier, and Yellowstone—all in the month of September. That was me. I did all that."

"Okay, Frank, you went to three national parks in September. May I ask why?"

"Sure, Detective," Frank said. "I can give you five good reasons."

He ticked them off on his fingers.

"First, I'm retired. Second, they're the 'local' national parks. Third, it's after tourist season. And fourth, it's before the snows make the parks impassable."

Frank paused.

"You said five. That's four."

"If you're hoping I'll say I was plotting Amelia Artaud's murder, you'd be wrong. My fifth reason is I've taken up photography. Now that I'm retired, Isabel thinks I need a hobby that will occupy my time and my mind. So I agreed, and I went and bought a new Canon digital camera. Would you like to see it? I wanted to try it out on my favorite subject—Mother Nature. Took some award-winning pictures, too."

"According to you," Isabel teased.

"Where did you stay?" Jimmy asked.

"When?"

"When you went to Montana."

"I stayed in a hotel in Livingston. The Comfort Inn. Why?" Frank asked.

"You went through Bozeman to get to Livingston?"

"Just like everyone else who's driving to Livingston from Seattle. Drove through Bozeman on my way home, too."

Maybe it was the Scotch, maybe it was the darkness that descended in the early evenings in November in Seattle. But Jimmy felt conflicted, felt sympathetic. A new and uncustomary feeling.

"I don't think I should finish this Scotch," Jimmy said. He stood up and gently placed his glass on the granite countertop. "Wouldn't do to have a detective pulled over for drunk driving."

"I'll finish that for you, Detective," Isabel said. "I'm certain the alcohol kills any germs."

Frank stood up and moved to the detective.

"I'm sorry that you still think of Isabel and me as suspects," Frank said as he walked the detective to the door. "We've always been good people, Detective Brautigan. We are still good people. We believe in fairness and justice—and we hope you do, too."

Jimmy stood in the doorway. The sliver of a moon peeked out from dark clouds. He stopped to inhale the chill November night air.

"Nights are getting colder," he observed.

"Yep," Frank agreed. "Thanks for coming by to tell us about Ms. Artaud. We're sorry? I know that sounds like a question, but we really didn't know her. And she never took the time to know us. It's too bad."

"Well, this is probably my last visit, Frank. I've decided to stop doing what I've done for more than three decades."

"You sound uncertain."

"Well, there are still some things undone, some questions unanswered. No one likes to end a career when things are unresolved."

"Kind of like putting a book down before you finish the last chapter, isn't it?

"Something like that," Jimmy agreed.

"Well, Detective, if you'd like to see how beautiful a home can be around Christmas time, stop by. Isabel's decorations will be lavish and fresh, our tree will be decorated, and every corner of the house will shout 'Christmas!' to all who enter. So come by. I'll lay in some more of The Balvenie if you'd like."

"I'd like that. Goodnight."

"Goodnight."

Jimmy took two steps out onto the deck, and turned. *I might as well ask now,* he thought to himself. *It's why I came tonight.*

So he asked.

"Are you done now, Frank?"

Epilogue

Last Entries In the
Last Notebook

Jimmy Brautigan
November 22, 2019

It is Friday, November 22, 2019. I gave notice and handed in my papers two weeks ago on November 8th. Today was my last official day on the force. It's been a long time coming. My "Bad Guys" Library—to date, 421 notebooks that contain my entire career as a beat cop and a detective—will be completed when I finish my final entry, the one I am writing this very minute.

Leaving the job I've had for more than three decades feels strange. As much as my partner, Steve, has bugged me about retirement for the last few years, he seemed genuinely surprised and saddened when I told him I was finally pulling the ripcord. I told him on November 6th, the day after I had my tête-à-tête with Frank and Isabel on November 5th. I'd gone to their home to question them about the news I'd received from Bozeman about Amelia Artaud. They sat opposite me in their comfortable family room and listened to what I had to say. They listened carefully, even respectfully.

Decades ago, I remember asking my first mentor, a detective named Karl Douglass, on the day he retired, how I'd know when it was time to retire. I'd worked with Karl for two years when he decided to "hang up his spurs." He looked at me and said quite simply, "You'll know, Jimmy. Don't worry, you'll know. There will be hints and signs that it's time."

Karl was right. When I walked out Frank and Isabel's front door, I knew it was time to call it quits. The signs were everywhere.

I'd knocked on their door, and Frank and Isabel invited me in, led me to their family room to warm myself by the fire, and gently joked with me about my kids and their kids—they have three boisterous, happy dogs that are their family. And three cats. Isabel poured me a very nice Scotch and both Frank and Isabel expressed their sympathies for Amelia Artaud when I told them that she'd been murdered in Bozeman, MT. They didn't flinch at all when I explained that we had evidence that the same gun was used in the Mick Walther and the Amelia Artaud murders.

They said they found that "interesting." Nothing more.

What kind of reaction did I expect from them? I'm not sure. Did I expect surprise? Did I expect them to act cautiously or defensively? Did I expect them to go on the offensive, and tell me I should let them alone? After all, I've been knocking on their door plenty over the past ten months. After thirty-one years as a policeman and detective, I should have known what to expect. Or be able to interpret what I was seeing. Once upon a time I could, but no longer.

I think that's a sign.

I saw neither surprise nor guilt. I wouldn't have been surprised if they'd offered a crime scene crew another opportunity to search their home all over again.

Perhaps I'm letting my own personal feelings intrude on my objectivity. Perhaps I've lost all objectivity. For the better part of a year now, I've worried that I've begun to question the strict "by-the-book" approach to law enforcement—especially when I think the law is wrong. I felt that way about marijuana for years.

You see, I know Frank Hannigan is guilty. I know it like I know my own name. Frank Hannigan killed three people. He killed Kelsey and Mick Walther, and then he killed Amelia Artaud. And I'm betting that his wife Isabel knows everything about those murders—chapter and verse. I'm as certain of that as I am that the sun rises in the east.

I'm also pretty sure that Jacob Forrest's disappearance fits into this Serrene Homes mystery somehow, some way, but that's the only part that's still a mystery.

If you ask me who killed Kelsey, Mick, and Amelia, Frank did. And he may very well get away with it.

And I may very well let him.

I think that's a sign, too.

As often as I've shared my suspicions with my lieutenant, he's always deferred to the need for hard proof. "Where's your proof?" he always asks before retreating to his office. Don't misunderstand me, proof is always required to convict, but the same proof is not required to suspect—or even to know. And I know Frank did it.

Truth is, the whole situation feels like justice gone awry. The lieutenant is always saying that we're in the police business, not the justice business. I've always been tempted to say, "With all due respect, lieutenant, that's bullshit." I've never surrendered to that temptation. However, my lieutenant's perspective is not only annoying, it is completely wrong. Who says we're not in the justice business?

From my perspective we have always been in the justice business—anyway, that's how I've always attempted to comport myself. The public wants justice. It's what they expect. They expect the rigorous application of fairness and common sense. Beware the day when the people we serve don't feel that they are being served fairly or with common sense.

After 31 years of police work, I just know Frank did it. I can feel it in my bones. But no one will accept a "feeling in my bones" as proof. Yeah, proof is our gremlin. No gun. No physical evidence. No DNA. Solid alibis.

If my bones could be entered into evidence, Frank would be in jail. But it's time I gave these bones a rest. You know those cartoons where the character has an angel sitting on one shoulder and a devil sitting on the other? The angel counsels obeying the rules while the devil counsels breaking the rules. Well, that's where I am. And quite honestly, I don't know which one to listen to. That's probably because I not only know what Frank has done, I understand why he did it.

As I left Frank and Isabel's on November 5, I stopped at the door to see if I could scratch an itch that I just can't seem to reach. I stood in the doorway, thanked Frank and Isabel for their hospitality, and asked, "Are you done now, Frank?" All he said was, "Goodnight, Jimmy." It was the first time he ever called me by my first name.

It was a simple question. I knew what I meant by it, and I'm pretty sure Frank—and Isabel—did, too. As I departed, Frank shook my hand, thanked me for stopping by to let them know about Amelia Artaud, and wished me well. He said that the holidays would be upon us in no time, and that I should stop by and visit the house sometime before Christmas, when Isabel's decorative skills are on full display.

"Christmas is our favorite time. The dogs love it, too. What could be better than having a tree right in the living room? Yeah, Miss Aria loved Christmas." He pointed to a picture on the wall—a rogue's gallery of sorts—with photographs of all the dogs and cats that had spent their lives with Frank and Isabel. "Miss Aria always wore a frilly collar, with jingle bells attached, in observance of the season." I looked closely at Miss Aria's photo—she seemed to be smiling.

I owned a dog, once. A mutt named Impy that Felicia had brought home as an eight-week-old puppy just after our second child was born. That's when I found out what puppy love really meant. Impy died two years before Felicia passed, and I was heartbroken. I don't know how I'd feel or what I'd do if someone was responsible for killing my dog...and I knew who they were...and they got away with it.

I've always sympathized with the people I meet—whether victims or perpetrators. My lieutenant has always given me a bad time about my tendency to identify with people—including the "bad guys." He said I sympathized too much.

That's a sign, too. One more reason to add to the pile of reasons to stop.

So, I've decided to stop. I didn't say retire because that word has all kinds of negative connotations for me. I remember my dad telling me that retiring was the worst decision he had ever made. Maybe it's just semantics—maybe stopping and retiring are really two sides of the same coin—but I've decided not to retire. No, I'm just going to stop. Stop being a detective. Stop nosing around in other people's lives—except maybe the lives of my children and grandchildren.

Nosing around—being a person my mother would have called "a butt-in-ski"—or looking under rocks, or in the backs of closets... or into the darkness of people's souls...seems to be in my DNA. But now I'm stopping. Sometimes I think I've stopped because I've finally come to understand the darkness. That's scary.

Maybe now I can live in the light.

December 23, 2019

What was it my mother used to say? Just when you think you're done, you find out you aren't. I thought I was done—not only with being a detective, but with writing in my journal. I certainly acted as if I were done, as if I were finished with my career in law enforcement.

After all, I quit. I turned in my badge and my gun. I started collecting my pension—my 401k can wait for now. Interest rates and the current rate of return on investments suck right now, but in four years—maybe sooner—I'll have my pension, social security, and my 401k. All that, and my house is paid for, my children are grown, and I don't want a boat. I can do pretty much what I want--and I can do it in style, too. I can read or travel or go to the theatre or watch TV. Maybe even date. Steve has volunteered to "find someone suitable for a well-to-do, eligible bachelor."

My daughter has encouraged me to take some classes in the use of the computer—and I'll be taking an evening course at Eastlake College just after the New Year. Truth is, it's rather nice taking a class that isn't required. Maybe it'll help me join the digital world.

But I digress.

Shortly after I quit—I went back and re-read all the notes I'd made since January, when Kelsey Walther was murdered. Well, not all my notes—just those that applied to The Serrene Homes Killer. What made me curious was Frank's avoidance of my final question as I left his home on November 5—the "Are you done, Frank?" question. Frank acted as if I hadn't even asked it—but I had, and I knew that he knew I had.

So, today, I took him up on his offer of a holiday visit. And

I decided to take him a birthday present because I found out his birthday is December 23rd. My birthday is Christmas Day.

When I rang his doorbell, his three dogs all crowded at the front door, barking incessantly, as Frank shouted for me to come in from the other side of the storm door.

The dogs greeted me enthusiastically and I greeted them in return. "Are those cookies I smell?" I asked.

Frank said, "Ah ha! Your detective's nose has found us out. The cookies you smell are my mother's favorite recipe. It's good to see you. Here, let me take your coat. I didn't know if you'd take me up on my invitation."

I had to remind him that I was no longer a member of law enforcement. "A detective, no longer," I said. "I'm a civilian now." "So, you have actually retired?" he asked as he threw my coat over the back of a chair. "It's a reality?"

"Yeah, I'm pretty sure. I'm not certain I know what retirement feels like—or what it's supposed to feel like. It's still pretty new," I told him. I handed him the wrapped present I'd brought. "Happy Birthday, Frank."

Isabel joined us in front of the Christmas tree.

"Detective—no...not detective...Mister Brautigan has officially retired," Frank said to Isabel. "And he's brought me a birthday present."

"How thoughtful," Isabel said. "How did he know it was your birthday?"

"We former detectives have our ways of knowing things," I said. "I wouldn't be much of a detective if I didn't know when your birthday was. When I found out it was today, I thought I'd kill two birds with one stone. Help celebrate your birthday, Frank, and see if your claims that Isabel possesses magical decorative powers at Christmastime are true."

Isabel smiled coyly. "First, let me congratulate you on being happily unemployed," Isabel quipped warmly. "That means you've got time to review my...what was that?...magical decorative powers at work in our home. Am I right? And you can share some of my ancient Scotch, too?"

"I'd love it," I said.

I must say, Isabel truly knows how to make a home Christmassy. Me, I have no gift for decorating. That's something my daughter laughs about all the time. But Isabel...she is definitely an aficionado. Greenery adorned with twinkling lights outlined all the window and door frames; nutcrackers stood proudly atop cabinets and at my feet. Her dining room table scape announced the holidays with a brilliant red cloth and holly-wreathed candles.

I told her how beautiful it all was.

I was invited into the family room to sit by the fire and enjoy another seventeen-year-old Scotch. Neat.

"Do I hear John Rutter choral music, or is that the Scotch singing to me?" I asked as I snuggled into the chair by the fire.

"Christmas wouldn't be Christmas without John Rutter's divine music, Detective," Isabel remarked.

"My late wife, Felicia, would agree completely. She used to say that this is what Heaven sounds like year round."

Frank handed Isabel a glass of Scotch—neat, as well—and he took a moment to sniff the brandy in his sparkling crystal snifter.

He asked me, "So, a detective no longer. May I call you Jimmy?"

I responded, "Offer me Scotch like this, and you may call me anything you'd like."

"May I open my gift?"

"It's your birthday," I said. "Please do."

Frank pulled off the red-foil wrapping paper, and held up the book I'd purchased.

"Look Isabel. Look. Oh, my, Jimmy, this is one of my favorite books," he said. "The Princess Bride. I've always loved this book. Thank you."

"You're welcome," I said. "I got it for you it because I

remember a conversation I had with my daughter—many moons ago—when she was reading it in high school. She wanted me to explain the final lines to her."

Frank smiled that knowing smile at me. "You mean when the narrator says that life isn't fair?" Frank asked.

"Yeah, that's the line. After all, your trees had their roots severed, then they fall on your house, kill your dog, and what? Nothing. Nothing happens. Life isn't fair. I've thought about that line ever since I met you and Isabel and heard about what happened here,"

I said. "Goldman's right. Life isn't fair."

"Yep, but he doesn't stop there, Jimmy, does he? Do you remember what the narrator says next?" Frank asked.

I paused a moment. Suddenly, I was back in school, and my English teacher was asking me an important question. "Yes, Frank. After he says 'Life isn't fair,' he says 'It's just fairer than death, that's all.'"

"Well, remembered, Jimmy. Well done," Frank said to me. Then his voice became very quiet as if he'd lapsed into a daydream. "I think William Goldman was onto something with that final line. He's suggesting that one doesn't have to surrender when life isn't fair." Suddenly, Frank broke from his brief reverie and said, "Thank you for the book, Jimmy. Until now, I'd never even seen a hardback version of The Princess Bride. Only paperback. Who knew?"

We all laughed.

Then, without missing a beat, Frank hoisted his glass. "A toast! To Jimmy, a man who now has the time to do whatever his heart desires. Merry Christmas!"

We all raised our glasses and became a contented chorus offering "Merry Christmases" to one another. I took a sip. Then I asked, "What may I toast for Frank and Isabel?"

Frank and Isabel mulled over my question for a moment, then Frank raised his brandy-filled glass. "To our noble, fallen trees."

I took another sip.

After a few quiet moments, Isabel raised her glass, her eyes glistening with tears. "To our beloved Miss Aria."

I looked at Frank and Isabel, and I smiled. I took another sip. Finally, I raised my glass. The light from the fire, twinkling and glistening through the cut crystal, was mesmerizing. They waited patiently as I struggled to find the right words. "To justice," I said.

"I can drink to that," Frank said.

"Absolutely," added Isabel.
I savored the final sip of Scotch in my glass.

Frank stared into his brandy snifter, swirling his ice cubes. "It's good to see you here, Jimmy," he said.

Then he looked up at me and began smiling and nodding. He stood up and walked to the granite counter gleaming with the liquor-filled, crystal decanters. He picked up the Scotch decanter and walked to my chair and refilled my glass. Then he returned the Scotch to its place and reached for the brandy decanter, removing its stopper.

"Let me answer your question, Jimmy," he said. He smiled at me as if we somehow shared a secret that no one else knew.

His comment took me by surprise. For the briefest of moments I wanted to ask, "What question?"—but then I knew.

He poured himself another brandy, replaced the stopper, and resumed his seat. He sat back, making himself comfortable, and looked across the room at me. I awaited his answer.

I could see from his smile and the slightly quizzical look on his face that he was searching for the right words. Once he'd discovered them, he leaned slightly forward, swirled the brandy in his snifter, and looked up. He made it plain that he was speaking directly to me.

"The answer, Jimmy, is yes," Frank said. He took a sip and then stared at the golden liquid in his glass. "Yes. I'm done, now. Pax vobiscum—peace be with you."

Certain moments cause our minds to erupt in chaos—that unsettling jumble of thoughts when clarity seems like a forlorn hope. I was having one of those moments. I took a deep breath and asked myself: What was I hearing? Was this a confession? Or was this simply a simple answer to my simple question? I just didn't know.

Then somehow the chaos ceased and peace descended with the simple realization: it was no longer my job to know. "Pax vobiscum," I said, raising my glass. "Peace to you and Isabel."

I took a sip of Scotch. It tasted wonderful.